Gerard McCann grew up in the north of Ireland and currently lives in Lisburn, County Antrim. He is a senior lecturer in International Studies and head of International Activities at St Mary's University College, Queen's University, Belfast. He has been an Erasmus Coordinator for fifteen years and in that capacity has worked in numerous universities across the European Union. He spent the past four summers teaching on courses in Poland and Hungary. He has worked in an advisory capacity at governmental and EU level, and has guest lecturing experience in the USA, Africa and across Europe. He has published a number of books on regional and international development. In his spare time, he acts as an advocate for the African diaspora in the UK and Ireland. *Lustration* is his first novel.

LUSTRATION

Gerard McCann

LUSTRATION

Vanguard Press

VANGUARD PAPERBACK

A CIP catalogue record for this title is
available from the British Library.

ISBN 978 17845 116 9

*Vanguard Press is an imprint of
Pegasus Elliot MacKenzie Publishers Ltd.*
www.pegasuspublishers.com

First published in 2016

Vanguard Press
Sheraton House Castle Park
Cambridge England

Printed and bound in Great Britain

For those who were never released
from history.

'The only writer of history with the gift of setting alight the sparks of hope in the past, is the one who is convinced of this: that not even the dead will be safe from the enemy, if he is victorious.'

Walter Benjamin

PROLOGUE

The river Wisła, which works its way through the heart of the city of Kraków, has been recently spanned by a leaf shaped metallic modern footbridge. Officially known as 'Kładka Ojca Bernatka', after a local Catholic monk, the bridge has the aspiration of linking the old Kazimierz Jewish Quarter with the emerging left bank. As a monument to the renewal of the city, it has become a symbol of cultural rebirth for the young in particular, who, in their thousands, have secured padlocks and other trinkets to the rails of the bridge – creating a light spectacle of glittering, shimmering hope. They call it simply 'Lovelock Bridge'. As with other similar bridges in Prague, Paris and Dublin, this moderate act of resistance has given young people a way of expressing a sense of desire and freedom that their parents and grandparents were denied.

The padlocks are inscribed with wishes and names. Some are simple with first-names or dates, while others are decoratively carved. In Poland they represent something more than they do in other regions of Europe. Many are cryptic and immensely personal to those who secretively secure their locks. Others make a defiant statement of solidarity for the future of Poland. At twilight the multi-coloured lights that stretch the length of the bridge catch the sparkle, brought alive by the illuminated water-flies attracted by the lights. This surreal flickering mass captures the eerie spectacle of movement, mist, life and frozen thoughts. Ultimately it encapsulates the melancholia of a young generation's frustrated hopes for a future still held hostage to the country's tragic past.

In the autumn of 1988, in the middle of the campaign to remove the Soviet regime, scores of young people, intellectuals, students and trade unionists were rounded up by state security services, interrogated and tortured. During the 1980s, under General Jaruzelski's regime, thousands were detained, dozens were killed and many were brutally treated as they fought to liberate Poland from foreign influence and internal collaboration. As with all the cities of Poland, the people of Kraków suffered terribly under that regime. Many of its people still hold chilling memories of the long terror that was visited upon them. Many still seek the truth of what happened through the closing days of the regime. The legacy of those days and the activities of its tens of thousands of military bureaucrats, continue to haunt Poland. The Lustration process has been the attempt by the country to exorcise this past.

***

Lubeka stared out of her apartment window. The perfect rings of smoke that she blew towards the glass obscured the boredom of the view. Initial thoughts of cleaning the window were replaced with the frustration of trying to blow the dirt and cobwebs away. This day offered her the chance of something new, a distraction from the realities of waiting for any something to happen. It forecast change, removed from the mundane pattern of not knowing where her days were taking her. The snow on the uniform lines of Nowa Huta's housing blocks had settled into its usual grey, merging with the drab discoloured tenements.

The lights still glinted with an orange blur, projecting the last gasp of the distillation of night. Lubeka watched and waited for the moment when she could break out; get moving, be alive, work to give meaning to the day. The smoke circles conferred a pattern, a rhythm and scent that were reassuring for her. It meant otherness, something different. The snow had been falling intermittently all week, its soft silence only disturbed by the occasional rattle of the trams as the earliest of the city workers, the cleaners and night security staff, started to make their way to and from the tourist haunts of Kraków's old town. She looked to the shifting bent figures, moving slowly beyond the street, black against grey, wet and struggling through an irregular light drift of snow. Then she joined them.

16th November

Kraków at night is a city of two faces – one of the visitors and the mischievous, the other of anguished fated spectres from a tragic past. The two play off each other in a daily tussle of visibility and presence. In winter the very concrete unites with the clouds. When it rains the greyness of the older buildings turns darker and angrier, exposing the menace of what they have witnessed through the city's long and painful journey. The weight of what had happened a generation ago, or two generations ago, that fight to escape the hurt, is always present. The heaviness of time sits uncomfortably with the lowering of the day. As the winter moves on, rain in this part of the world only gives way to the bleaching of the sleet and snow.

Each family, each house, each creaking door and cobbled street has a fated story to tell. Most often the stories are not those of two generations past and the horrendous terror that families had to endure under the swastika, jackboot and concentration camp. Often the stories are alive with more recent injuries. The scars are just below the surface and suppress a collection of memories that rarely change: charged with rumour, fear and the legacy that ideological zeal bestows. The more you get to know the place the more the weight of time increases. From the cafes and bars of Kazimierz to the hallowed ground of Rakowicki cemetery, the Krakowians know their history and carry tragedy instinctively.

The November evening had brought the mist from the Wisła River to the city centre streets as the taxi cautiously bumped along, slid and nervously navigated its way through the empty streets to a bar. Łuka Gabreski had survived the flight from London without temptation, but on landing felt the urge to return to his usual comfort zones of alcohol and reading. Still damp from the dash to the heat of the airport taxi, he felt as if winter had instantly closed in, leaving him to seek warmth and solace where he could. The tyres wheezed as the car pulled up. The taxi driver offloaded the bag, fiddled with the notes he had just received and stood to watch as Gabreski disappeared into the antiquity of a candlelit bar in Plac Nowy, the old Jewish market square.

Gabreski needed anonymity to cover his habits, discretely moving to an unoccupied table in the almost empty establishment, safely positioning his bag under the table. Ordering his beer he proceeded to work away, his face illuminated by the brightness of his tablet. In this isolated existence, pub life had become a window into other worlds and a lifeline to the only companionship he had come to know in later life. It was his world and through all the bustle of soulless city life, the bar, its staff and the routine provided him with a lifeline, a refuge.

Things seemed uncluttered at this point in the evening, seven p.m., as the bar staff shuffled around the tables relighting flickering candles and wiping away the damp of the last customer. The usual clatter of faithful evening patrons appeared, to secure shelter from the sleet. Smoke stained walls and ill-matching tables were perfect for Gabreski and his non-perturbed mood. Pictures of long dead socialites covered the walls, together with browned newspapers depicting Kraków before the world was turned upside down in September 1939. He periodically glanced around to read the fading script in the yellow glow, relief from the glare of the tablet's screen.

In his own world Gabreski had experience of the peace before the storm of the eighties. He knew of a Kraków that was once silent. As a child he would play on its streets and knew of it as home. He was in the bar to hide in a half written article on the Tupolev-154 plane crash that killed many of Poland's political and military establishment in April 2010 – and a triple whiskey. As a semi-feral academic this was as good as it would get, refining pieces of work that may never see the light of day, reworking commissions, drinking whatever inclination would draw him onwards, but mostly observing. As with many of his ilk, he was always running away from something or towards something else, never knowing which direction would be better. It was an inquisitive existence, tiring but never dull. In a way, movement had become the purpose of his life. He liked the uncertainty that academic travel could bring, the excitement of the unknown and usually chose the commissions and places which would bring him closest to the front line, to the anger of the street.

The bar in Plac Nowy was usually the first place Gabreski would resort to when going through Kraków. Its depth and the labyrinthine network of rooms meant that he could disappear into the dark and remain until things had settled in his mind. It may only be two hours of solace and may have had the hint of desperation, but it was calming; away from the circular world of flights and hotel rooms, debates, public scrutiny and detached lecturing. This bohemian environment remained sanguine and familiar. He searched out its like in whatever city he was rushing through, registering the places and times as if to collect a list of caverns where he could hide. These moments gave him time to take stock and reflect.

Gabreski struggled with the pressure of being an academic adviser, as they all do, but found the instability motivating. He had built his reputation as a specialist on state transition, social memory and reconciliation as a process. While history was his discipline, security and peace had become his trade. He wondered at communities struggling to get through history in the making. His specialism had become topical again with the debates around the Arab Spring and the new Cold War. His interests predated the ongoing turmoil in North Africa and Syria, but his real focus, the trigger that shifted his mind immediately, was the Eastern European trauma of transition from authoritarianism into an uncomfortable, uneasy democracy.

Tensions in the East had dominated his work for ten years or more, and with this badge of knowledge he had become an academic personality of sorts. With minor celebrity status he was able to gain leave from his university almost at will, to assist in the discourse around transitory processes for peace building, whenever he was called. The themes had become part of his make-up, shaping his way of thinking and his diplomatic personality. A historical reference was always close at hand, an anecdote or name. The threat from old regimes followed him as he rolled through city after city. This world left him in an obscure void between institutionalization and celebrity, a form of nomadism, shaped by residency in a sequence of hotels across the world, regimented and impersonal. At this stage he could not envisage an alternative settled life, but constantly and jealously hankered after something less impersonal.

Gabreski had tried to settle once. He had lived in Tervuren outside Brussels for a time while working at the Business College, a popular hub for policy hacks in the heart of the city. The data processing he was involved in at that point in his life had become intellectually sterile. A nine to five routine within the prison of working towards a pension. Although exciting at the start – being a part of that mixture of power and ego that had become the European Union's life blood – by the end it had come to weigh him down. The bureaucratic humdrum of researching statistics and demographic trends almost killed him. It destroyed the spirit and left a void that gave him pain with every spreadsheet he faced. He began to spend more time in the pubs off Grand Place than in the office, picking up a taste for strong Belgian beer and Irish whiskey. He eventually began to despise that round of seasonally exposed tram journeys and turned it all in, deciding to look eastward for a world to live for rather than a job to die for. It took him five years to extract his life from Brussels, sparking a new and increasing interest in the political changes that were occurring across Europe. The big break came with a university post and an opportunity to get back to London to rebuild from there.

***

Just before his precious two hours in the solace of the bar were complete, his smart phone jumped from the table. The silence and reflection had been a welcome relief, but Gabreski knew his calling would always kick him back into the realities of his world when the gmail beeped or the melodic invitation of the ringtone picked up volume. The texts and calls seemed to collide this time. The message was all too clear – there were people waiting and he should get back to work.

"Professor Gabreski, where are you? We are standing outside the hotel."

"I do apologize. I got distracted. I will be with you in twenty minutes. I have a taxi waiting." Gabreski felt that he had been exposed doing something illicit. He could feel his heart beating again, his mind kicked back into the purpose of his trip.

In a clutter, the whiskey glass emptied, the phone disappeared and tablet slapped shut. His coat and bag all sprang into life at the same time. Emerging from the pub, the sleet was lighter but still fleeting onto the hardy souls who tried to venture out into the cobbled streets of Kazimierz. As he emerged from the pub, the taxi driver who had helped him beat the tourist scrum at the airport was still sitting there. They entered into an awkward exchange on loading bags and causal rumour. Gabreski's interest in rumour was genuine. He thought that he could be unguarded in his comments and at the same time offer a sense of honesty to the driver.

The taxi industry appeared to be doing well in the city, kept alive by the hordes of tourists who flocked in the summer to visit the sites, the concentration camp, be religious, or follow the obsequious 'stag' from one club to another.

Settling into the taxi, Gabreski worked to get the sombre embattled driver to lighten up: "So what is happening in Kraków these days?" Straightening the rosary beads around the mirror, shuffling in his seat, the driver seemed to be preparing himself for an official answer. He glanced wearily at Gabreski, measuring him up.

He was around the same middling age as Gabreski and seemed to have kept himself well given his sedentary occupation. It crossed Gabreski's mind that had his mother been at liberty to stay in the city, this profession could well have been a part of his own life experience. He felt a bond of sorts with the driver, but wondered how the experience of staying, of fighting for a living in a depressed world of work, had affected him. As the conversation revolved it became confessional.

"Football fans and stag parties took over the market square on Saturday. They were dancing on the sculptures and teasing the police all night. It brought the city to a standstill… There was no movement, no fares. The police were doing nothing as usual. If I had my way, we should lock half of them up and whip the rest. Usually the police are tougher than that. They can put up a good fight when they want to. They would never have allowed that rabble before… Well… You know what I mean."

"So you didn't get much business from the fans? Bring it back to the good old days. Send in the troops, eh?"

"Give me a state that knows what it is about any day."

The driver shrugged without committing more. It was clear he was not happy with the day to day struggle of this new world. Gabreski realized that he may have hit a raw nerve. As with many Eastern democracies the role of the police had been contested, if not politically then certainly among the ordinary citizens. Some, indeed, saw the past as a safer place to be.

Life prior to the freedom of the nineties was, for many, a comfortable moment in history. Nostalgia was the unspoken dislocation for the society. This bi-polar dispensation could be seen across the former Soviet bloc. Poland was no different. The silence between him and the driver exposed the possibility of differing judgements about this new awkwardly-formed country. Liberation had brought with it hardships that many who stayed had to endure for decades. It was tough and begged the belief that the old world, for many, was a better place to be. Nostalgia was a refuge, whispering its way across many families. The short journey around the old city walls from Plac Nowy to the hotel by the Galeria focused Gabreski's mind somewhat for the more formal reception that he expected to see from his university colleagues.

Poland had changed enormously since it had achieved its freedom, with many of its brightest and enterprising searching out opportunities elsewhere. The haemorrhaging of the young in particular annoyed the older people, who had come through war and occupation without relief for over fifty years. For them freedom was not about emigrating. It was supposed to be about building and doing justice to those who had resisted and suffered. The contradictions were divisive and generational. Movement remained a rite of passage for the young and gave many regions an unexpected exiled diaspora, draining the youth from society and the economy.

Gabreski too had been a victim of diasporatic circumstance. His mother escaped from behind the Iron Curtain as it closed for a generation, settling in London, yet trying to live the often austere life of the Polish *intelligentsia* abroad. Their home was filled with the sobriety of Chopin, the wisdom of Władysław Reymont and the visions of Czesław Miłosz. His mother's world was informed by the hopes of Solidarność and a Polish Pope. It gave her a context within which to struggle and held her passion for the country long after it should have been a fading memory. Gabreski's world was caught between Highgate Hill's Polish orthodoxy and socialization marked by student parties, anti-war protests and a Britpop soundtrack from the nineties. Kraków and north London sat uncomfortably together for two decades of his life.

For Gabreski and his mother, returning 'home' was an obligation, a rite of passage for émigrés. It was one which had become an anti-climax when it eventually did happen in the mid-1990s, visiting relatives who had forgotten them, touring streets in the Kleparz district of the city that were no longer recognizable, and reminiscing, continually reminiscing. The memory sustained the identity, but it was of a city and a people that no longer existed for many in the diaspora. Gabreski came back occasionally, but his world was that of Highgate and no matter how he tried to empathize with his mother's experience of displacement, it was not his. If anything, he missed the energy of London in the nineties. That was his youth, his moment in time.

As the taxi pulled up to the front of the hotel he could see a small reception committee had already gathered. The smoking conventions introduced by the government to ban it in public spaces had driven avid smokers, the diehards who shunned the 'e-' imitations, to vacate buildings periodically. In Poland, it meant a regular mass exodus of staff and sympathizers from buildings whenever anything pressing was about to happen. He almost forgot the silenced driver – still nonplussed – as he opened the door to dive into the small huddle under the canopy at the entrance. "Twenty zloty… Twenty zloty." He had paid six the last time he had taken this short journey, but accepted that this is the price of new 'rich' Poland and a disgruntled driver. Dodging the drift of sleet and the increasing chill of winter, Gabreski ploughed straight to the lobby, fluttering a wave, chased by two of the smoking party. He felt it was a bit assertive, rushing on, but wanted to ensure that the etiquette of meeting colleagues was properly followed. Being drenched was not a professional look.

“Professor Nowak, Piotr, I hope you are well.” Gabreski stretched his hand out. The handshake held to emphasize the tenure of the friendship, staring straight into the gaze of his former colleague as if to reignite a trust. Nowak and Gabreski had been collaborating on research for a number of years. They had been working on the state’s transition after communism and had built up something of a reputation as troubleshooters in the field. As a team they would often have been called in to advise state departments on good practice in transparency. Nowak fitted well into the Polish academic establishment with his intensity and conservative disposition. He had always been bookish and in later years had attained a priestly demeanour to match. Unlike the British and US system where performance had come to shape academic personalities, the old school of scholastic academic rigour remained a priority and was still currency across Polish university life. The two men stood as exemplars of their respective cultures.

As young academics Gabreski and Nowak had the wherewithal and arrogance to address the Chicago economists who were being forced upon many countries in Europe at the time, condemning the ideological salesmen, chasing after these evangelists of greed as they tried to convert Eastern states to their new faith. It had often involved hastily organized seminars in cities as diverse as Budapest and Gdańsk, but enabled them both to build up an expert knowledge of the changing Eastern bloc and to cut a profile on the academic circuit that would provide opportunities to build international reputations as specialists on the former communist regimes. Their collaboration finished when Gabreski bailed out to take up the Brussels post and while they had kept in touch, working at times on joint projects, research had become a supplement to friendship. Consequently, the threads of friendship were constantly referenced by the past, rarely the present.

Now older and wiser, their more recent work had evolved into the sensitive area of historical enquiry and retrospective analysis. This was a new enough field – premised by an idea of conflict resolution as practised in Rwanda, South Africa and Ireland. These methods and its rationale had never been discussed as a way of dealing with the complicated recent history of Poland. It would mean the monumental task of following up on events that took place during the Soviet period to decipher the facts of controversial incidents. Closure was the desired result, for communities, families and individuals. As with the other countries, searching the past would prove to be politically sensitive, even though in other places restored social memory had gained popular support as a means of dealing with community trauma.

The chance to present at a symposium on the topic was to bring the pair together again for the first time in some years. The series of conference lectures at Kraków's University also provided a good opportunity for Gabreski to lend support to Nowak in the esteemed position he had been elevated to.

"Łuka. Welcome back, I hope your journey from London was pleasant. My apologies for the miserable weather. The Kraków we know and love, eh? It's good to see you again."

"Yes, Piotr. We had a short delay of fifteen minutes in Stansted, but we made up the time on the way over. It is great to be home… back to the scene of the crime." Gabreski looked around to survey the lobby, conscious of the fact that the last time they were resident some accompanying students had noisily awoken the establishment by partying half of the night. An exchanged glance between the two referenced the chequered anarchic history, a smile all that was needed.

"God, yes. I don't think anyone recognizes us these days. Time has served you better than me." As the friendly banter broke, the presence of another colleague carried the discussion in a different direction. Beside Nowak was a ponytailed dark haired woman who had been responding to the jovial exchange with politeness, pitted with the occasional nervous reciprocal smile. "May I introduce Doctor Katarzyna Lubeka, the conference organizer and an authority on Cold War narratives and documentation. Kasia has been the brains behind this whole initiative. She has been able to locate some of the missing Mitrokhin files in Warsaw relating to the transition period. They have given us a great insight into Russian-controlled activities and the rank and authority of operatives during the Martial Law period. Her work has exposed the extent of the collaboration. Kasia has been able to prioritize activities in a way the infamous Wildstein List never did. Obviously…" Nowak scoped the two people listening. "The material is sensitive, but Kasia assures me that it will rattle a few bones when we display it at the symposium." Nowak smiled with a sense of collegial pride.

Gabreski's interest changed immediately from guilt on getting raucous students released from the hotel bar some years ago to acknowledging that this woman had gained access to material that he had been trying to locate for a decade. Closed Russian files that had been lying dormant somewhere, their value was only known to a handful outside the SVR, the powerful Russian foreign security service, the Sluzhba Vneshney Razvedki, and the ever elusive Polish old guard. His first instinct was to view Lubeka with suspicion, questioning why she had been able to get to the core of an issue that he and others could not, even with the weight of foreign academic impartiality. His suspicion begged an answer. Did she get the results by brass and hard work? Was it insider knowledge? Or was it sheer luck? Caution on such issues at this stage of his career had become intuitive.

Lubeka's openness puzzled him. She showed honesty through her mannerisms. His view softened on the realization that Lubeka was here to share the outcomes of her own years of work and considered that she was here at his hotel because she seemed to trust his judgement in assisting her to scrutinize the material. She did not have to approach him. The whole Russian academy would be only too willing to help her to manage information such as this for public consumption. Also, her deference to Nowak and nervousness exposed her as someone who had not been trained to tease out intelligence from others. There was none of the starched introductions or arrogance that comes with that ilk. Gabreski had come across many from that world in London and knew their ways, the dependencies, their lack of nerves and the false egos. Lubeka was a researcher, her insecurities were very obvious and her awkward interest in his work suggested that she was either a new type of operative in that game or she was telling the truth. Gabreski decided to read her as genuine. Stripping it back, listening to the ongoing exchange, he sensed hope in Lubeka's tone and that was never a trait that came with the cynicism of the intelligence or academic worlds. As the conversation gathered so did her confidence.

Helsinki Watch, Snowden and Wikileaks had been able to release information on the activities of the secret police from the old era over a number of years, but detail – particularly on the Polish Służba Bezpieczeństwa (the SB) and the Urząd Bezpieczeństwa (the UB), the Security Service and the Ministry of Public Security – had always been sparse. Information was the key to their power and as time elapsed, sensitive and detailed insight had become more and more difficult to track down.

The transition in Poland had been so prolonged that it gave the former regime's security hacks ample time to clean up histories and rescript the lives of many of its people. Identities shifted and people moved on, or out of Europe altogether. Other operatives had retired to adjoining states, disappeared into the civil service or switched their uniforms for suits to take up positions in the emerging and chaotic private sector. Crucially, there was still a constant fear across the country of the shadow of what the media called the 'secret collaborators', the 'TW', who were to varying degrees still involved in running aspects of Polish society. For this old guard the transition had become an opportunity to build new empires and forge a different type of link with other emerging regimes in the East.

Colonel Vasili Mitrokhin, a senior Komitet Gosudarstvennoy Bezopasnosti (KGB) operative based in Moscow, had defected in December 1992, along with twenty-five thousand pages of evidence of ongoing KGB activity at that stage of transition. It was a visceral shock to the system, the old guard. Files connected with the Polish secret collaborators could not be located, had already been siphoned out or had been destroyed. As a consequence, evidence of the KGB's role in the transition of the state from Martial Law – which ran between 13th December 1981 and 22nd July 1983, to be formally lifted on 30th January 1990 – remained scarce. Across the East, among intellectual and opposition groups, it was generally accepted that it was the Russians who were pulling the strings in the early transition process. The closest the Polish civil society and media organisations had been able to come to the truth about those years was with the unexpected and explosive leak of the Wildstein List in 2005. This was a list of almost a quarter of a million agents of the secret police who had been working for the communist regime. They were the ground troops of Soviet repression. Wildstein paid for the revelations.

As a seasoned journalist Bronisław Wildstein had gained access to the Institute of National Remembrance in Warsaw and walked out with the list which came to bear his name. He ceremonially posted the list on the internet. His website became one of the most visited in Poland as people tried to check on relatives and neighbours, looking for reasons for events that may have occurred decades ago. For a while it was a Polish national pastime. It sparked a political crisis due to the obvious scale of the Soviet involvement and the fact that post-liberation there was still an active core of the old regime across political, business and social life in Poland. In Germany, where a similar leak occurred, two million people had been able to view files that had been complied by the hated Stasi. In Poland, the government had permitted only fourteen thousand specific requests for access to files, mostly from establishment figures, until, that is, Wildstein broke open the files for public viewing.

Across Poland in the late 1980s there were an estimated ninety-eight thousand working in a security capacity, spying on their own people on behalf of the satellite regime. After 1990 many of the operatives had been integrated into the new system, quietly subsumed within a new bureaucracy, disappearing, or starting private sector initiatives where they could profit from the knowledge learned from years of keeping the population in check. Wildstein suffered for his boldness, his career ended almost immediately. He was vilified by elements of the press and establishment for dividing the country and removed from his job with the national daily newspaper *Rzeczpospolita*. This victimization of such an advocate of free speech was, for many, further evidence that the TW were still alive and functioning. The great fear was that this demonization of the rights campaigners was being driven from outside the country.

Gabreski's memories of his mother crying at the footage from Poland from the transition period, fears for their family caught up in the struggle and the desperation of not being able to participate, had remained a motivating force for him. Memories of the disappeared and stories of torture were standard whispers throughout family life for Poles across Europe for decades. 'They' may be listening, or someone may say something that would fall back on the families at home. 'They' were always there, in the walls, in the schools, in the shops, in life itself. As he learned more of the internal workings of the People's Republic of Poland, the more he wanted to know where this state apparatus and its functionaries had dissolved to. As he got older and his confidence in challenging bureaucrats grew, his academic life had come to be shaped by this drive to get through to the raw uncomfortable truth.

Lubeka still held the aroma of her last cigarette. Patient and intense in her scrutiny of the visitor, she moved to get introduced to the newcomer. Gabreski and Lubeka shook hands.

"A pleasure to meet you, Kasia. It looks like you may have opened up a Pandora's box. I don't know how you got to those documents, but well done. Working from Moscow to Warsaw as opposed to the reverse may prove to be very fruitful. We will have to compare notes."

Gabreski was distracted by a bluish discolouring at the side of her temple, which she had tried to flick some hair over and cover with some skillfully applied makeup. Caught looking at the bruise, and realizing the sensitivity of the glance, he pulled out a stock line to overcome the embarrassment. "A sporting accident?" Lubeka responded in a manner that she seemed to be used to – without breaking a smile. "Something like that." The silence hung a second. She felt that it was her obligation to change the subject.

"We have a packed week, Łuka. The speakers are from seven different states and the discovery of the new archives will put a spark into the whole event. The media has also picked up on its importance. We will be working directly with ŻYCIA, the magazine, and a number of other researchers from the university. The magazine has dedicated some of its journalists to work with us on public relations. The material is explosive if we can manage it right. What we are hoping for, ultimately, is a media splash. It would be nice to have a political ripple as well, but you know what they are like. What do you think?"

"Excellent. That sounds like a fight." Gabreski sensed the enthusiasm and the grit of the rapid-fire of ideas. It gave him the impression that Lubeka was a person who knew the importance of the topic and that she wanted her research to take her somewhere else.

Gabreski knew that for many in Poland, as with other peoples in former Soviet bloc states, memories were very much alive about the years of repression, the Martial Law and summary injustice. He was old enough to have participated in the various human rights campaigns that were set up in London to highlight abuses and to prepare for democracy. His family in London had found a Polish political voice at that period in the 1980s, protesting together and shaping what *his* diasporic experience would become – second generation, demanding change, radical in a peculiarly English way.

With the lucidness of Lubeka's introduction out of the way, he again realized what he suspected, that through the distractions of the new dispensation there was a generation gap in attitudes about the comprehensiveness of the transition. For many of the older generation there was still fear and suspicion, the old system was still residual, lingering. For some the Soviet era carried nostalgia, a hankering for the sureties of the past that could be seen across the eastern states. Some even longed for a return, without the terror, but with the security and the jobs. For the young, the memories of oppression, the pain, or alternatively, the security of the past, were not there. In this space the social memories between old and young diverged. For a small minority, the simmering war in the Ukraine was their battle also, the fightback had begun.

"Okay, let's get some rest and we can reconvene in the morning." Nowak interjected. "We have a long week ahead of us and I'm sure we have to finalize notes and take stock of the scale of the issues we are dealing with." Looking at Gabreski still standing with his bag and coat in hand. "Kasia has a file which you may want to look over, to show you where we are at in the analysis of the archives. We have kept any explosive material away from direct electronic circulation as a basic security precaution. If it is traceable assume it will be traced. The trail we are looking for is the KGB's reports to the Central Committee of the Communist Party around the start of 1988 and the possibility of a historical enquiry. Kasia has been looking at the expressions of opposition at that period and the manner in which culture was forced underground to express resistance. Our task, Łuka, is to examine the outworking of the secret police through to the liberation. An easy task, eh? I'm sure you are the best man for the job." Nowak smiled as he set out what was expected of them. Gabreski had not seen the documents and his Russian was rusty. He returned the glance and nodded to Lubeka in a reassuring manner.

On the exchange of the grey heavy bound folders and smiling their way through the clarification of roles, the three parted company for the night.

Gabreski was still feeling the warmth of the whiskey from the bar. Checking in, he had fought to negotiate a room that overlooked the medieval Barbican and city walls. Happy with the results, he pounded the sturdy, duvet free, patterned heavy blankets of the bed, before he proceeded to extract an airport bottle from his bag to return to the haze of the night. For him he felt he could manage the whole bottle, which he took as a challenge to his stamina. He poured the whiskey as if medicine, treating the administration of the shots clinically, to ensure sleep without the paranoia and desperation that cold mornings could bring.

The experience of dealing with sensitive material over the years had brought with it habits that, although tedious, were both cautionary and peculiar. With the tablet opened he videoed the documents before emailing the video-clips to himself, linking immediately to the secretarial pool at his department in the University in London. For Gabreski, it served the purpose of securing the material as well as giving him an alternative electronic version to work with later. The primary reason was more mundane. It meant not having to carry around bag loads of papers. He had the comfort valve of knowing that the material could not be located easily by others, but if need be it could be recalled easily from his colleagues. The technology was annoying at times, but increasingly he had come to realize the importance of circulating and revolving sensitive research material. Wary of Nowak's caution, he also knew that this format was not easily traceable or deleteable. Page after page he scanned the script, speeding up as the effectiveness of the process became more familiar.

With that completed he could resort to semi-sober reflection. Locked in the splendour of a hotel built to celebrate the dissipation of the Great War, with its rococo style furniture and all the mustiness of time, Gabreski's room impressed him as a place that had witnessed the full flows of the city's history. His mind wandered to the plight of the returning Kraków volunteer legions from the trenches of the East after the Russian revolution; or the hatred of the Wehrmacht and its disciplined sadism that was to weave its venom through to the hell that was Auschwitz on the outskirts of the city; or the hundreds of Soviet tanks that rolled though the city until the 1990s, to impose their might. The room was unlike any of the usual ubiquitous hotel rooms that Gabreski had drifted through recently. He loved Poland for that. It expressed its bohemian predecessors, its character, albeit cramped and aged, warmly antique. He felt at home in this environment, it reminded him of his mother's living room in London.

Sleep never came easily. He had a tendency to mull over every detail of every day before finally deciding that things were clear enough to get to the next morning. He had a tendency to recall the smallest of flaws, to get to solutions that could be followed up in the light of day. A hang-up of academic rigor, the bottle of Bushmills helped ease him into single thought, obsessive, unconsciousness. As Gabreski drifted off his last visions were to reflect on his quest to look to the past to inform what could become a future. He saw his task as a search for moments of truth in the sea of media, misinformation and cover-up. The pain that often accompanies social memory remained one of the unanswered tensions of this transitory society.

People across the Eastern states still hurt, he knew that – they just had to look to the Ukraine – but many were still angry and still carried unexpressed suffering. Revealing simple truths from the past could provide a semblance of justice. What a legacy this would be for those who marched, were beaten, imprisoned, tortured or killed. "The only writer of history with the gift of setting alight the sparks of hope in the past, is the one who is convinced of this: that not even the dead will be safe from the enemy, if he is victorious. And this enemy has not ceased to be victorious." The words of sacrificed philosopher Walter Benjamin had haunted Gabreski for most of his adult life. It was the epitaph of many émigré families.

The implications of revealing lived experience in all its emotion and rawness had the potential of constructing a canvas for forgiveness. If it could be achieved, it had the potential of releasing any generation from a crucified past. Behind this quest there lay a passionate belief that freedom and truth move around each other, one cannot be complete without the other. Listening to a moment in time, with all its noise and confusion, provides a sequence of experiences in the course of history and at least, at least, the approximation of hope. "The nourishing fruit of what is historically conceptualized has time as its core, its precious but flavourless seed."

17th November

The morning dropped abruptly for Gabreski, with the mobile phone rattling as the door was being diplomatically knocked. "Good God, what is it?" Tackling the door first he heard Nowak's disarming calm. "Could you come down as soon as possible? We have a bit of a problem." Nowak had obviously been up and out at the first light of dawn. Gabreski opened the door and came back to him with a curt:

"Ten minutes and we are out of here." All against the rattling soundtrack of the phone. Gabreski finally answered it.

"The files have gone. The files have been stolen." Lubeka, obviously distressed, overcame an inherent reticence in addressing the stranger to ask him for help. She trusted him and went straight to him for assistance. Gabreski again wondered why he was the recipient of that trust. Lubeka started lowly, the frustration building as she relayed the sequence of events: "When I went to our office this morning at Gołebia, beside the university, I found some of the Mitrokhin files were missing. Only the ones with the pictures in them. Only the pictures. We have only just been able to get to these files. We did not even have time to copy a batch. The bastards. It is as if they have been watching us do the work and then came in to take what they wanted, when they needed to. That was four years work. Four years work. The police are on their way... for all that will do. We have gathered up what is left and need to get out of here. Can we meet?"

Gabreski listened but remained distant from the urgency that was being vented by Lubeka.

"Take what you have and get out of the office. Make sure that you are in full public view with the material. We can meet at the café beside the clock tower in the market square at eight a.m. Give me fifteen minutes."

Nowak was at the lobby of the hotel as Gabreski reached the bottom of the steps. Nowak spoke on the move. "We can catch some coffee with Kasia and that ŻYCIA journalist Marianna. We'll get an idea of what is going on. The journalist is safe, she has been with us from the start and has been working on the restricted information." Lubeka had already texted Nowak.

From experience of travelling in states where the police were overly zealous, Gabreski knew only to leave those things in hotel rooms that were expendable and accepted that given the sensitivity of the work that was being done, he was likely to be on a burglar's list somewhere. Everything he needed he uploaded to the Cloud, regularly reviewing material to be absolutely secure. The process had become compulsive. Only essential work, personal documentation and cards, were necessary for travelling these days, everything else could be purchased en route when needed. On leaving the hotel with Nowak, he understood that the theft was the starting shot from the other side of Lustration.

***

Nowak's mind was on other things. He was very conscious of the fact that two hundred delegates from fifteen countries were arriving that day for an international symposium on the transition period, based at one of the city centre college halls. Irrespective of the importance of Lubeka's research, or its loss, he saw it as his task to keep this gathering as busy and as organized as possible. He had been over at the offices earlier and considered Lubeka's reaction to the break-in to be unprofessional, panicked. For her, the risks were immediate and meant more than just another series of articles never to be seen in the outside world. She wanted answers in a very political way. Some of her peers were uncomfortable with this disregard for the establishment. For some, she was far too Western.

The relationship between the two academics had been strained from the beginning. It had become increasingly obvious as Nowak had moved into good favour with the university's vice-Rector. Beyond the hub of university politics, Lubeka struggled daily to get on with every aspect of academic and professional life. She had worked steadily through the ranks of university life from an undergraduate, had excelled as a postgraduate researcher and was considered to be a hard working, dependable lecturer, who was taken for granted by her mostly male colleagues. On occasion the head of department would request her to do secretarial work on his behalf, leaving her vulnerable to jibes from other members of the department who thrived on rumours of a relationship. Lubeka always dressed down to dissuade the chatter, but her slender shape and dark complexion left her susceptible to petty jealousies and inappropriate comments. Her head of department, Jan Szolnoky, revelled in the rumours, taking it as a sign of leadership and popularity, without acknowledging the imposition within which it had placed Lubeka. Nowak had done little to interrupt these tensions since his arrival, always tacitly complying with the inference of a relationship.

Passion for her work had been her release, her saving grace, from the discomfort of the environment. She had worked harder than all her colleagues to get to the point where she was and for her a fight was only to be expected to maintain her integrity – to give her a way out. This attitude had brought her from the hardship of a Soviet-era block of flats, the struggles and communitarianism, into the privileged environment of the old city. Her deportment gave it away, as did her accent and loyalty to her community culture, family traumas and church rituals. For her, the university job gave her options in life which she herself could control. For people such as her, having options was liberty in its own right. It also carried her away from her own personal circumstances that belied her twenty-eight years and the pressures of a different and harsher world. This world rushed back each night when the university security guards ushered the remaining staff out of the buildings.

Brought up in Nowa Huta, the model Soviet town of tenements and the site of the vast derelict steelworks, Lubeka was of a post-communist generation who had seen little of the benefits of liberation. In the labyrinth of flats, the young were reared initially for the steel industry, then for emigration. If lucky they could secure work in the growing tourist traps of the old city. Her family legacy was that of obedience to the church, urban myths from the street demonstrations of the 1980s, vodka and an early marriage that was bitterly maintained. As with many in the rows, the apartment where she and her husband had been living for the past eight years were frozen in a different era. Where there once was a young couple not knowing where their decisions were taking them, there now was the claustrophobia of community that often sustains the urban poor.

When she left the university for home each evening, she returned to this world of the past, dreading the battles of the weekend. She often retreated on Monday mornings with physical pain and social humiliation. Their apartment had, as its most prominent characteristic, a clear view of the Chromy crucifix – eight meters high to remind the population of what it had come through and to mark the spot where the martyred Bogdan Włosik was murdered in 1982. Life for many in the estate never seemed to move beyond such austere and poignant moments. A traumatized community rehearsed these memories regularly as if to freeze the current desperation in the violence visited upon them in the past.

Before going to the office each morning, Lubeka joined the silent queue of women, young and old, who gathered after the early Masses at St Mary's Basilica in the main square. Lighting candles for release in their lives, the tradition had been in train since the doors of the gothic masterpiece opened. For many of the women the prayer was often the same, but no one would dare spell it out to the others.

Some would nip around to the side of the building to make the sign of the cross on the head of one of the bronze skulls supporting an ornate weighty baroque chair; myth having it that the tortured women represented by the skulls could intervene to change lives and deliver hope to those who paid their respect. Lubeka watched the track of older women, but had never pushed belief into this simple act of surreal adventure.

As she made it across the square, she navigated her way through the industrial army that emerged each morning to clean up the litter and rubbish left after a weekend of stag parties. She braced herself for the ritual humiliation of department life. Eight a.m. and a second cigarette before the day could begin.

This morning all Lubeka's fears had come crashing in on her. The weekend had been tougher than usual, with a blow to the temple from her husband for working on Sunday evening to meet Gabreski and Nowak. She had got used to the routine and had long learned to look through those who stared. She had been excited that her research would get a hearing and that the symposium would give her work a profile way beyond what Szolnoky wanted of it.

Lubeka needed results and was not shy of annoying people to get them. Nowak habitually ignored the evidence of domestic violence, viewing it as a private concern. He was more concerned with the prestige of the events to come. For her, it was the potential recognition of years of work and her steadfast belief that others would give her answers to the question of how to get out of the cage that had become her existence.

The intensity of it all had collapsed in on itself on arriving at the office to find that data sheets and order code lists from her files had been taken. The theft seemed very carefully executed. It would not be noticed by a casual glance at the office or the desk. Lubeka ritually placed files in the cabinet, had her PC files backed up and tidied her desk as though she was leaving the office each day for good. It was a small world that she had control over and she was particularly cautious to ensure its order. She could see immediately what had happened.

The arrival of the ŻYCIA journalist, Marianna Wójcik, was a relief. Wójcik had been tracking the Soviet nostalgia movement for a number of years and knew exactly the level of sensitivity of the issues Lubeka was dealing with. Wójcik was slightly older than Lubeka, and although from Warsaw, she had sparked off a deep friendship that had ensured a working relationship that was often monotonous, but occasionally fun. There was always something happening with Wójcik. She exuded movement and urgency, her hands trying to talk as intensely as her mind worked. Wójcik had been behind the drive for Lubeka to continue her research against general political suspicion of anyone looking too closely at the past – including her colleagues at the university. It was Wójcik who had used her journalistic contacts in Warsaw to get access to the Institute of National Remembrance's archives, the celebrated but struggling IPN. Their cross-referencing from cultural events to security files through thousands of historical records had enabled them to build up an in-depth knowledge of a residual political influence which they suspected remained across most eastern states. The Ukrainian war hung like a volcanic night over Eastern Europe, an example of where external interference could draw many states back to the depths of the Cold War. Poles feared the past as much as the despondent Ukrainians, the border villages arming themselves in the event of any spillover.

Wójcik suggested getting out of the office immediately. The police were informed. As they moved, a message was left on

Szolnoky's answering machine and Nowak was texted to warn of possible consequences to the symposium. Her dealings with Nowak were always formal: *Professor Nowak, the office has been broken into. Some material has been removed. I have told the police. We will have to alter the schedule. Can we meet?* Nowak, as a matter of course, rarely replied. If he felt it was urgent enough he would phone directly, his dislike of social media and the world of Twitter coming from a grinding suspicion and knowledge of the total lack of security. In an act of faith, and indeed courtesy, Lubeka also decided to inform Gabreski. In this case the response was more active. They were all to meet at the clock.

First to make it to the clock tower in the market square were Nowak and Gabreski, where they settled down to warm up with piping hot coffee and take in the morning air. Against Gabreski's better judgement the business of the week took precedence over the urgency of the break-in that morning. The sleet that had been periodic throughout the early morning had cleared, but there was a bite in the air that suggested something colder was on the way. The square had recovered its equilibrium after the social chaos of the evening before and the clamber of the early morning recovery. The residue of the damp and cold anesthetized the air. The greyness of the cobbles and the lowness of the clouds presented a timelessness that, in that spot, could have made it 1989 or 1979, or any year post-war.

"Do you think the TW are still active around here?" Gabreski presented the question bluntly. Nowak cupped his coffee for the warmth and leaned towards him.

"Well... in Russia the KGB simply put on suits and became businessmen or presidents. The state was so pervasive that it naturally struggled to survive in some form or other after the revolutions. The mentality of state 'bean counters' is not that easy to change. Remember that as late as the 1980s most of the senior civil servants in Italy were former fascist officials, appointed under Mussolini himself. It should not be blown out of perspective though. We have a system now that is, by and large, together and surviving to an extent by avoiding this type of question. And anyway, if Kasia is implying that there is something more to the transition than a move into democracy, then we have to question her academic trajectory... That is, where is she going with this?"

Gabreski sat for a moment looking around the square. The hustle and bustle of the morning echoed around the buildings. He returned to Nowak.

"Forgetting may not be enough, Piotr. Russian society was destroyed in part by those who needed power without conscience. Power is addictive and it can come in many guises... as you know. Poland may not be as bad as it was, but there is still something corrosive here from the past. And anyway, Kasia has the right at least to ask the question – where are they now?"

Nowak knew the line of discussion and realised that Gabreski had been out of the loop for some time. Poles simply did not want to ask these questions. He worked to close the conversation down. It was not an issue that could be dealt with without raising voices. As the invitation to a full blown political debate lessened, Lubeka and Wójcik lurched towards the table, all bags and scarfs.

"Please sit down, can I get you coffee, or something stronger to calm the nerves?"

"Can we smoke?" Wójcik was as forward as Lubeka.

"Of course, we are not in London." Smoking across Poland was, for many from the younger generation, an indication of a person's challenged economic background or a bohemian lifestyle. The women could claim to have feet in both camps. In unison they hurriedly searched for battered packets of Marlboro and the ubiquitous Chinese red lighters that the world of smokers had come to depend on. The clutter of paper that came with them gave the impression of a hurried flight from the office.

"What did the police say?" Nowak enquired.

Lubeka jumped in first with a rapid fire, confession-like series of comments. "We have lost photographs of UB operatives, data sheets and order code lists with names that matched. The door was not forced opened. They stripped the computer drive and took any mobile drives lying around. They were very discrete. They knew what they were up to and only the research was targeted. All the older documents were left. We have names, given the volume of the copying and the years of sourcing... the briefing papers remain. We have incidents spanning the years of Martial Law now with no pictorial evidence. I have seen the pictures and have worked though the papers myself, but the connection between incidents, names and faces, has been lost. They knew exactly what they needed and where we were in our research."

"Surely you can return to the source of the Mitrokhin files in the Warsaw state archives."

"That would take months, and if they have gotten this far I would think they have scoured Warsaw as well. They knew we were about to shoot, we had them, we had it." Lubeka seemed to be enlightened by the realization that the break-in justified the path her opposition had taken. Her years of silent, tedious research spooked them and in that it seemed to suggest it was all in the right direction.

Wójcik interrupted: "We have people in Warsaw who can search for the documents or at least get access to the archives. Let's see if they can get to it before anyone else." As a general ripple of approval went around the table, she hurriedly proceeded to text a colleague in thc capital, to book time at the Institute to check if it was possible to relocate material or at least salvage what was left. Lubeka's mobile phone buzzed. She leaned away out of habit. Dipping back into the conversation she muttered two words, "the police", looking towards the phone.

"Maybe they can shed some light on all of this. We need to be moving on to other things." Nowak resumed.

After a series of quick exchanges, Lubeka returned to the company by repositioning her chair. "As expected, the police are unconcerned. They are more intent on letting me know the problems of foreign football fans than our burglary. They fluffed for a while before suggesting that it was most likely a theft from the inside. That is, that it was not criminal, but industrial. Someone from the university who could get into the room. That was it. A professional investigation – I don't think so."

"Don't expect much from that enquiry," Wójcik interjected. "It was probably their second visit to the office today."

"Forget about them. We can recover material. We have to work on irrespective." Gabreski looked around to catch a glimpse of the square. The urgency of the impromptu meeting had shocked him out of the slumber of being somewhere different. This was an obvious place to meet, but they could be viewed by just about everyone in the area. Maybe they should be more discrete in the future. He assumed that they were in all likelihood being observed. As with the old days, he thought it would be wise to take being watched as a given. Surveillance was the most intrusive feature of the regime for ordinary people. The means may have changed, but the motivation, he was sure, was still there for some. It was prudent that they assume they were being monitored.

Gabreski had travelled across North Africa in recent years, trying to get an understanding of why the Arab Spring was so ineffective in changing the geo-political composition of the region. His trips had been for an article commissioned by a UK newspaper. It would look good on his profile and he thought it would not distract too much from his ongoing research. The danger of dealing with Islamist warlords had also seemed to play to his boyish sense of adventure, another thing that he had missed while in Brussels. With political observation as his remit, it brought upon him immediate and constant surveillance in Egypt. Three weeks of being followed in the summer gave him some insight into the way in which people could be marked for surveillance. He learned to be paranoid very quickly. The game he played was to keep the state security in view while working away, to get results irrespective of their presence.

Gabreski learned to drip feed information, change arrangements erratically and provide windows for misinformation which could carry investigations in an anticipated direction. Misinformation was ninety percent of the game; the other ten percent was disinformation. By the end of that trip it had become playacting for him, albeit dangerous. In Cairo, the surveillance was a bit more subtle, the secret police there had bundled him into the back of a car when they saw him stray from the old tourist tracks, only to return him to the luxury of his hotel.

In Kraków his mischievous nature had stirred again. He accepted that, given the seriousness of the issues being dealt with, in all likelihood conversations would be monitored and they would be targeted. The webcam network across the main routes of the city centre, similar to those across European cities, had technological sophistication that could now indulge in private conversations as well as survey the activities of the rowdy unknowing tourists, picking out faces, studying the unwary. Monitoring was easier now than during the communist era. As if George Orwell had written the script, people had, by and large, been convinced that being continually watched was in their interests. People could be tracked around the city without leaving the comfort of a laptop, access to conversations could be gained through most mobile phones and common household devices. With relevant applications, streamed video could be taken through the phones of the monitored themselves. He looked to Nowak and Lubeka, and was wary of the context.

"I should have some material which could help here. Helsinki Watch has secured some reference to the TW from Moscow that they released last year. We can collect it later. We just need to take on board that there are people out there who don't want this information in public view. We can deal with the situation as it evolves. The time we have should enable events – whatever they may be – to evolve." After a short pause Gabreski flagged up his concerns by pointing to the buildings at the edge of the square. "We really need to move."

Lubeka and Wójcik seemed relieved that Gabreski was there and could do something, even if it was only to reassure them that their work was legitimate. It was an outside voice which could not be pressurized in the way others could who lived in the city. Nowak, eager to continue the conversation, packed up as the rest manoeuvred bags. He voiced the immediacy of his concerns.

"Excellent then. Let's get on with the symposium. Kasia, we have people arriving all day and we need to locate and confirm their registration. We need to do this urgently. Painful as it is, you need to put the break-in behind you and move on. We all have material to work with and I am sure, Kasia, that your paper on the transition period will be illuminating. We have to be pragmatic. Let the police sort out all the other stuff." Lubeka's face registered a sense of being dismissed. For Gabreski the change of direction was perhaps what was needed. As they walked the short distance to the college for registration, Gabreski was able to catch Lubeka alone for a hurried conservation.

"Kasia, we need to test the severity of this... as a threat to the research. Do you remember the people in the pictures? Do you have an idea of who is who?"

"Yes. I have been working on them for so long. I know faces, some names and some activities. Some are dead, many migrated, but there are others – and I think they are still pulling strings." This admittance placed her in a peculiar situation. She was perhaps the only person outside the state security services to have the knowledge to place the activities of a group of largely unnamed state security personnel and their images to events that occurred over twenty-five years ago and more. It was imagery at best, and would need hard evidence, but it was leading a trail nevertheless.

In the silence that followed, they were both aware that accusations would remain just that, accusations subject to denial. It was also the reason why Gabreski suspected that Nowak needed to assertively close the conversation down. The protection of the rule of law still applied to all. Speculation was dangerous.

"Kasia, keep this to yourself. This will roll out or collapse depending on how we deal with this. You know the price."

***

The rest of the morning was spent in the humdrum of academic administration. The delegates arrived in chattering rows, to meet a small army of embattled administrators and nonchalant academics managing the throng into the gothic façade of the conference hall. Szolnoky made a rare appearance to welcome the foreign dignitaries, ignoring Lubeka's correspondence earlier that day, he made the most of an opportunity to sell the institution and the city in an evangelical manner. Bad news was not in his market. The cap of two hundred delegates had not been reached, so the invite had been extended to local postgraduates and political advisors, who would obviously find discussion on the transition informative. The flow of people covered all aspects of regional life, together with a stream of international security advisers and academia.

Wójcik stayed close to Lubeka. From the body language it was obvious that they had known each other for some time. The ease with which they communicated and signed to each other gave the impression of either a childhood connection or a personal relationship. There was an intimacy and sensitivity that was more than work, and ultimately this conveyed an atmosphere of trust between the two women. The way they linked arms when forced out for a cigarette was more Polish than sexual. Wójcik fixed Lubeka's collar in a motherly way, their whispering tones occasionally drifted into the lobby where the delegates gathered, verging on the conspiratorial, the exchanges between the two were never complete without a sprinkle of laughter.

The routine of this type of event was monotonous for those organizing. The symposium was opened by Adam Pasternak from the city authority, who awkwardly, but loudly, recited a city tourist brochure in English with Eastern formality. It was coupled with an invitation to the region's beauty, while downplaying the legacy of past occupations – the history that most Europeans knew the city for.

"In an era of free capital flow, Kraków has become an attractive place for locating investment. Attractive areas, rich offers of the property market, as well as a developed sector of business services and scientific-and-research facilities are just some of the arguments in favour of selecting Kraków as a place for investment."

This was the all new Kraków that the delegates were listening to, at the centre of the European project and on an anticipated road to consumeristic prosperity. The rebranding was all but complete, bar evidence of the other, Soviet constructed, marginalized and impoverished sides of the city. Pasternak finished with the sentiments of the political enigma, Lech Wałęsa: "My most ardent desire is that my country will recapture its historic opportunity for a peaceful evolution and that Poland will prove to the world that even the most complex situations can be solved by dialogue and not by force." Szolnoky complimented this relief with a caution to the academics, telling them not to act like the football hooligans who had romped through the city during the Euro Championship. "Respect our city, respect our peace." It was subtle, but the sentiment was self-evident, the delegates were not to rock the boat. Given that many of the speakers were specialists in state reconstruction and the breakup of the Soviet Bloc, the wish was hopeful. For a few, Gabreski included, the message that was to be delivered would have to be politically sensitive, otherwise what would be the point of such a gathering in the first place. For Lubeka, it could prove to be her moment and that of her kind. Her experience was different than the rest. She had stayed and had the voices from the past still very much in her mind, those who were oppressed then and continued to struggle in the new dispensation.

With the welcomes over, the issues from earlier in the morning were reemerging for those who knew of the break-in. As everyone dispersed into the cafés and bars of the city, Gabreski saw an opportunity to group with his immediate colleagues to get an update.

"Well, Piotr, that went splendid. It will be hard to keep this lot marshalled. The delegates seem eager enough to get into the whole debate." After a short pause, he questioned: "Have you heard anything regarding the break-in? I am sure Kasia would like to know."

Nowak was still buoyant at the success of the plenary session and side stepped the direction of the question. "Outstanding. The city seems happy. The Rector seems happy. This is a good start. Don't let the incident with Kasia spoil it all. The police are working on it. They left a message to say that they think it may have been someone within the university. Just papers were taken. It may have been the cleaners. Why should they be concerned? As with all of us, they have other priorities. I hope that is the end of it. Kasia knows what has to be done, she can relocate the lost material another time. She is the best we have and I am sure she will be able to get her thoughts together for her paper. She can just rework what she has and get on with it. Trust her, Łuka, trust her." He punched Gabreski lightly on the side of the arm in an encouraging manner. "I'm off to the restaurant with some of the delegates. Do you want to join us?"

"Piotr, I think I need to lose myself somewhere else. I will see you back at the hotel."

"Łuka, you will have to get to grips with that before it becomes a problem." The long term unsettled mind-set that Gabreski periodically slipped into was obvious to some, but he was cautious to conceal the depths of what he no longer considered a problem. In this, he had managed to play Polish and English cultures against each other. It was where he was at.

"Piotr, you are only one bottle behind me." Gabreski smiled in a mischievous manner.

Gabreski felt that Nowak was perhaps understandably trying to avoid reference to the break-in, but at this point of the day his demons called and he needed to hide in the twilight of a bar. One last pang of conscience before he moved. He felt that he needed to reassure Lubeka. There was vulnerability within her that he had to respond to. She was still with Wójcik, enjoying the company of Swedish and Dutch academics, who were intently discussing the post-war period and the lack of knowledge the west of Europe had about this period in eastern European history. As with many conversations of this type among relative strangers, each in turn tried to draw it into their own world of interest, hoping to get an insight into the company in a more meaningful way. On the outside of the discussion, Gabreski registered the familiarity of Lubeka and Wójcik and wondered about the bruise. They both glanced and smiled. He stood for a moment not wanting to be a part of this newly constituted forum, but needing to get an acknowledgment from Lubeka to reassure him that she was fine. He briefly interrupted to ask if they were okay and bid his farewell for the evening. He touched Lubeka's arm and she broke from the immersion of the group.

"Kasia, I will look through your briefing document tonight to see why they needed to silence it and let's continue our conversation tomorrow. Are you okay?"

"Yes, yes, yes. Tomorrow." Obviously engrossed in the other conversation, it seemed to be the trauma of the day was over for her. The word 'resilient' came to his mind as he slipped away. Gabreski left, reflecting on the two faces of the day; the panic of the morning and the laughter of the afternoon. His instincts again kicked in. This was real. He knew of the pressures that the former regime's people were putting on human rights activists in other countries. The Ukraine collapsed with the old attempting to kill off the new. Why would Poland be any different? There was the potential danger. People had been running the gauntlet of this danger for so long that they seemed to take it for granted, moving from one difficult situation into another, treating each as just another part in a sequence of interconnected experiences.

Gabreski braced himself for the chill and started to walk, somewhere different so as not to become too familiar with the staff of one place or another. His walking took him into Szeroka in the Old Jewish District. He knew that there would be only tourists in that direction and he could find a table to hide behind to refresh his mind and relieve his needs. Snowflakes fell steadily but softly on the hallowed streets around Szeroka. The cold started to bite as the light grey buildings turned gun-barrel grey in the damp.

18th November

Lubeka took a taxi home to the apartment in Nowa Huta. The gentility of the snow had arrived in Kraków to replace the harshness of the sleet, giving the roads a release from weeks of intermittent rain. Slowly the streets were turning whiter as the taxi worked to navigate through the growing lines of slush along newly formed tracks on the roads. They drove through to the development, silent and imposing. The apartment blocks were large numbered concrete constructions, row after row, lifted out of a modernist textbook from the 1950s. Once domestic freedom for many, now dated and oppressive, in a society where everyone knew there were other places to be. What it had going for it was the same list of hopes and failures that exist in all the ghettos, tenement blocks, and housing estates across Europe. Community was everything.

Families colonized streets, the older matriarchs and patriarchs had always been there. The tenements held the family histories and stories of hard and good times; narratives of struggle through domesticity. For the young, it had easy access to the excitement of the city centre and the airport. Everyone knew everyone else's business. It seemed safe, yet was claustrophobic at the same time. Threats, however, were largely from within, when doors shut and night fell, that was when the tensions of life spilled over.

Lubeka's experience was a familiar one. An early marriage coupled with a family feud. Her husband, Andrzej, had lost his job in what was left of the steelworks soon after they got married, and although doing a sequence of odd-jobs around the city, he was never able to get back to steady employment. It got to him early. He had spent some time on the emigrant labour trail to London, working for months at a time as a builder on the London Olympic sites. Each time he returned he had become more estranged, having addressed his bitterness and loneliness in the usual way for many migrant men, through litres of vodka and pent-up anger. By the time of his last job away he was no longer in the right state of mind to work. His manager would no longer tolerate the danger of having him on a building site. He returned to use his sacking as an excuse to beat his wife.

Lubeka's ideas of marriage and children, and the sense of hope that they at one time briefly shared, came to an end when the beatings started. Vodka hazes and violence merged together in periodic extremes. They were rare at the start, but as the dizziness of time and space caught up with them, it became almost ritualistic in her household. By the time she realized what had been created, it was too late. She dreaded going home. He used to wait up until she did. It seemed like obsession mixed with entertainment for him. He did not like her working and him unemployed. For little reason, she held on to hopes which were no longer possible and everyone else in the family knew it. She could handle the shame. Many women were caught in the cycle. It was harder to deal with lost dreams. She still hankered after what they had for a time and hopes they once shared. They had had their moment. The fake tortoise shell framed pictures of a newly married couple that hung in the hall seemed like ghosts of different people living in a different time.

Coming home this evening seemed no different to all the other nights of dread. Lubeka tried to stay out as long as possible to avoid confrontation. She even took her time to have another cigarette outside before bracing herself to go up the stairwell. The bleached smell of the landing took her aback, the mental closure settled in with every step upwards. The grasped luxury of a night out with friends and meeting new people was at an end, the reality was here again, smoke stained and wet, cold and concrete, and she hated every minute of it.

As she approached the front door something was different. It was after twelve and all the lights were on. Andrzej would never drink with lights on. His drift into a stupor would be too stark and painful for him. As she opened the door a shiver took her. It was too bright, too artificial. As she moved through the hall, the taut cable of a vacuum cleaner could be seen to be looped around the door handle. As the moments sped up, Lubeka knew instinctively what it was, but needed to see. Pushing the living room door open, the weight could be felt immediately. Andrzej was strapped to the door, his neck twisted, the noose tightly distorting his flesh. His colour was what shocked Lubeka, grey lifelessness with dark blue lips. His loose tartan shirt and jeans were hanging as if on a small child, the black belt she had bought him for his last birthday bunching the trousers to the side. Lubeka felt the blood drain from her body. Calmly, she stepped backwards to the couch to look on at the grotesque spectre in front of her.

"You selfish bastard... You selfish bastard... You selfish bastard." She punched the sofa.

She felt as if her life and soul had been stolen from her. Through all of those years when she stood by him, no matter what. And what about the dreams that young couple once held? He had even taken that from her. She could only think of the past few years as she stared, the bruises still visible, the throbbing pain on her temple: the time when he locked her in the bedroom to stop her going to her graduation; when he lied to her parents about why she no longer visited them; when he followed her into teach one morning, only to accuse her of playing up to the male students in the class; when he hit her with a cup; when she had to lie – always lie – about a fall, a bruise, the spontaneous bouts of tears. The experiences lined up almost to demand that she should feel no pity. She could not give the moment emotion. She could not be the one to cut him down. She sat and waited, and waited. As the chime of the clock sitting above the gas fire chimed three a.m., it was over. She lifted the phone.

For once the police beat the ambulance to the apartment. The brightness of the room got to Lubeka as the body was laid out. The neighbours were already alerted by the sirens, but huddled at the front door of the apartment awaiting approval to get a better view of the body. Lubeka joined them and responded where possible and where sensible to the volley of questions, her mental exhaustion leaving her with a series of stock answers. "What happened? How did it happen? Was it an accident? Why? Why? Why?" One elderly neighbour began to recite a decade of the rosary as if there was a need to bring the gathering dozen or so into the world of the dead. Some responded, some stayed silent, some just smoked and watched.

A few of the immediate neighbours were there to stay up all night with Lubeka, to resort to a tradition of just being there at a perceived time of need. Their role seemed to be to whisper the virtues of Andrzej. Everyone, though, knew the real narrative of that apartment. Lubeka for her part stayed silent, still refusing to shed a tear.

As daylight broke the orange winter sun appeared, the brightness of the snow cleansing the horror of the night. Lubeka, although exhausted, for the first time in years, in that room, felt the newness of the day. Her first movement since the chaos of the early morning was to leave the neighbours in the apartment to go into the fresh snow. She phoned Wójcik to let her know and to ask her to inform the others.

"Mari, Andrzej is dead. He took his own life. That is that. Please let people know. I need to get on. I need to fight this." She paused and the silence lingered: "My mourning for him finished years ago. It's over. Please let Nowak and the college know, I intend to get back as soon as possible."

"Jesus, Kasia, is there anything I can do? Do you want me over? Is your family there?

"No, no, no. We can sort this out here. The police and ambulance people are here. They need to do their work. The family will bury him." The space held for what, for Wójcik, seemed like ages. "Please continue our work. For me that is important. We need to fight if no one else will."

"How did he die?"

"He was hanging from the door… with the lights on." This last thought took the full toll of emotions and Lubeka pulled the phone away, biting her lip and forcing strength. "Please Mari, do what you have to do." Lubeka broke down and fell grappling at the soft purity of the snow.

***

Gabreski had returned to the hotel late. Unsteady on his feet, his time check was obscured by double vision and the haze of the room. He crashed onto the uneven curves of the bed, only to be abruptly awoken by the television alarm. Six thirty a.m. Margaret Thatcher's nights comprised of a bottle of whiskey and four hours sleep. Gabreski could never match this, but on occasion he tried. Sleep was something that he found hard to get used to. The urgency of life carried him through to the mornings and when it came he packed it out, too busy to think of other things. It compensated for failure in other parts of his life.

The shock awakening brought the realization that he was to speak at the symposium that day. In order to do that he would need to get his act in order. He remembered also that he promised Lubeka that he would check through her report. Both exercises would have to be rushed over breakfast. For him, intuition and experience would have to kick in. He knew the topic like no one else and knew that once he got motivated, he would demand of himself a good performance.

He surveyed the hotel room and in a way was a bit disappointed that there had not been a break-in or some form of disruption, having suspected that they were being watched throughout the previous day. "What kind of secret police are you? The least you could do is break-in." He said it aloud as if to speak to some saint of hidden conspiracies. He took his regimented twenty minutes to clean and freshen up. It had become a process which was, at this stage, monotonous, a habit from his days of catching the tram from his apartment by the Royal Africa Museum outside Brussels each morning. He no longer needed a count-down, but retained the minute by minute routine.

The television blared out the topical issue in Poland for politicians that week, the Unmanned Aerial Vehicles (UAV) Act, on the extension of the use of armed drones within the state boundaries for surveillance purposes, and for sale of services internationally. It meant the growth of a new market but also, as Gabreski thought out loud: "Here we go again with the government wanting to keep an eye on everyone." With this, drones could go beyond the battlefield to be used to monitor crowds and suspects. With the Act, private sector organizations, beyond the state, could get access to them for the first time.

"The Unmanned Aerial Vehicles Act is being debated in the Parliament today with the question of private sector lobbying causing some controversy among politicians. If passed, the act will give licences to registered companies to manufacture, sell and use drones within the state borders. The police have voiced concern about the drones falling into the hands of terrorists, but those supporting the liberalization of the use of the equipment argue that it will bring thousands of jobs to Poland. Spokesman for the Confederation of Polish Security Industries, Bolek Janowski, had this to say..."

A balding demure authoritative figure came on the screen, staring awkwardly between an interviewer and direct eye contact with the camera. "This is about creating jobs and keeping Poland as a world leader in this industry. We expect contracts from across the world, civil and military contracts, as soon as this gets through the parliament." The TV anchor seemed to be uninformed about the issue and uncharacteristically held out from making any opinionated judgements. He moved on without further comment.

At breakfast Gabreski was finally able to glance at the Mitrokhin archive report from Lubeka. Rambling at times, the document took up where the Wildstein list had stopped. It selected only those who were perceived to be in positions of authority or those who were engaged in activities that were obviously contravening international human rights. Much of it relied on the research of Father Tadeusz Isakowicz-Zaleski, who, in 2007, published a book which lifted the lid on the role of a hundred and thirty priests, eight bishops and Archbishop Paetz of Poznań, who were all engaged in the communist security network through to the collapse of the system. Even the second most important post in the Catholic Church in Poland, the Archbishop of Warsaw, was not immune from the accusations, with Stanisław Wielgus having to stand down due to his Soviet secret service background.

Isakowicz-Zaleski had been Lubeka's parish priest in Nowa Huta and obviously there had been a deep affection between the priest and his community. It was where she had picked up an interest in the topic, citing him continually as the authority on that era in the city. She mentioned in detail his incarceration and torture, and suggested that a subaltern establishment existed in Kraków in the 1980s, and although it remained marginal, it was nevertheless intact after the 1990 liberation. She cross-referenced the Wildstein and Isakowicz-Zaleski's research through the lens of the Mitrokhin archives to link names to incidents. Images and footage stills were referred to but missing, which could have visibly placed individual secret service agents at specific events. Gabreski could now see why Lubeka had been so animated about the material she had lost, and also why the images were so dangerous that someone had to get rid of them. The details went on and on:

> Ryszard Witek – 1974-1980 SB - Kraków – order code 87467
> Stefan Stefannowski – 1949-1990 UB/SB – Bydgoszcz – order code 89928
> Konrad Szumacher – 1975-1990 SB – Bydgoszcz – order code 83788
> Jozef Suliński – 1961-1990 UB/SB – Bydgoszcz – order code 78390
> Bogumił Różycki – 1970-1990 SB – Bydgoszcz – order code 89309
> Marian Wojtas – 1981-1990 SB – Bygoszcz – order code 87659
> Marek Rasch – 1979-1990 SB – Bydgoszcz – order code 66673
> Perek Jerzy – 1975-1990 SB – Bydgoszczy – order code 73672
> Eugeniusz Grwroński – 1975-1990 SB – Toruń – order code 99773
> Henryk Watroba – 1975-1988 SB KWMO – Toruń – order code 67467

Page after page of names, dates, locations and key operations. They linked times and places with the perpetrators of activities and where the orders were relayed from. It amounted to a catalogue of secret service activities in certain regions and cities at specific periods throughout the 1980s. As he read through the document, he began to appreciate how important it was to be a resident of the city.

The cold helped speed up the walk past the Barbican and around the outside of the Market Square to the college. Gabreski was able to absorb what Lubeka was implying, but felt that the scale of the task was beyond what was feasibly possible for a handful of wishful academics. What was being highlighted was the fact that in post-communist Poland there remained, in certain areas of power and influence, a cabal whose members were dedicated to the protection of their own interests, personal histories and legacy. If it went to the highest levels of the powerful Catholic Church, the most influential civil society organization in the country, where else had the fledgling democracy been compromised. It had collapsed the Ukraine into a bloody civil war. Could this be Poland's fate? As Gabreski trudged along through the park deep in thought, Nowak caught up with him, looking grey and dishelmed.

"What is up, Piotr?"

"Kasia's husband died. They think it was suicide."

"Christ, Piotr. That's terrible."

"Marianna Wójcik phoned to say. He was dead by the time Kasia arrived at the apartment. I asked about helping out with the funeral arrangements, but his family want to do this. It will be on Wednesday morning. I have no idea how she is, but there is a large family network and if we are needed I have left all the details."

"That's quick for the funeral."

"Yes, the coroner's office has already finished with him. They must have needed to clear up the morgue."

"Anyway, I may have to go at any time if called upon to help out. We have got to get on with things. These unfortunate tragedies happen in people's lives. People's minds are very fragile. Life must go on."

In a reflection, Gabreski quipped. "Are they sure it was suicide? It is a very Catholic side of town."

Nowak looked perplexed, knowing of the growing problems related to suicide and its prevalence across the county among young men, irrespective of what side of the town they came from.

"Pretty sure. I presume the family know what they are doing. It is usual enough in this side of the world to bury people quickly if possible. It will not prolong the grief. It is good for Kasia and her family."

As they reached the college, the chatter around the local staff was of the death. There also seemed to be stoicism about not letting the foreign guests know about the incident, hiding it even from the colleagues Lubeka was with the previous evening. The word was that she would be joining the symposium after a family funeral.

Wójcik was darting between Nowa Huta and the city, bringing back updates on how things were going. Gabreski felt on the periphery of a community in shock, trying to keep abreast of all that was going on amidst a cloud of whispers. The delegates milled around the coffee machines, with different personalities from the various regions of Europe competing for noise, exchanging notes about the beauty of the city in the snow and the strength of Polish beer. Group by group they made their way into the auditorium and noisily settled in.

Szolnoky was first up to introduce the day. He avoided the fact that the coordinator of the whole event was no longer present, almost suggesting disapproval of Lubeka's grief. His intention was to sell the university and its legacy, holding aloft the weighty catalogued history of the institution. His stand and demeanour were dictatorial. It was obviously why he had reached the dizzy heights of the university authorities.

The first academic to speak, as the symposium got underway, was a Cold War specialist from Cambridge who had spent time in Moscow through the 1980s and into the 1990s, and had witnessed the transition at first hand. Richard Knox knew his stuff, but tended more towards apologetics than analysis. The chronology of the period was clearly enough stated as a picture of the immensity of the events that occurred were revisited. Forcefully and analytically he presented the evidence of a dislocation process that was still continuing.

In European terms, the transition into the European Union was epochal, breaking decades of oppression across the East and, in certain regions, liberating peoples from centuries of being pawns to various power hungry neighbours. The freedom that arose with the break-up of the Soviet Union and the option to participate in the European Union, notwithstanding the economic imposition, was generally recognized as liberation in its purest sense for the peoples of the East. It was marked first and foremost by the freedom of movement, even if this meant the wholesale rush of the young to the West.

Knox was followed by a Czech academic impassioned about the literary material that was to emerge across the East in the period of transition. Poetry, popular music and the novels of the time were elevated to heroic revolutionary status, reflecting on how this inspired people to challenge the state. The brilliance of Václav Havel, the playwright and poet who made it to the lofty position as the first president of the Czech Republic, was introduced to a new audience. Many were too young to remember the Velvet Revolution of 1989 in Czechoslovakia, but could relate to the inspiration of an imprisoned artist who had challenged the might of the Soviet Union. Gabreski listened intently. Some of the names and the lives he had not heard of in years. It stirred a moment of reminiscence, taking on board the sacrifice that many ordinary and not so ordinary people had made to resist the repression.

"You should never, it's true, calls motherland insistent, in twilight's advancing gloom be the least resistant."

The past seemed alive in the middle of the fora, the sense of achievement palpable. Inspired by this sentiment from Havel, Gabreski was up next.

Gabreski was nervous speaking to large academic audiences, but he understood that this had a disciplining effect. He was obsessive about taking care of the message being delivered, ensuring that every word could be sourced, authenticated. His message was the focus. His introductory habits were, however, the same whether speaking to the rowdy first years at his own department, or the esteemed professors of another university. He removed his coat and placed it behind the chair beside the lectern. He placed a bottle of water at the lectern, never trusting the water that was there, often not drinking his own. It was merely assurance, breaking the seal and leaving it as a control. He needed some measure of management over his own space. He looked around to assess the pitch of the audience, noticing a number of new additions from the previous speakers and a gathering of suited men at the back, in the way that in his undergraduate lectures the football teams would colonize seats so that they could deal with questioning in scrum formation. He removed his watch, placed it beside the speaker, shuffled the pages, felt the silence in the room, took a breath and then launched into his paper.

Gabreski's stance was straightforward, taking in the theory of historical memory, selecting examples from where it had worked and contributed to peace building elsewhere and noting where historical enquiry has had innovations in practice. Ultimately, Gabreski wanted to do justice to those who were subjected to the repression, yet did not feel that justice had been done. Freedom can bring its liberties, but the pain of the past can frustrate the very sense of liberation that others had fought and often died for. Rwanda, Ireland, South Africa and more recently Spain had been providing examples of dealing with past hurt within these respective societies. National identities have been shaped by the needs of the population to resolve hidden historic truths. His thesis was that collective memory can move to heal, without compromising the integrity of various sectors of society. For him, truth commissions could be helpful in overcoming issues related to past injustice.

Gabreski knew that investigating the past was a sensitive issue across the post-Soviet countries, but his belief, the idea that he had brought to this conference, was that societies that have come out of divisive and oppressive environments can only expunge their ghosts when they present truth and hope in the same light. *Lustration*, as it had become known in Poland, had evolved as a political tool for many. In this it was perceived to be a witch-hunt. What was needed was an agreed way forward in the desire for justice through truth. His tone was evangelical.

"Poland, as with the other states, has a duty to those who suffered under the old regime. Irrespective of political sensitivities, if you believe in getting to the fresh air of the future, you need to clear the bad air of the past. People must have faith in where their society is going. To resist this by holding back on past calumnies is to rest from moving forward. There are ugly pages across our history, but we must remember that they are marked with the demands of people past and present. These demands cannot be ignored... To conclude, I will draw on the thoughts of Martin Luther King and his words about what can be demanded through the revelation of history. He commented, that in our present state our society 'owes a debt of justice which it has only begun to pay. If it loses the will to finish or slackens in its determination, history will recall its crimes and the country that would be great will lack the most indispensable element of greatness – justice'."

There was a moment's silence at the conclusion of Gabreski's lecture. He had voiced these opinions before, but had never had this length of collective consideration by an audience. As applause rippled out, the smiles from his colleagues caught his attention. He was satisfied that he had made his case carefully and apparently successfully. Nowak jumped up to congratulate him on the performance and circumvented any questions by pronouncing boldly that: "Due to the consideration of time, history in a way, I am sure that Dr Gabreski would be only too happy to take any questions during lunch. And of course, he will be around for the rest of the symposium. Thank you." The clapping released the worry of challenges. Gabreski was relieved in a way, although he thought it was unusual not to permit that long-standing tradition of public humiliation of academics after lectures. As he moved out, he noticed one of the 'suits' from the back of the hall discretely breaking rank.

One young man had lingered behind at the back as the others had left. He veered towards Gabreski and the small chattering party gathering around him. Gabreski thought it was an approach to dispute his thoughts on truth commissions, or the Ukraine, and braced himself for the questioning. Others surrounded him, enquiring about his travels and trivia around the diversity of the topic. When the man made it through, he leaned close and in a whisper went straight to the point.

"Doctor Gabreski, my name is Stanisław Kaszowski, I would like to speak to you about the files." Gabreski was relieved. This was an unresolved matter in its own right. This man may have answers he could carry to Lubeka.

"Yes, of course. One minute, please." Gabreski politely disengaged with the group around him with a sequence of handshakes and business cards. He moved with Kaszowski to the cleared side of the room. The others were slow to get out, but nevertheless Gabreski felt comfortable enough in the safety of the public environment.

"I work for the Office of State Protection in Warsaw. I am interested in your work and have been trying to look at the possibility of searching out perpetrators of crimes against the nation in the last years of the old regime. My concern is that there are a number of organizations that still act in a shadow form. They are not state, although some seem to work for the state indirectly, despite restrictions on post-Soviet involvement by these people. Some are active in this city, as well as in just about every other city in Eastern Europe."

Gabreski was once again curious about the need for this man to release information to him, a relative outsider. He knew that the old guard still existed, but had largely stepped into the background of private life without too much resistance. Poland was not like Russia.

"I have been chasing down some senior Zomo members who we fear have regrouped to put pressure on the government regarding the protection of their vested interests. I have been working on this largely unsupervised, but think that the problem is bigger than we ever thought. My superiors have instructed me to look into the possibility of a group emerging from within the former secret service and Zomo. The original orders for this went down with the presidential plane in 2010. Coincidence or not, that has unfortunately left me with the poisoned chalice."

"So what do you want to do?" Gabreski was hesitant at engaging in the question of conspiracies, believing that his remit was largely to enlighten government representatives to the value of truth commissions, but not to expose malcontents within or outside government. It was also the first time he had heard of a Zomo concilium as a potential threat to the transition. The Zomo had been a paramilitary group set up by the old regime to investigate and confront popular movements, and to violently suppress dissent. It was a significant wing of the state apparatus right up until the collapse of the system. They were known for beating and torturing protesters, they were uniformed and irregular, as these units tend to be. He wondered what Lubeka knew about this.

"You are on a path which will come directly into conflict with the interests of the old guard. Lustration has been tough enough for them, but someone advocating the wholesale opening of files and the scrutiny of past events. This will cause them big problems. Anyway, listen carefully. Be wary of local police and a number of senior civil servants. I want to get back to you with more detailed information on who the possible threats are, but I need clearance from Warsaw on this. The media need to be secure in their understanding also. You have better links here than we do. Many people do not trust us. Detective Mazur from the Kraków police is with us, he can be trusted. He has been posted to Toruń, but is contactable. Watch out for the private security sector and surveillance. In particular be cautious of Bartek Securities. This is where my enquiries have led me up to this point, but I've hit a brick wall. I would like to cross-reference material at a later date. You might want to do this also. Ok, anyway, we can meet again. Good luck with your work."

Kaszowski's hand swung out as if a deal had been struck. Gabreski responded although unsure of where this would lead.

Gabreski knew the information was sensitive, but struggled to get some appreciation of the scale of the problem. As he watched the civil servant move quickly to catch up with his colleagues, he held his thoughts a moment to reregister and name-check – the Zomo concilium, a Polish registered firm protecting financial assets, Bartek, and Mazur. He felt there were a lot of very committed people, passionate about the idea and ideal of democracy in the country, yet they were being caught with a suspicion that something was taking place behind the scenes of government that was a threat to the very fabric of the democracy.

Gabreski joined the rest of the party as they made their way to the university canteen. He knew that this would do him for the afternoon, deciding to face the fluttering snow again to clear his head. Like a magnet to metal, the draw caught him and he resigned himself to a wine cellar off the Market Square. The isolation of this world sometimes dragged him in, on other occasions it was to hide from the pressures of being in the continual spotlight of intellectual enquiry. His space was precious. This time he justified the resignation with a need to collect his thoughts. He liked the pressures and responsibilities, but hated being forced onto a gruelling treadmill of thinking on his feet during very public academic interrogations. It had given him a complex of aspiring to unobtainable perfection when it came to delivering the information, a bit like the veterinary surgeons drawn to the job for the love of animals, yet spending their working lives putting them down. There could never be a successful completion of work or thoughts.

Staring at the red brick wall of the bar, Gabreski snapped out of the hypnosis of thought to come back into the responsibilities of the day. The whiskey shots rocked his sense of place and were just enough to bring a focus to the context. He sat and watched for a while as the expectant tourists came and went. He monitored the square deco clock behind the bar, increasingly obsessively, as time caught up with him.

***

Gabreski was sufficiently recuperated to rejoin the symposium for its evening reception in the salubrious state rooms of Wawel Castle. The splendour of it, he felt, could really not be missed. It was also a unique opportunity to get privileged access to one of the most iconic representations of Polish architecture. With the snow resting on the roof and grounds, and the chill pacifying the noise of any traffic in the surrounding streets, the atmosphere was perfectly gothic.

The splendour of this medieval sky scraper held the secrets of the Martial Law period when the communist authorities used to meet to discuss how to suppress the movement for democracy. It was where the Nazis would cynically snipe down on the beleaguered local population, or oversee the pogrom against the poor-fated Jewish families. The gas fired heat of the interior was unlike the air conditioned comfort of the university in that it dried and burnt the air, leaving the environment warm, but unnatural. In contrast to the snow, it was an optional, artificial alternative.

The event was typical of institutional receptions, adapted for every gathering of university or government people outside the Islamic world. It comprised of a wine reception profiling regional vintages with a recital of the works of local musicians. In this case the sombre work of Chopin, his *Krakowiak Concert Rondo* seizing its rightful claim to global importance. The sophistication was a fitting elevation of the skills of the organizers of the symposium, a point where the interacting transnational guests could network with the conference's personalities. Gabreski stood to the side, fearing that his afternoon's indulgence would be offensive to anyone who had to endure his overly politicized conversation.

The piano sounded around the building. Gabreski smiled and engaged where the friendliness of the other guests at the reception demanded a response. He was interested and polite, but kept the pain of Lubeka close to mind. He wondered how she was coping. The participants had thinned out somewhat from the earlier attendance at the lectures, but the conversations remained the same as the previous evening, built around the antiquity of the city and the weather.

Out of the corner of his eye, he glimpsed Lubeka and Wójcik. They moved to the back door and stood, studying the body language and deportment of the delegates. Gabreski felt that he should be with his two colleagues, and went to enquire as to their wellbeing. As he moved towards them, they started to work their way towards the exit. Not seeing him, Gabreski suspected that they would not be far from the front door or the nearest cigarette bin, and as he caught up with them he noticed how ashen, gaunt, weak and fragile Lubeka looked. The anxious pride from the other night, the glow of confidence he was greeted with, had been drawn out of her. She seemed broken, the bruise on her temple now yellow, her clothing darker than the red or blue university uniforms that women often wore in that type of environment. Her features were symmetric, her figure statuesque, and with a halo of smoke around her, she looked distinctly Eastern.

Gabreski considered her posture to be remarkably similar to that portrayed in the portrait of Queen Jadwiga which hung on the front wall of the lecture theatre at the college. Pretty in melancholy, both women, separated by over six hundred years, donned similar crucifixes and courted glances in a distant manner. Wójcik, alternatively, was from a different cut. The manicured deportment stood out in total contrast to Lubeka's: less aloof, more intense, inquisitive and unassuming. Wójcik's journalistic career showed through and one could tell she revelled in intrigue. She scanned environments as though reading a page, gathering information out of habit. The jeans and black boots that she seemed never to be without were part of the makeup, her movements reactive, but discrete. She knew how to garner sources, to play the game of information – and to take risks.

Wójcik had been working for ŻYCIA for a number of years, but was continually looking for the story that would give her the confidence to move through to the more mainstream papers and an international remit. That was her goal. She had been inadvertently drawn into the investigation of the pre-1990 period by Lubeka, attracted by enthusiasm and political passion. The risk element excited her and, with a fondness for her academic collaborator, working this story was where she felt she should be. Together they looked like a formidable match.

"Kasia, how are you? I am so sorry to hear about your husband." It was an opening refrain that Gabreski knew would be a way of breaking into the conversation. His silence held in case it was inappropriate. They both paused, their gaze connected and then Lubeka engaged him. She was exhausted by the experience of the previous night, but seemed to fall into the duty of responding in a way that was clinical and respectful at the same time.

"Thanks. We will have the funeral tomorrow morning. You're welcome to come along. He was not feeling well. What can you do? Everyone has been supportive."

Gabreski sensed her disbelief and despondency. "I needed to get away from the family. I am not very good with grief. I don't have the DNA for it. I would rather be here." Wójcik stood listening, waiting to intervene whenever the discussion became too sensitive for Lubeka.

"What are your plans now?" Gabreski had the words out without thinking, then realized that in a state of bereavement there is an obvious heightened sensitivity. He lowered his eyes in deference. He also was aware that saying stupid things to the bereaved was a universal problem. She was professionally responsive.

"No, please. It is okay. I can talk. Thank you. We need to get on. The Warsaw office of the journal wants us to return to the archives again to try and retrieve any lost material. My suspicion is that they will have got there first, but we need to try and log what is there and what is missing. I think the missing material may leave a trace in its absence." It was what Gabreski wanted to hear. He knew this was a tough woman who would not be intimidated by circumstance or context, not even by such crippling events. He pushed the questioning one point further to address a thought that he had had about the timing of Lubeka's husband's suicide. Judging the control that Lubeka had over the conversation, he responded: "Was your apartment okay?" Lubeka's pause in answering gave the impression that she was not willing to dwell on this subject, but needed to get through to an answer. She stepped forward to close the conversation to anyone who may have been in earshot.

"No. The lights were on when I got back to find Andrzej. We never put the lights on, never. Nothing seemed to be missing, but I know one thing, Andrzej was too angry a man to kill himself. That's it. There is nothing we can do." Wójcik nodded and put her hand on Lubeka's shoulder. The observation she made hung in the air. For

Gabreski, it highlighted the stakes that Lubeka was playing with and the risk that the women had been carrying.

"When are you going to Warsaw? May I come along? I have never been to the archives." Gabreski knew he could bring an added international dimension into the enquiry. For Lubeka, a foreigner may provide some protection. He also suspected that there was a danger there that should be shared. This was not only a fight for Lubeka and Wójcik, it had a far wider significance to all who were affected by the Lustration process. Instinct suggested he act on this, their experience also. Before he could move to emphasize his role in the whole affair, Wójcik forced the point.

"We go on Thursday morning. We can cross-reference notes and take a breathing space on the journey. If we are drawing in the *nomenklatura* [the state elite] we must be doing something right. Be prepared for a few cold days in Warsaw."

The snow was moving in on eastern Poland and he knew exactly what to expect. After saying goodbye to the women, he decided to opt out of the ongoing college hospitality, and went on into the snow of the city towards Szewska's jazz clubs. He was intent that he would help out in whatever way he could. He had made his commitment to Lubeka and Wójcik, and felt he needed to escape the imposition of the moment in anticipation of an unexpected trip to Warsaw.

The snow was soft and settling, not having the bitterness of the late winter drifts that come through from Siberia. It reminded him of the time he visited Prague in the heart of winter only to find that he was caught in an unprecedented freeze. It kept him locked in an unwanted cycle of hotel rooms, bars and airport lounges for a week. That round of hapless and fruitless journeys to the airport outside Prague still made him cautious of any flurry of snow. He felt the winter in all its rawness for the first time since he had arrived. Warsaw it was on Thursday.

***

Jazz brought Gabreski into a world he never thought he would occupy. The music was a part of the attraction of the clubs, but it was also the people who seemed to revolve on the fringes of that type of intellectual society. It was a space where the disaffected could congregate, lifting minds through free-form playing that – as with the audience – presented a different aspect to life unrestricted. It was for those who could not be caught by structure, or institutionalized. Its chaos was its freedom and this audience, as with Gabreski, found flight in the movement and intensity.

Many of the jazz musicians who had flocked to Kraków in the early years of the century, found the city's clubs to be liberating for their genre. As a consequence, it rapidly attained a reputation for gathering world class musicians. There was no hierarchy in the city when it came to this industry and being good, or excellent, was what brought people to listen, beyond the mediocrity of the popular market. Jazz, as it evolved in Kraków, was quite punkish, which followed through from Gabreski's earlier musical interests. There was anarchy to this subculture and he felt comfortable there. A visit to any of these clubs was an experience for him each and every time, and they were also usually packed with fellow drinkers. All were cut from the same cloth.

The snow was crisp by the time Gabreski stumbled from the bar, the cold air aggressive enough to take his breath away, as the freshness of the evening shocked him into the need to get back to the hotel quickly. Insulated by the libation and charged by the music, with the swagger that comes with having an enjoyable evening, he navigated his way back to the hotel through the streets of the old town. The snow crunched under foot and with the slight wobble that he brought to it, in his mind, the rhythm continued.

The hotel was warm and inviting, the heat of the halls and rooms providing relief from the shutter of minus ten outside. His room was untouched, unmade and as he left it. Again he wondered, was the Cold War on or not? Collapsing onto the bed, coat and all, with his tablet still intact in the inner pocket and the smell of smoke from his coat polluting the linen, he caught the remote of the television and was startled to see Kaszowski's picture on the screen. He sat up.

"The body of a policeman has been found in the Wisła River near to the Ojca Bernatka footbridge. He was dressed in civilian clothes and was last seen at an event in the old city before leaving to walk back to his accommodation. His death is being investigated and a crime has not been ruled out at this stage. The police would like any witnesses to come forward."

As his body floated under the bridge, crowds of young Krakóweans had been gathering for their nightly celebration of the best of the new city, to promenade across the discoesque façade of the snow covered structure, reading messages of hope lovingly inscribed onto the thousands of locks flickering on the grills. Some simply read 'freedom'. The city of old briefly but violently interrupted the vibrancy of the city of the young. Past and future collided.

19th November

Lubeka had returned to her apartment with Wójcik. She knew that she would have to work on the delicate choreography and ritual hum of a Catholic funeral. When they had arrived earlier, the family had already let in Father Chorabik, whom they had known for years. Her husband's immediate family had called in briefly to agree the order of ceremony and to ensure that the circumstances of his death were not talked about at all. This was Catholic Poland. The stigma of a suicide in a local family still blighted many in the community. A lot of families were affected. The painful nature of the death was unmentionable and the circumstances were an uncomfortable reminder of the depressed world that many people from the tenements were trying to cope with on a daily basis. The priest's approach was a business-like exchange. Lubeka hoped that this would be the way of things throughout the process.

"There will be no flags, popular songs, impromptu speeches or unorthodox prayers. The family will remain in the front seats until the Mass is complete and the readings will reflect the dignity of the sacraments. Is that understood, Kasia?"

Lubeka could see the reasons behind the severity of the priest's message. She nodded. Exhaustion prompted her not to challenge the orthodoxy of the arrangements. She just wanted the whole thing over, finished. She was compelled to go to back to work prior to the funeral to get on with her life as soon as possible. It would take her mind away, but she knew this could be a last duty to her past. The remaining hours were a matter of waiting, and waiting, the chain smoking acting as an alternative timing mechanism to clock watching. Her mother had arrived and stayed briefly to give her a maternal hug, sitting and patiently listening to the stipulations being directed towards a stunned daughter. Wójcik responded when the window allowed, out of politeness, filling the awkward spaces that Lubeka left unfilled. While Lubeka's family huddle slipped out after the business of the Mass and burial were completed, Father Chorabik sat on and occasionally interrupted the bouts of silence with an exchange of coffee and lighters. Wójcik went to the kitchen to tidy up for the morning. Sitting on the sofa with Lubeka, Chorabik held her right hand and absorbed her emotions. "Are you going to stay in Nowa Huta, Kasia?"

"I don't know. I have never lived anywhere else. This has been my world for so long. I would find it difficult." She held the sentence, unable to finish. Her eyes filled up with tears. For one part of her, this was the end of her childhood and youth. It was a breaking point in life.

"You have a good career in the city. Would that not bring you closer to the university? Sometimes we need to renew our lives, make a move." The smile from the priest was genuine, and momentarily relieved the emotional charge. For him, it was not encouragement to leave what had been her home, it was a suggestion that she was in a position to do something radically different now. He knew of her circumstances, everyone knew of her circumstances. It was just that the cloak of silence over domestic violence, alcoholism and suicide, was resolute within communities that had been terrorized by all three. Moving provided one answer, migration of sorts, but it would be a hard decision for her to make. The priest broke the thought.

"Kasia, did you know that Andrzej's index finger on his right hand was broken. The police mentioned it to me."

"No."

"It seemed to have been bent back, possibly after he died."

"How could that have happened?" Lubeka struggled to get the energy to think this strange comment through.

"They don't know. It was as if it was bent back and then straightened again. Strange. It could have happened when he was cut down. That seems to be the police conclusion. I just thought you should know."

"Thanks. They never said." The priest changed the topic again, pointing towards the window.

"This place works well if everything is as it should be. It is for families who are working, people with kids in the school, families that have got their act together. Money. If you do not have enough, it can become a prison. It can be very lonely."

"There is more to life, Kasia, than this place." Wójcik interrupted.

"I know, I know."

Lubeka sat with her coffee mug with 'hers' emblazoned across the front, a legacy of Andrzej's trips to London. She caught her memories at every glance around the room. She had promised Andrzej she would clean the cup circles from the arms of the brown leather sofa; the cobwebs at the corner of the room needed dusting; the curtains needed to be ironed; that alarm clock. Intermittently she fixated on paying the funeral director what he was owed. As time moved, the dawn caught up with the wake. The priest discretely departed when he saw the two women drifting in and out of sleep. His place was elsewhere at this point. The snow clouds had finally lifted to illuminate the morning with a crystal clear sky on a carpet of pure new white snow.

The mourners started to gather after eight a.m. at the tenement, frozen puffs of breath hanging like a mist over the black-coated congregation. Lubeka and Wójcik struggled to change into the conventional black skirts and neck-scarfs of those in mourning, while acknowledging the rumbling presence of the others in the living room and out through to the landing. The silence was the most striking thing for both of them. No one spoke in the apartment or as they started to make the short journey to the church. They could hear the clatter of feet, the odd whisper and the shuffle of coats gathering in for the procession.

***

Standing discretely to the back of a group of mourners, Nowak and Gabreski waited at the front door of the church. They maintained their place in line, as attention from all was directed towards the demure, statuesque Lubeka. As she made it to the front door, the hearse arrived with the coffin, crunching up the snow as it pulled up. Lubeka took her place with the small gathering outside the church while the undertakers, Andrzej's brothers and former work colleagues carried the heavy wooden coffin, with a solid crucifix on the top, into the farewell room at the side of the church, the 'sala pożegnań'.

Lubeka knew what she had to do. She had been to many funerals before in this church. It was her turn to be the focus for the community and the roles were well defined by tradition and experience. Everyone awaits their turn, dreading the day, but knowing that it will be them someday, on one side of the soil or the other. In a dream-like daze she asked the undertakers to remove the lid. The others left the room as she stared at the corpse. Numbed by the whole experience she lingered, gazed and caressed Andrzej's forehead. "Why did you do it? Why did you do it?" His face was grey, his eyes sunken, but no answer came back to her in the same way as she received no answers to that same question in life. The door knocked. She knew it was time for her to give him up, the ghost offered no answers, the circumstances again bringing up the thought that with him bringing her to this moment, he was continuing the torment. Her mind could not help taking her back to the boy and girl who stood in that very church professing vows. Where did those two people go?

As she opened the door the undertakers moved quickly into the room, the coffin lid closed in seconds, abruptly, and his body was carried through to the main marbled aisle of the church for Mass. The sombre tones of Chopin's *Marche Funèbre* sounded the requiem, the rituals of the Mass bringing the all too disturbing circumstances into the realm of the surreal. Incense filled the church.

The brightness of the morning illuminated the stained glass through the greens and blues of the lens, as the mourners emerged from the church. Lubeka again had to take the focus away from the congregation, taking brief condolences from a tight-knit community shocked at yet another young man from their world committing suicide. It was as if the whole of the community came out to walk behind the coffin, an event which was obviously intended to be an act of solidarity. It drained Lubeka in its lack of intimacy at this point of life and death.

Father Chorabik led the invocation at the graveside. The snow fluttered again and the bite of the wind carried his hymn in waves: "Wieczne odpoczywanie racz Mu dać, Panie" ["Eternal rest grant unto Him, O Lord"], to be met with the hypnotic response from the mourners: "A światłość wiekuista niechaj Mu świeci" ["And let the perpetual light shine upon Him."]

At the conclusion of the prayers, Chorabik solemnly anointed the coffin with holy water, splashing a torrent of cold water across the crucifix. In a final act of ceremony, soil was thrown onto the coffin as it was lowered into the ground, the thud shocking the peacefulness of the moment: "Prochem jesteś i w proch się obrócisz, ale Pan Cię wskrzesi w dniu ostatecznym. Żyj w pokoju" ["Dust you are and to dust you shall return, but the Lord will raise you on the last day. Live in peace."] Led by Chorabik, the mourners whispered the funeral hymn 'Witaj Królowo Nieba' as soil and gravel were shovelled into the open grave. Lubeka watched at the head of the grave, stoic in going through this final act of her marriage. Her duty was complete.

20th November

The morning maintained its chill, the weight of the grey clouds sitting just above the city. Snow free, the train station at the Galeria in Kraków was bearing the lights of a winter schedule. "How are you feeling, Kasia?" Gabreski whispered as he hugged Lubeka. "Shit." "It will take time to think it through. You have good people around you." Gabreski alluded to the extensive family network and the friends, impressed by the community that surrounded Lubeka in the previous days. "It's done, Łuka. I need to get out of it. That was my life, and it was difficult. I need to work myself away from it, or die trying."

Wójcik moved to greet Gabreski, showing a lighter side that lifted both her travelling companions. "I have brought some good old-fashioned spicy bagels for the journey. It may be a bit of a trip until we get to Warsaw central. Are we all okay for taking a few days to sort this thing out?"

Gabreski was first to confirm. "I have told Piotr and my own department at the uni in London, so we can have support while we move if we need it. The symposium will close itself. Piotr is good with that. We have done our best there given the circumstances, and anyway, this is infinitely more important. We need to keep up the pressure."

The EIC3108 at 7.45 a.m. from Kraków to Warsaw was a bit more comfortable than the other trains. It usually carried enthusiastic tourists or lacklustre business commuters. Few of the railway stock across Poland had been reconditioned, but in matt grey and emerald green even the newer stock looked as if it had been running since the post-war reconstruction of the rail networks. While losing out on high-technology, the solid frame and aluminium sliver lines of the train fitted perfectly within the plastered façade of Kraków's neo-renaissance central station. The carriages were warm, maintaining a musty smell, carrying the dust of age and the history of smokers gone by. In the sharp cold of the morning, the blown heat of the carriage was a comfort of sorts. All elbows and fumbling, Gabreski, Lubeka and Wójcik shed layers of coats and fleeces to settle into the trip.

"How was the hotel, Łuka? Was it ready for the snow?" Wójcik was aware of the fact that with the weather being so changeable he should have felt the pinch of the cold in the hotel.

"It was fine. They seemed to have the place well insulated for any eventuality. It was solid. I was hoping the staff might have put on Christmas refreshments to get the season started, but I suppose we will all have to wait another few days for the festivities to begin."

"Not like in London then."

"Well. We begin Christmas in October these days. I do not see why they just don't have a year round festival. It would save the shops taking the decorations down, and keep the children happy."

As the three of them settled in to the soft talk, the train glided gently out of the station. The carriage rocked slightly as speed picked up and the cluster of passengers regained their slumber. Lubeka stared out of the window and was the first to break the developing comfort zone. Her mind was obviously distracted as she struggled to come to terms with the past few days. The other two sensed the anxiety and were cautious only to enter into dialogue when she was ready.

"Who killed Kaszowski, the policeman?" The sharpness of the question was a wakeup call for the other two.

"Did you know him, Kasia?" Gabreski returned.

"We interviewed him in Warsaw in the early stages of the research. He gave us some direction, but you could see he was under pressure to stay away from certain people and topics. He gave us too much for his own good." Lubeka had a link of sorts to the dead policeman. She was determined to make a connection to her work.

"Why did he end up approaching us?" Gabreski felt that they were becoming a cog in a bigger chain, realizing as he reflected on the fact that he may have been the last one to see Kaszowski alive.

Keen to get into the discussion, Wójcik leaned forward and pointed to the suburbs of Kraków. "He came to this place to give us direction. There was no need to put his life at risk unless he knew we could have an influence on the *nomenklatura*. He had something that we need. Maybe he was too close to offering it up." Gabreski intervened.

"Do you know he approached me at the end of my lecture? He said a few things and seemed willing to put himself at risk to meet me. I still don't see why we seem to be the focus of attention. Someone is trying to tell us something." The two women sat up in anticipation as their new colleague appeared to be shedding light on the complex.

"In hindsight, I think that he, and whoever his colleagues are, have broken ranks to try and drip feed information into the public domain. We seem to be a target, for whatever reason. I think it was a dangerous move for him, and I would think his accomplices also."

"Dangerous for us to be involved with!"

Lubeka carried her stare from the window. "We know it is dangerous, we have been living with it for years, Łuka." Wójcik shuffled on her seat and directed a glace quickly between Lubeka and Gabreski.

Gabreski continued: "Kaszowski mentioned a few things which he insisted in passing on. He seemed to feel that certain companies and individuals were unhappy about the type of society that has evolved in the country. I caught three words from our conversation - Zomo, Bartek, and Mazur. Kaszowski's urgency was that the leadership of the first could still be active, the second is a security firm of some sort and the third is a detective who can help. We need to get to him."

"Lucky we are getting out the pressure pot of Kraków. There will be more room to manoeuvre in Warsaw." Wójcik was less than reassuring.

"Kaszowski is dead. I have buried Andrzej. What if he was killed also? What if he was there instead of me in that apartment? Who commits suicide with the front door left open? He never tried it before, why should he want to now?" The other two looked stunned, but held to the logic of the thought.

Silence awaited Lubeka as her recall linked the dialogue. "Bartek is one of the most successful security industries in the Eastern states. It took in former military commissioners when it began in the 1990s. Its success is based on its knowledge and reach into the various administrations. It also makes millions from basic security, private sector... all barely regulated and very lucrative."

Wójcik chipped in, looking at Gabreski and acting to back up Lubeka's line of investigation. "Even as early as the break-up of the old regime, thousands of small and medium sized companies were established to absorb the elite into the business sector, to carve up whatever market benefits that were to filter through from the West. New Poland resembled old Poland except that uniforms were exchanged for power suits and rifles for Filofaxes. And where do ex-military people usually end up? Drunk, in security firms or finance."

In sequence, Lubeka responded, speaking at Gabreski: "Exposures come occasionally – such as with the FOZZ, Orlen and PZU scandals. These were military intelligence units from communist times simply searching out state funds for their own enterprise. Or with BIG, the Bank of Economic Initiatives, badly organized and obviously set up to siphon off public funds. They learnt their lessons with these early attempts to walk into business. The later efforts were more sophisticated and, we think, embedded within the very fabric of the system. They are still there." Lubeka gathered up Wójcik's interest to reinforce the point. Gabreski looked out of the window to view the snow driving in sheets diagonally across the laden fields. The information was intriguing, but the question remained in his head: "What do we do with it?"

The vast stretches of farmland in the middle of Poland looked bleak and battered in the depths of winter. The heat of the carriage was unnatural and stuffy, but gave the perfect vantage point to see the fields, broken by the occasional hedgerow or desolate cottage. The shutter and clutter of the tracks brought the drama of the conversation to a melodious pause. Lubeka discretely went through her satchel for a packet of cigarettes, leaving the carriage to find a place to smoke and think.

Within seconds, Lubeka rejoined her colleagues, who were both patiently watching the countryside being sprayed with a blizzard of white snow. A young man appeared at the room door to enquire about a seat. His demeanour was unassuming, his cropped hair not out of place in the teams of office workers who commute between the cities each morning. Without waiting for an answer he was seated, and in accepting the fate of unwanted company, the three fell silent. Lubeka was agitated and fidgeted for the remainder of the journey, her glancing expressions telling of her discomfort at the man's presence. The other two hypnotized themselves by staring out the window at the dazzle of whiteness, the rattle of the train and the dry heat being blown into the carriage. It helped them to drift between a light sleep and an anti-social fixation with the winter. The bagels provided a distraction, handed around as with a school outing silenced by the one who misbehaved.

Gabreski knew that there was danger in the search for the answers that the women were looking for. He felt compelled in part by a new profound loyalty to carry through with the journey started by the women. As for the women, as with millions of ordinary citizens of the East, they were already implicated in a political maelstrom not of their making. All they were doing was joining the dots and hoping for a positive outcome. It was their instinct to search for justice. It was bred into them. Consequences were not a part of the calculation.

The train arrived prompt at ten forty-five a.m. and cluttered its way into the industrial labyrinth of the Soviet monolith of Warsaw's Central Station. On packing up, Lubeka became obstructive to the additional passenger, loudly proclaiming, "excuse me, sir" and "do you mind" to the man who had remained frozen to his seat. The group shuffled by. Her point was made very bluntly, with everyone's assumptions exorcised quite forcefully. The man did not flinch, but stared at her intensely. The implication was that the two Polands had just come face to face, and neither liked the other.

As they got down from the carriage, Lubeka uttered to the others. "He spotted me and followed me back in." Gabreski did not answer back, finding the aggression of the act somewhat disconcerting. Wójcik was more philosophical. "Maybe he fancied you, Kasia." Lubeka proceeded to wrap her black woollen scarf tightly around the collar of her long black padded coat.

***

Warsaw had become the beating heart of the new business-focused Poland with its packed concrete boulevards merging with unnamed concrete apartments, blockhouse estates, glass fronted shops and offices. Its post-war reconstruction was built out of desperation and need rather than architectural vanity. The weather always seemed more severe in the capital than it did in Kraków, or indeed elsewhere, the roads marked by lines of slush, coloured grey from the trams, the oil and the congested traffic.

It was still early enough to search around the city for accommodation. At this time of year the choice of hotels was not going to be difficult. Tourists tended to go to the south of the country, leaving Warsaw to the business traffic. With the end of the summer festivals and the inclement weather through autumn, tourists did not come through to the northern cities. If anything, it was Kraków that had won the struggle for the tourist trade hands down. Warsaw faltered in its attractions in competition with the other cities, drawing in the politicos and history buffs. For those coming to the city more recently, it meant that hotel rooms were freely available, particularly in winter.

"Should we stay with my ŻYCIA colleague, Beata, or break the trail by cold-calling a hotel?" Wójcik assumed that the other two would much prefer to keep moving where possible, even though there was an open invite by her journalistic colleague that they could hole up in her apartment whenever necessary.

"Let's book into a hotel, it will be a bit more discrete. Plus, it is our choice of base. I am sure Beata will understand. If they are arrogant enough to send someone to sit beside us on the train, they are bound to be watching the ŻYCIA people in Warsaw as well." Lubeka felt the need to justify her rudeness on the train.

"I also think we should divert our journey to find somewhere... Does anyone know a hotel close?" Gabreski was unfamiliar with the city and felt that the women would be best placed to decide where they could hide for a few days.

"Zofia. The hotel. It has apartments. It's good. It is like a hotel without the flow of strangers. I stayed there before and it is walking distance from the Institute of National Remembrance." Reinforcing the recommendation, Lubeka commented: "It is as discrete and as safe as it gets in the city." Lubeka had been coming back and forward to the city for years for research and academic work, and on occasion had secured the expenses to get to know the hotels around the centre of the city. She knew where they would be safe.

"Okay, let's get a taxi." Gabreski broke from the women to lead a charge to the taxi rank at the front of the building.

Central Station was cluttered and alive with the pulse of commuters, its dystopia marked by movement and dislocation, bags and disorientation. Fighting through the constant flow of people, the smell of winter mixed with the stench of diesel, giving an industrial harshness to the corridors and shops that occupied the underground walkways. On being released to the exit, a couple of taxis sat waiting for custom, hoping for tourists who would provide some added entertainment for the day. Even though it was only a few kilometers away, behind the imposing façade of the Palace of Culture and

Science, the thought of trudging through the slush to get to the hotel confirmed the decision to opt for the laziest means around to get to their location.

The taxi struggled to get through the traffic to the impressive Aleje Jerozolimskie Boulevard which cut through the centre of the city. The two minute journey seemed to last an hour as the old BMW shunted and halted, the driver pointing and directing other drivers as he crunched through the slush and the traffic. Turning into Chmielna it was smoother to drive through, with the hotel visible from the end of the street. The three sat patiently, bags on laps and pensive not to open up a conversation. The taxi pulled up. Lubeka, on opening the door, stepped out and threw a question at her colleagues.

"Marianna, do we need to contact Beata to let her know where we are and when to meet?"

As they made their way out of the car into the sheltered frontage of the hotel, Wójcik was tapping away on her phone, oblivious that Lubeka had been speaking.

"Beata, we are here, when can we meet?" Wójcik's voice was distinct, loud, the question direct. Wójcik had developed the irritating habit of staring through people while talking on the phone, something that Lubeka in particular found frustrating. "If that is Beata, tell her to go straight to the Institute. We can get there in forty minutes." Lubeka's keenness to get on with the job was a bit unsettling to Gabreski. He would have liked to settle in. "We are here to get a job done. The sooner we get to the files, the better."

"How will we do the rooms?" Another conversation opened up with Gabreski wanting to get the bags left off and arrange the paperwork.

"It doesn't matter."

“We get two adjoining rooms then?” Gabreski, walking towards the reception desk, went about the administrative task as if going to a supermarket till.

Wójcik shouted her goodbyes down the phone to Beata, the loose ends of the various comments being brought together. She interjected with: “Yes, two rooms.” The reception was an immediate and warm comfort zone and, for a brief moment, the new residents looked about them surprised at the salubriousness of the choice of hotel.

“Two rooms, please, together if possible.” Gabreski used English to impress upon the receptionist that they were there for business. He had a departmental account and card which could be used in emergencies and for extra-ordinary circumstances. It was useful when changing, or being forced to change, travel plans. In Egypt, it was helpful to alter flights and move when the towns he was visiting were becoming too risky for Europeans to do business in. When the paperwork was completed for the rooms, they went to drop their bags into the adjoining respective suites, individually disengaged.

Gabreski searched out the minibar, fiddling to pour miniatures of whiskey into a beer glass, before being interrupted by Lubeka and Wójcik. Both were obviously impatient to get to the Institute, knocking quickly but lightly on the door while trying to whisper his name through the wood at the same time. Gabreski sipped on the glass quickly, embarrassed, before noisily ordering his notes and loading what he needed into a satchel. Against his demons, he killed off the temptation to indulge more in the mid-morning drink, returning the unwashed glass to the fridge.

Away from the heat and luxury of the rooms, the process of gearing up for a walk in the snow brought out a sense of steeliness in them all. The Institute was a short journey from the hotel, down Prosta and on to Wołoska. The snow in Kraków seemed fluffier and whiter than in the north, but it was easier to get around in Warsaw with the footfall of others leaving grey mushy tracks down the paths. The grip gave even the most careful walker traction. Layer on layer, scarf on coat, the ritual of snow proofing distracted the three for the moment, the women having the added complication of 'snow fashion' to attend too.

"Is that Mercedes with us?" Wójcik looked causally out to the snow and assumed that the others had spotted the black car sitting across the road adjacent to the entrance of the hotel.

"It looks like it. It didn't take them much time to locate us." Lubeka was not as candid in her observations, glancing across the road. The car remained with its engine gently running, the two silhouettes in the front barely visible behind the darkened glass.

"Just keep walking. They know where we are going. They are just making sure that they know we are here." Gabreski was pensive as the three trudged quickly along the path. The car glided slowly twenty meters and pulled up, far enough away for them not to get a glimpse of the occupants, leapfrogging periodically, but ensuring a menacing visibility. Ignoring the obvious sense of threat, Lubeka again brought minds back.

"Ignore them. We have only two days here. We need to work through them. We need to get to the issues as efficiently as possible. May I suggest that we get as locked in as possible to get to the material in the Institute? It may be an idea to keep your phones on and stay alert to any information that could be transferred as soon as we locate it. Record everything. Would it be okay to bank information with your collegues in London, Łuka? We can transfer it automatically, I think."

"Sure, Kasia. Any sensitive information we need to transmit we can do it. Just image or video, it can go straight there." Gabreski responded.

"Should we divide up the tasks to make it more manageable?" Lubeka panted as she struggled to deal with the inhaled freeze, the conversation and the briskness of the walk. She had obviously thought the process through. "We need to get to the Muscovite files first. Any Mitrokhin material that has been left unanalyzed – or not stolen. This should give us names at least. Most of the key figures in the Zomo would have moved back and forward to Moscow. They were probably trained there. The secret service may also have planned the corporate transition there. Activities should have been documented at some point. New material coming through from Moscow is a priority. They should have reached the older material at this point. They've been trawling and changing the Wildstein files for years now. Most of the older stuff may not even be authentic. Beyond that, let's look for the command codes and links. Pictures. I forgot the damn pictures. These should give us the villains and heroes."

The process seemed straight forward enough to Gabreski, only too pleased that Lubeka was taking a lead.

"It will be great to have Beata to help. She has years of experience with these files and helped with the opening of the Institute itself." Wójcik then went about the tricky task of navigating through the slush while texting to let Beata Krolas know they were nearing the door of the Institute. The Mercedes moved again and on the other side of the road. The three tried to ignore its presence, the dark windows obscuring the shadows inside. The message was clear and all knew it. It was the prelude to a confrontation of some kind.

The Institute was an impressive bunker-like modern building sitting in the centre of Warsaw. Its concrete and glass design was different from the surrounding buildings in that it showed architectural flare and a utilitarian grid-like shape. It was intended to be bureaucratic and nationally important at the same time. Instytut Pamięci Narodowej, the IPN, had been able to gather some of the most sensitive documentation in Poland since the war with Germany began in September 1939, but was also a repository for millions of documents that had been amassed by the communist regime until 1990. It was, in a way, the paper heart of Poland, the place where oppression and suppression had been catalogued and filed away. Although only opened in July 2000, the wealth of the organization lay in the respect that the population held for the very idea of a library for national remembrance. The biggest fear which the directors of the institute had was theft, infiltration by the *nomenklatura* – the TW, former elites from the SB and Zomo – who were intent in altering history or eradicating their presence from history. In this, all the others knew that there was a race on to get to the truth before it was erased or warped into something totally different.

Waiting on the steps of the archive was Krolas. A stalwart of radical journalism in Warsaw, looking older than her fifty years, with a flow of grey hair and a dress sense locked into the 1980s. She had been there through the thick and thin of the transition and delighted in the demise of an old regime which she, as with most Poles, felt was the last vestige of the hatred of the war period.

"I have secured a room where we can work. Hello. We have two days if we can take it, to process the new material that has arrived. We are very close. This is great... Look, they are everywhere." Krolas seemed enthused at the thought of being under surveillance. The energy was brave and infectious. She hugged her three accomplices, accepting Gabreski without question or discomfort, simply because he was with her two colleagues.

Krolas pointed to another Mercedes located beyond the Institute. She had already spotted the black one following the others. This seemed to be an adrenaline kick for her, a reminder of earlier times and the thrill of working in confrontation to the system.

"Come in. Get out of the cold. We have a lot to do." Immediately, with her confidence, there was an assurance that this was someone who could face various threats without too much difficulty. It was empowering. Like a tour guide, Krolas led the team through the various checks and stairwells and into a maze of file blocks and cabinets. The halogen lights on the roof picked up the dust from aging documents, and for all there, as they went further into the archives, there was a realization that this bunker-like environment was as protected and as precious as it was going to get. With the authorization of the president of the Institute himself, Krolas acted as if the rooms were her own private domain. If checked by staff she waved the authorization around like a winning lottery ticket. Doors continued to open.

"Here we are." The party halted abruptly at a glass-walled room with a secure code locking system on it. It was bedecked with newly fitted wooden furniture, unlike the other more utilitarian stacks that they had passed on the way. The locks were obviously not as much to keep people out, but to keep the material in after the incident with the 'walking' Wildstein files.

"Excellent, Beata. This is exactly what we need – some time and security. A bit of space for once." Gabreski had kept up with Krolas and was the first to get to the designated room. The background chatter of Wójcik and Lubeka bounced around the hallway. Krolas hammered a code into the door-panel and pushed, letting the lingering duo in last.

"Okay, we have Wi-Fi and access to most of the documents. They must be addressed at the cabinet where they are located. Larger files need to be signed out if they are to be moved from their location. Only I can do that, and we should not take more than one file block at a time to the room. A lot of this is new."

Gabreski's research instinct was alerted to the restrictions of this system, but there was obviously a security precedent. "Let's get to the Moscow files first and then select the most important. With the other material, take notes on the move and, where possible, photo or video material that would be of use. Keep the live feed mode on your phones so that we can interact as we go."

Lubeka added: "Also, we are looking for codes and photos... cross-reference... and may I suggest restricting the trawl to a number of years at the end of the communist regime, 1985 to 1990, maybe." Lubeka knew where the names would be catalogued chronologically. Not for the first time iPhones appeared as the new weapon against an imposing adversary.

"'Eighty-five to ninety it is. Is that what you were thinking, Beata?" Gabreski looked for approval for the plan. He could see Lubeka's logic in that the controllers of the late communist period would also be the architects of the new securocratic system after the regime. This period was where it happened and any mistakes that they made would surely have come through at that point.

"It sounds right to me. We need to get to the most active and most senior, which will have a tendency to be doctored or misplaced. Do not take order for granted in the files." She paused. "Let's get to work." Krolas's enthusiasm was as fired up as Lubeka's, the energy palpable as the four broke up into rolling back steel doors and searching files.

All four knew that the scale of the task was haphazard, but they needed to relocate a few hooks by which they could hang the system. The SB alone had files on ninety-eight thousand people working for the state in a security and spying capacity in 1988. That also meant there was a similar number of official traces. This was vast numbers of people in the pay of a security fixated bureaucratic system. It was no wonder that after the regime collapsed it was the work that the old guard retired to for a livelihood.

The government, and to an extent the archival skills of a few at the Institute, had kept the documents long enough for conspiracy theorists, with some justification, to accuse the post-1990 administration of hiding the truth of the situation and the truth of where the police state had dissolved into. It was also enough time for the former agents to replace files, destroy or change details to distort the truth of the extent of former police involvement in the evolution of the new state. Changing names, dates, events and photos was as destructive as losing files altogether. Unfortunately, the vetting office of the Institute was somewhat late in its response to the infiltration by the private security firms.

Only in March 2007 did the office start looking at those who should be banned from public office or working in sensitive state security related posts. It was later than had been hoped and many suspected that it was too late to curtail the activities of the old guard in protecting their own histories or rewriting their own personal involvement in the regime. In 2012, one journalist, whose name the state released as 'Robert W.', was charged with removing photographs and a document on the secret police during the communist era. The practice had become commonplace.

Files were catalogued in yearly rows, the columns showing a spread of regions and the extent of state activity. Some material, doctored or not, had been put online to make it as widely available as possible, but new material flowing through – particularly material from outside the state that the Institute had secured from other post-Soviet governments – was acutely sensitive. It was in a process of being vetted, but remained both secretive and open to adaptation, or theft. The race was on to locate and distribute the original material, list what was possible to list and build the case. This was what Krolas was keen to get to first. Her knowledge of the involvement of the foreign security services in Poland was second to none and her interest only increased when evidence was gathering of continued links between the elder gentlemen of the old services across the Soviet bloc after its collapse. Her role as a journalist offered her some protection, but she was ecstatic that her often lonely world of archival research had been interrupted by such a glamorous delegation from Kraków.

"Check for the Russian and Bulgarian references first, anything that looks on date and newly stocked." She whispered loudly across the stacks. At times the four seemed frantic in their search. On occasion, a whisper came out to acknowledge a find, some of the material was still apparently there. It was a matter of targeting what could lead to the core.

> 'Wrocław 01.05.87. File 783930987. Illegal gatherings in university campus. Zomo intervention, 11 arrested and interrogated. Photographs of main protagonists. SB involvement. Command, disperse and round up leadership.'
> 'Wrocław 03.05.87. File 78938900. Parade in support of Solidarity. Zomo intervention. Monitored and sought homes

of organisers. Church clerical involvement. Photographs. Testaments and related statements. Zomo statements. SB statements.’

And so it went on; notetaking and scanning, numbering and translating. Krolas was more discerning, her technique more candid with her use of an old digital camera and a notebook. Three hours into the trawl and scan exercise, Wójcik could not help but break the silence with an excited yelp “Bartek, 1988, Kraków”. The alert stopped the search to listen to the intervention. “I have a catalogued Russian file here. It is short and looks as if it was altered years ago, but it is hitting all the right notes, what I remember from the old files. I am finding it hard to get through some of the Russian but it gives... yes, dates and times, политической, допросить, извлекать информацию устранить угрозу, ‘political, interrogate, extract information, eliminate threat’. I need to video file this one. It has locations, personnel, links and some grainy photos from the eighties.”

Locating this file brought some of the material Lubeka had lost into context. She realised immediately the importance of the series of photos. “These are documents and photographic evidence that profile the main agents of Soviet security at that point. Get this into the Cloud before they get us into the ground.” The trawl moved onwards without drawing too much more in evidence. Gabreski’s phone hovered over the files. Krolas occasionally leaned over his shoulder to snap choice pages. Some photos of rioting across various cities and details that were largely in Russian. File after file, some of it could be transferred, but the volume of the material was overwhelming for the four researchers. On occasion, one piece of information could be cross-referenced with another piece. They drew from a sparse knowledge of the language, needing Krolas to return with words that the others struggled with.

The Russian files were more scrupulous and detailed than the standard Polish files, which was unusual given that the Służba Bezpieczeństwa, the SB, in particular, were reputed to be meticulous in their documentation techniques. As with so many security organizations, the operatives were also afraid of the system and wanted to document as much as possible in case something came back to bite them. They never thought their world would collapse.

Gabreski knew that the clear out of files during the 1990s was formidable, but the sophistication and scale of the alternations were way beyond what he thought could have been possible. Hundreds of thousands of Polish files altered or disappeared in order to hide the identities of those engaged in the activities of the regime. Where the Russian material differed, was in the manner in which the data seemed to be almost complete. It included the names of the officers involved in certain actions, the link codes that could identify the people to the actions, and what they were up to on specified dates. It was all there. Even with his basic understanding of Russian and a reliance on the others to fill the gaps, he knew there was a vast amount of information here that could lead through to identify agents of the regime and the foreign interlocutors of the day.

The pictures in themselves told a tale of suspicion and fear. The greying faces were soulless and distant. The ages of the victims of interrogation was perhaps the most shocking aspect of the files. They all seemed to be very young, as if this was an older world deliberately targeting the spirit of the young at the time. Their faces represented the ghosts of a generation that had for decades hoped for freedom. Other pictures showed the spying that went on against the ordinary people of the country, jazz musicians and comedians, writers and students. He knew they were all favourite targets for surveillance, but these images showed more than that the scale of it was limitless: shopkeepers, artists, clergy, along with the trade unionists – in the great workers' republic – being singled out for particular attention.

Gabreski took pride in the fact that he recognized some of the academics whose names were mentioned as being under surveillance. The years fitted the fashion and the demeanour of those in the photos, the distanced details of their lives were of a people who were trying to etch hope out of authoritarianism.

More alarmingly, the files went into the detail of the interrogations, the personnel involved, the unfortunate individuals who were subjected to psychological and often physical torture, and the outcomes. One file stood out for Gabreski. It covered June 1988 in Kraków. The SB had brought in five students for questioning. They had all been at a protest against the Zomo and had links to the various student organizations. Each student was interrogated separately, held without food or water for two days and in cells of white light. By the end of the process, the SB had extracted details about their families, colleagues and staff at the university; personal details, trivia, political aspirations, feelings. It reminded him of the interrogation of Sophie Scholl.

It covered their lifestyles, what it was like to be age twenty in 1988, the Western rock music they were listening to, what it meant to them and how they perceived the West. The questioning was intrusive and forceful, the answers honest and innocent. For Gabreski, the contrast between the interrogators and the prisoners was what stood out the most. The former hard bitten cold warriors serving the state for personal survival, the latter hopeful enthusiastic young people caught up in a political vacuum not of their making. The Independent Students' Union had provided a forum for students in those days to work on human rights issues and campaign for democracy. Their leaders took as severe a hammering as the leaders of Solidarność.

Many of the student leaders escaped to Western Europe prior to the collapse. For the students, and particularly those who were intimidated into giving personal information on their parents and neighbours, it was a violation that would be carried by the young people for the rest of their days. He wondered where they were and guessed that at least some would be similar to himself, part of a diaspora who would never be able to fit into Polish society properly. And this, from the simple harsh narratives of five young people in June 1988, five in amongst tens of thousands, multiplied by trauma and hurt.

As the day moved on, the darkness of the evening could be faintly glimpsed through the only skylight in the room. Although the day flew, the returns on the research may have been minimal but important, lucrative enough to get agreement on the need to tie up and get moving. As with all such exercises, the clear up was infinitely faster than the set up arrangements. Files were replaced and shuffled as the team regrouped back in the small quiet room at the end of the shelves. They arrived at the same time in a line, tired and quiet, but waiting for the silence to be broken to exchange opinions on what had been discovered.

"Well, what did you get?" Krolas was keen to get to the answers. Lubeka was first to jump in with a lead. "They have stripped even more from my last trawl. The new material is really where it is at. It is good, if it is real. Their problem is, I suspect they have teams drifting in and out of here without targets, just trying to clear up. You can see it with the number of pictures that are missing. Much of the Polish material has been corrupted."

"And then, there is all the Russian material." Krolas interrupted with a sanguine comment to try and bring the group to the point they were all eager to get too. "And then, there are the Russian files." Lubeka refocused to get to the point of interest. "What we have is a bank of unrifled material. Pictures, codes, data, and dates, everything. I will give it a life expectancy of weeks."

"Especially after we get it into the public domain." Wójcik had remained silent throughout most of the proceedings, but wanted to plant a flag in the ground for the journalistic worth of the finds. "We need to get this out there. The files we don't have knowledge about will have meaning for someone."

Lubeka, wary of the eyes that were keeping them at bay, felt that much more was needed. "We have got to get more material from this repository. We have got to get it saved before they close this source down also."

Gabreski had been sitting listening to the concerns and in standing up drew the group to his uncomfortable body language. "Go for targets. We need leads and actions, and if we get to a few of these people, others may come out of the woodwork to protect their own interests. We need to drip feed the material into the public domain. We have to learn the lessons from Wildstein and Mitrokhin. They were here, they walked off with information and the volume of it swamped the system and the media. It was the starting gun for a cover up of historic proportions. Every SB and SA operative in Poland was at that door looking to get rid of files and histories. This needs to be strategic." Gabreski pointed to the end of the files at the locked door.

Lubeka's inclination was to challenge just about everything, but on this she held back. She knew the costs and the losses so far and agreed that a strategy was key to the way forward. "What do you think, Beata?" she said, searching for any advance on Gabreski's plan.

"There does not seem to be any other way. I was here when Wildstein did his swoop, and Łuka is right. The material that went missing after that was vast and the material coming out from Wildstein's website left everyone snow-blind. We have a lot here already. We have dozens of files in the Cloud, photographed and noted. We need to select, focus and move on. It is the only way."

"I would also say that as soon as we walk out that door, they will know exactly what we have, so be wary." Gabreski still had the fate of Stanisław Kaszowski in mind.

"Okay, 'Bartek', what do we have?" Sitting with her elbows on the desk and head in hands, Lubeka did not want to think about the repercussions.

"The name came up a couple of times across Kraków and Warsaw." The journalists' notes of Wójcik were as concise as she could make them, the recall of the videos on her iPhone emphasised the point. "This might save us going too far into the other videoed material for the time being. An SB operative with the unusual second name 'Bartek' comes up in a number of files. I copied the ones that I felt had him in specific places at specific times in the eighties."

"Is he from Kraków?" Lubeka questioned, wondering about the name, scanning the others to get an answer.

"He seems to have been based in the SB headquarters in Kraków. There is a picture of a younger operative, but out of focus pictures of someone looking like this other guy overseeing a Zomo unit. The Russian over the pictures refers to Solidarność members, local rights activists and, interestingly, foreign agents." Wójcik passed the phone around and in turn each surveyed the picture to get some semblance of where it was and whether, in vain hope, they could recognize anyone. Local interest made them instinctively call out places they recognized.

"Look carefully, the Russian notes two foreign security people, one MI6, whatever he is doing there, the other Bulgarian. I wonder if they are still around." Moving on, Lubeka commented: "There are others, perhaps six or seven similar photos with annotations and references." As she flicked through the video, she paused, and then passed it around the table. At each stage, the others chipped in with background knowledge drawing from the various worlds they had each emerged from.

"June the twentieth 1988, that was a student protest at the university."

"The seventh of February 1988, that was a riot against the imposition of food price rises. That one, I know, was a way to try and mobilize Solidarność members in the city. Protests were used as a way of coordinating activities. Most of the main decisions by the trade unions were made at the fringes of these marches. It is obviously why the SB considered it so important to monitor all of these events." At that time it was the usual form to round up the ring leaders and hold them for interrogation for forty-eight hours.

"That one is from Lenin Steelworks. My father was there." Studying the zoomed-in distorted images from the still, Lubeka could just about recognize some of the workers being dispersed at the march. Social memory took over. "From what I can remember, they were forced into a confrontation with the Zomo at that time. There was a lot of tension around the city, and what I remember them saying in the family, was that there was anger that Zomo from other parts of Poland were being drafted in to take on Solidarność. My father was bruised, others were trailed away and tortured. I used to remember the names of the leaders. As children we considered them heroes. I suppose they are patriots. I am sure someone remembers."

"Well, we now have grainy photos of perpetrators, details of their command structure and the roles they played in the activities. We have evidence of sorts, and that is what we came looking for. Our problem is that we will not be able to get more material in the time we have been given." Gabreski was despondent at the enormity of the task given to them and the need to get material into the public domain as quickly as possible. It went against every academic muscle he had, knowing that material needed to be counter-checked and verified, reinforced with unquestionable reliability. Even his thought processes were shocked into the new reality of journalism. He rose and paced the room.

"We have got to take a call on this. Get it out there as quickly as possible. There are families around still suffering from these actions and they need to know whatever we can deliver. This could finally get the Pandora's box opened." Wójcik was impatient. She also had an editor with a demand to complete the assignment.

"But what happens if we release some material and we lose the rest?" Gabreski continued to test the possibilities and suggest a longer trawl.

"You know, Łuka, the Wildstein method was not effective enough. It was not targeted enough. He did what he could within the chaos of the times, but things have changed. The old guard have embedded themselves in the system, they need to be drawn out. You said it. We need a hook or they will not respond. And anyway, they know already that this is a live issue again."

Without saying it, the death of the detective remained an unanswered threat to the whole investigation. Wójcik was starting to get animated and agitated at Gabreski's suggestion that the process should slow down. Lubeka had been sitting listening to an increasingly tense altercation. Her mind returned to the death of Andrzej. This was the endgame, someone has been spooked by their research and it could, if handled right, open up in the coming days. She jumped into the conversation in an attempt to try and link both sides. Gabreski was standing with his hands on the desk in front of Wójcik, looking at her for an answer.

"Marianna and Łuka, there has to be agreement here. And there is no point falling out over it. We are on the same side. We just need to work out a strategy to carry this forward. They know we are here, they know what we are doing, and do not kid yourselves, they are here with us. Why they have not stopped us at this point, I do not know, but we have stumbled on something they want. Maybe they are using us to locate material or to set up someone. I don't know. We are already in this, like it or not. You two either have to bottle it up and continue, or run. There are four of us. We can continue the search and get some material out there to see what happens. Beata can continue in the Institute, and we can get the relevant press releases together to create that hook."

"With Bartek as bait." Gabreski withdrew to the young woman's logic.

"With Bartek as bait." Lubeka replied.

"I have already started with the logging of material from the perspective of Warsaw and Kraków. I have a load of files on interrogations and the torture of Warsaw's civil rights activists in the late 1980s. I was afraid that I would not be able to get to key figures. I've already been working on what I felt we could focus on. I even have some of the original files at home, the ones that have definitely been removed from the archives." Krolas brought the tone of the conversation onto a different light with reference to the fact that she had "borrowed" some of the files when the Russian batch originally arrived. Her focus had always been Warsaw, given that it was her era and town that was affected, but she also had a soft spot for the dissident movement in Kraków. Her illicit act was because she wanted at least to have evidence that could be examined at a later date. She was also aware of the speed of theft of the files.

Her caution was that of the experience from previous releases of material and, as mentioned by Lubeka, any release needed to be planned and focused. Her fear was that the flow of material would again snow-blind the public, carry too much into the public domain at once, and this would merely play into the hands of the securocrats. It happened with WikiLeaks – with the results being negligible.

"Kasia, we have to get it out there, and we need to do it right this time around."

On that, there was a shuffling of the notes that were taken, sheets ordered, notepads closed and a silence which suggested that they should move on.

"Okay, Beata can stay with her precious archives and we will track down anyone who can shed light on the files we are working with, and Bartek."

"That sounds like a plan, Kasia." Gabreski could see that while time in the archive would be useful to get a thorough survey completed, this would have to wait. His world was very different from the urgent journalistic world occupied by the rest of his colleagues. They needed information immediately. He could spend the rest of the year working away on the obscurities of the issues that his training would drive him towards, producing a number of detailed articles which would get lost in the smoke of academia. The two journalists and Lubeka were more impulsive in their needs;

locating, packaging and distributing were their goals. "Getting it out there" was the constant refrain between them.

"Let's find some dinner." Gabreski thought that it would provide a more congenial environment to work out how they were to process this type of information. The movement of chairs was enough to get everyone on the same message.

"Where will we go?" Wójcik did not get up to Warsaw that often and wanted to see what was new or what was happening.

Krolas had an answer almost before the question was asked. "I know where we can go, where it is noisy enough not to be heard talking, but quiet enough to give us space to think. I have my car around the corner, if that helps. We could walk, but with the snow and the Zomo it may be handier to drive." After a smile and pause, she reloaded the thought with: "It should have enough to keep Łuka happy for a while at least." Gabreski's eagerness to get something to eat registered with the others. He smiled in acknowledgement of a gender weakness.

"Let's go, pack up what we have and we can process the material later." Lubeka was still impatient about moving the issue forward. They knew that with the technology they now had available to them, the material would be there waiting to be retrieved. This was a comfort of sorts given the vulnerability of the files, but it was also a problem for an academic researcher, who usually only felt content with hard copies safely tucked away.

"I hope this is all safe." She patted her notes as she put them into her bag.

"We have it, Kasia, don't worry. We have as much as we can manage at this stage and we have the freeze frame technology to retrieve it all when and where we want." The scanning process meant that they had gathered volumes of files, most meaningless, but others hung there in the Cloud waiting to bring out skeletons. As they moved along the corridors and through to the lifts, there was a sense of satisfaction that some progress had been made.

"Murphy's. That's where we are going. Off Nowogrodzka. We can find a quiet spot and get our heads out of this for a while." Gabreski was perhaps the most impatient of the group to change the topic. He had been processing the material for days at this stage and needed space to get back to a staging post. Krolas's car was parked around the side of the Institute. She had left it there in anticipation that they would eventually need a lift somewhere. The Mercedes was still there when they descended out of the building and towards the car. By habit and experience, Krolas circled around her old faded red Volkswagen Polo in a security sweep. The snow had not been broken and the papers she had left leaning against the driver's window were still as they were. She carefully cleaned the soggy snow from the windscreen and let the passengers in. It was like a fridge. Almost in sequence, the four of them voiced their coldness. The engine ticked over first time around and as the heat filtered into the car, Krolas slowly pulled out, followed by the black Mercedes.

In the slush of the evening, the car crunched its way through the city. The night was still and the occasional flutter of snow was caught in the orange glow of the streetlights. The parking places outside the pub were mostly taken by a row of tightly packed hatchbacks, bar two spaces together near the front of the building. As the Polo pulled into the parking space, the car was lit up by the green glare of the floor to roof opaque windows, with Murphy's Irish Pub emblazoned across the front. The Mercedes followed to pull up beside the Polo. Again, Lubeka had come close enough on her side of the car to be able to stare aggressively at the occupants of the other car. The two leather jacketed men remained motionless, looking ahead, waiting.

They were obviously there to intimidate them, arrogant enough to keep the group conscious that their every move was being watched. Lubeka reacted, finding her way out of the car and standing at the door of the Mercedes.

"Have you something to say?" She shouted authoritatively through the window, tapping on the driver's door. "Have you a problem?" She stared intently at the two men, gestured and walked to the pathment to join the other three who had assembled, cautiously watching. Gabreski was more intent on identification than provocation. "Do you recognize either of them?" Lubeka responded "No."

"Someone, take a picture of these two muppets. We may be able to get an identification if we eventually link in with the police on this." Krolas's trusty camera was first to take a snap, followed by Lubeka, who was keen on letting the car occupants know of her frustration.

"That will never happen, Łuka." Lubeka, obviously still annoyed, registering her distrust of the whole establishment.

In the bar things settled, as they were able to talk discretely without interference. The elderly checked-shirted men at the bar had obviously been here since the place was opened and the smatterings of customers were intently focussed on the highlights of a local football match being screened. Gabreski went to the bar for an order.

For the first time since Kraków, after venting her anger in a confessional manner, Lubeka seemed to get the whole experience out of her system. She had relaxed enough to talk beyond the events of the previous few days. She sipped a glass of stout and seemed to find some solace in being surrounded by her colleagues. "How do you feel, Kasia? It has been a tough week." Wójcik glanced around the small cramped table wanting to open up the conversation to more than the two women and sensing that a conversation could possibly bring out opinions that had been closed since they met Gabreski in the main square in Kraków.

"I feel numb. It is like a new world to me. I feel as if I have been struggling out of a train crash. I have lost so much so quickly. It is a big shock. I know that I have found a kind of purpose in struggling through it. It feels like a different life. No more staring out of that window in Nowa Huta, hoping for something else. My better life is a Cold War warzone and that's it."

"It has been a traumatic experience." Gabreski paused to see if there was an emotional response, but the frustration that Lubeka was carrying was holding her focus. "Where do you see this going, Kasia?" Gabreski wanted to get meaning back for her and to see if Lubeka knew what to expect.

"It is not over until this job is done. We have to face it down, hit them where it hurts and then, I suppose, run." Lubeka saw the damage as possibly being greater than what Gabreski anticipated for all of them and was keen to caution everyone as to the road that they were going down.

"It could be very dangerous to take this to its logical conclusion, Kasia. We are small fish in the bigger scheme of things. We down one of the old guard, and we will need to be very conscious of the fact that his comrades are there to pick up where he left off. Anyway, we need to have an out-clause, a way where our lives are not damaged by this."

"Łuka, we have been working on this for half a life time. This is it. You need to see how dangerous these people are. They are outside because they feel we have something." Wójcik was leaving the group in no question about where they were all placed. "Marianna, relax, we need time to chill out here. This place is beyond their control.

Łuka, what's your favourite pub?" Krolas interjected to break the tone of the conversation. A reticence descended on the table.

"Where do I start?" Gabreski was suprised with the question and change of direction, but rose to the challenge. "The Archway Tavern in north London is where I find myself most Saturday nights at some point. I suppose it has become a spiritual home. Beyond that, the Cuban bar off Grand Place in Brussels serves rum measures that are large enough to keep you there for the week. It's a great place Kasia. Where is your favourite place for a night out?"

"I suppose a small pizza restaurant in a town called Krosno in the south of Poland. We went there many years ago. The bar opened and closed depending on whether the staff were having fun or not. That is a good way to run a bar. It looked like somewhere in the Pacific and felt like it was in the Mediterranean. That was a long time ago, a different life with different people. I think I liked it because it was a peaceful time for me. I had peace of mind there, and it was very cheap. Cheap is very important when you are a student."

"Me." Krolas busted in. "Anywhere does me. As long as they know that I am a waking nightmare for anyone working in those places." A chuckle rippled around the company.

With the table's occupants suitably relaxed with each other, the night took over, interrupted occasionally by one or other diving for a mobile phone to text or, in Lubeka's case, vetting the texts and shutting down incoming calls.

On leaving the pub, the Mercedes was away, the shift seemingly over. The four, still glowing with the evening, stomped through the snow to the car. Krolas undertook her now habitual round of the car and, after some repositioning, the four settled in for the short trip back to the hotel. As they moved, Gabreski took a call from Nowak. The volume of the ring tone shocked everyone. The cabin-like environment accentuated the tones. Gabreski tried to present an official partially-sober update of progress.

"Yes, Piotr. We are just coming from the Institute. We have made some progress. The archives are a gold mine, I could spend a year there if you are willing to give me a research grant… It's worth a try. I hope all is going well with winding up the symposium… Excellent. And the policeman's funeral? Okay… Yes, Kasia, is still here. Okay. Okay."

On finishing, Gabreski relayed the conversation. Lubeka was visibly hesitant at Nowak checking up on her, but took the reference in good faith. The placidity that descended on the car brought each to a collective sleepiness. On arrival at the hotel, Krolas pulled up at the front door and offered an animated farewell.

"Okay, people, ten o'clock. When I get back to my place I will have a look over the material we gathered and will send through a statement of what I think should be in the press release. We can do a bit of damage tomorrow. If we can bring down a kingpin, they will be shaking. It is what we have been working for." She made a clenched fist salute, lightly punching the air.

At that, the other three pulled themselves out of the car and fought through the snow to the heat of the lobby of the hotel. The Polo pulled away into the night, wipers occasionally striking the featherlike flakes that continued to drift onto the Warsaw streets. Lubeka and Wójcik dug deeply into their handbags to find what was left of the Marlboros. They had both struggled through Murphy's to stay away from the front door and the possibility of confrontation, but now, on return to the hotel, both were intent in making the most of the open air.

Gabreski watched on, checking emails with one step in the hotel lobby to get the heat of the doorway without giving up on the women braving the cold for a final 'nail' of the day. On finishing, the two women immediately and politely excused themselves from Gabreski. He moved towards the reception at the side of the lobby. He, again, struggled to discipline his habit and bid farewell in an uncomfortable realization that they, too, were aware. The receptionist directed Gabreski to the lounge, where he sat alone with another overly large glass of whiskey. Back to his zone and once again in a space where he could recount the weight of the day. The lights of the lobby were strong and intrusive, but the moment provided some pause to take in events.

By the time he reached his room, the day was just about at a close. The newness of the hotel was disconcerting, given the hotels that he had recently stayed in, and preferred. The room was perfectly modern, the furniture from a boutique catalogue rather than from history. As he rushed to get his coat off and to the final check of the midnight news, the first image to meet him was the police-uniformed picture of Kaszowski.

"Captain Kaszowski will be buried with full honours in Kraków. His death has been confirmed as suicide by the coroner. His family are being supported by his colleagues." The video-shot went to his young family being comforted by police officers. Gabreski was annoyed, digging out the note he had made with Kaszowski's directions to Bartek. With the television on, the flickering TV the only brightness left, he lay on the bed, bag roughly unpacked, and drifted off.

Lubeka and Wójcik were still alive to the issue. Lubeka's phone continued to ring and she continued to hammer the tone off. Wójcik noted the regularity of the phone and was concerned that Lubeka was still struggling to overcome the trauma of the past few days and dealing with people at home. "Who is phoning, Kasia?"

"It's no one."

"It must be someone."

"It's just some prick with a one line threat."

"What? Who is it?"

"I have no idea. I didn't want you to be bothered by it. I have had these before. It seems to be their idea of fun."

"Let me deal with it the next time, Kasia, it will give you a break. I have a line or two that the usual phone perverts turn off to."

"Okay." She threw the phone on the bed beside Wójcik and walked around the room surveying the newness of the furniture. "You know my Andrzej would have loved this hotel. He worked on hotels in London and took pride in helping with the designs when he was asked. He used to tell me about the suites he fitted out in Bloomsbury and the glitz of Marble Arch. He was really proud of his work. That's before he went and screwed it all up."

It was the first time since the funeral that Wójcik had heard Lubeka referring to him, the only time in months that she had heard her referring to Andrzej in a softer way.

"Kasia, they killed him."

"I know." Her voice sounded defeated.

"And that is why we need to fight on. They killed him. He is not the only one. They killed the hopes of a generation of ordinary people like us everywhere."

Lubeka was sitting on the bed staring at her phone, willing it to do something. The loneliness was obvious and crippling, and even though Wójcik was there and talking, the emotional block was very evident to both. For once, the phone remained silent. To break the moment, Wójcik linked her phone up to her tablet, immediately transferring files from the Institute's archives.

"Let's see what we have." As the transfers opened through to dozens of videoclips, each of a file detailed enough to read, she paused to pick up images and codes. "This is what they have all been pushing for." Lubeka composed herself enough to spark some spirit. "We are going to down these bastards. We will do enough damage that they will not be able to recover." Her voice changed as she restated her resolve. As the two sat side by side pausing and zooming in on the images, on occasion they froze file images to mail them to a network of research and media safe addresses. "This will secure the material this time."

Some of the images could be enhanced to clarify faces, car registration numbers, street names and shops, people whose lives were caught in a desperate time. The night lost the women as they worked to process what they felt was evidence and voices from a different era and place, the pain in the faces of the people on the edges of the events, the pictures from the Zomo shots, stark, anxious, violent.

21st November

Gabreski was first to wake. Shocked by the cold and aware that he had not changed before going to sleep. He undressed and struggled to make his way to the shower. The heat was refreshing and the fragrance of the gel made him feel at least clean, if not fully awake, hangover intact. The hypnotic effect of the streaming water was calming. He considered the layers of information that he had been processing over the previous days. Something was driving this forward, but he could not pin-point it. They were following a trail that could not be of their making, it was too direct. They, surely, were being influenced for some reason, given a pathway. As he showered, the name of Mazur came back to him. He moved around the room and voiced the name "Mazur" as a link that they had as yet to cover. "Mazur in Toruń".

The brightness of the snow outside lit the room. The floor to roof windows with light muslin curtains did little to keep the wall of cold out. His standard British academic uniform of Marks and Spencer jeans, polo neck jumper and sturdy leather shoes had served him well, but at this stage of the week he felt grimy. He knew also that a change would have to wait and, dress code aside, the job would have to be finished. He moved around the room to dress, making thick coffee while keeping an eye on the weather channel. His mobile kicked in with its melodious tone for the first time that day.

"Yes. Gabreski."

"Hi, it's Beata. I have a press release ready. I will send it through to Kasia. I have not been able to get through to her and Marianna since I left them last night. Is it worth a check?"

"Okay, Beata. They are just down the corridor. I will go and wake them up. We should all meet."

"How about the café at the foot of the Palace of Culture and Science. We can get something there and it is touristic enough to keep us in public view."

"Okay, let's say eight thirty to give us time to make it through the snow."

"Great." He fiddled to get the call closed.

Seven a.m. seemed a bit harsh given the late night and the weather, but there was a lot to be working on never mind navigation through the city itself. He checked to see if the snow was still as heavy, pushing the muslin back to unveil a winter perfect picture of white trees and solid roof snow. His quick glance out of the window done, he was ready to join the working throngs at this stage of the day. He packed his tablet into his raincoat, scarfed up and made his way to the room where the two women had encamped.

"Kasia, Marianna, it's me. We need to get moving." Gabreski knocked the door gently. He heard a shuffle of activity as the door opened. Lubeka stood in a tee-shirt and in the background Wójcik covered herself on a double bed. Both had obviously been in the same bed. Gabreski turned his head. "Give us five minutes. We will see you in the lobby." As he waited, he reflected on the friendship of the two women, but also on the vulnerability of both given the stress of the past week. His mind was opened, but as an academic of long standing, sensitivity was the main emotion that came forward. It was good that the two women felt safe together, in whatever manner.

There was a silence as the three joined the rush-hour to walk down Chmielna and past the monolithic Galeria Centrum. A hub of commercial life in Warsaw, the settling snow did not diminish the determination of the population of the city to get about its frantic daily life. The Mercedes emerged as a reminder of the task at hand, always within eye-view, menacing but manageable.

***

The Palace dominates the centre of the city, its imposing imperial structure giving an uncomfortable repost to the aspirations of communist life. It was a 'gift' from Stalin to the city, yet it also represented the imposition of Stalinism, oppressive and authoritarian. Word was, that on the fall of the old regime no one quite knew what to do with it, use it or demolish it. In Warsaw they know it as *Pekin*, Beijing, and *Pajac*, 'clown'. It stands as a monument to paradox. Krolas stood outside the café at the bottom of the ominously grey, powerful skyscraper.

"Good morning. I thought it may be useful to go to the ŻYCIA office in the Palace. It is well out of the reach of our friends and can give us a place to gather our notes. We can get something to eat up there. Do we have all we need with us?"

A round of agreement responded as Krolas led the group into the ornate facade of the lobby and towards the lift. The corridors were dark and windowless, and give the impression of a warren of rooms, floor after floor. The whole place was perfectly dated with its deco-style lamps and its aura of chequered history. The office rented by the journal was on the thirteenth floor, just above the university that dominated a number of floors of the imposing building. On entering the office, the first thing that struck Lubeka was the view. She was visibly taken by the vista and a glimpse of the river, a blanket of white covering the city. Coming from Kraków with its renaissance architecture and its moderate height, she felt a rush of acrophobia – for her, it was exhilarating.

"I saw Leonard Cohen play here in 1985." Krolas could not wait to reveal that credential from her past. "He played for three hours and never mentioned the occupation once. We were all waiting for something. It was all a bit of an anti-climax. But at least he made it here for us. Most didn't care. He was a singer. We all tend to forget that."

"Did you ever expect anyone in the West would do anything for us? They left this city to die in 1944 and kept it frozen in time until business resumed in the nineties. We are Polish. We had to do it all ourselves. That is the big lesson of our history." Lubeka made the point glancing around to make sure she had an audience for her patriotism. She then returned to staring out of the window. Time had stalled from the day and hour the city was rebuilt. As they settled around a small desk, others from the office shouted across greetings. They were all aware of the role of this new team who just arrived, and were intent in offering a sign of solidarity.

"Do you want the good news or the bad news?" Krolas sat waiting to share some information that she had been working on overnight. She perched with the authority of a school teacher. The selection of tablets, smart phones and netbooks were placed on the table. Gabreski was first to reply. "Bad."

"Well, we have a problem with the release of material. We can handle photographs and files from the Institute for research purposes, but we cannot upload the material into the public domain. The Robert W. case is the precedent and if we release the material, even through WikiLeaks, we could each end up in prison for eight years for a breach of state security."

"Let's do it and see how they react." Lubeka was angry, adventurous, and searching for justice.

"That helps no one, Kasia. Look at where the rest of the leaks and exposures have got those involved. Where are Wildstein, Mitrokhin and Robert W. now? It won't help the issue, providing the system with four more prison mouths to feed." Gabreski knew that systems swallow people up when they are exposed to the state, wherever it was. The rest sat quietly.

"Well, Beata, tell us the good news and let's hope it has an answer to this."

"We can use some technical detail. The codes are not included in the censure. Also we only have brands, not names as such. We can use the detail from the codes to get our statement out and then wait." Krolas proposed an answer of sorts, but did not see any other way to engage with the question.

“Do we have any further options?” Lubeka was getting impatient.

“Mazur in Toruń. It is the only other name that we have, and Kaszowski lost his life to give it to us.” Gabreski felt that he had a sense of duty to the dead policeman, to bring him through to the conversation. He felt that Mazur may be able to facilitate them with a lead into the codes. There was no other name on the table.

“Okay, Łuka, how about we find Mazur. Marianna and Beata can stay with the Institute archives. At least we will have someone there to keep an eye on any new files. How does that sound?” Lubeka looked around the table for questions, but the silence again suggested agreement. She got up and went to the window, this time looking upwards towards the heavy grey clouds that were closing down on Warsaw.

“What else do we have in the files we caught yesterday? I saw more than Bartek. That Russian material needs to be translated better.” Wójcik spun Lubeka’s tablet with video shots of the files running. The others came around the tablet relaying additional pieces of information, single files and snippets of Russian, which filled gaps in translations or were of perceived interest. This began a process which was to last two hours, going through the material. Lubeka periodically typed in codes and dates, key names and words. “’npemaxBaHe Ha’, ‘eliminate’, why is it in Bulgarian continually?” The mix of words and meaning meant losing some of the detail. The pictures of interrogated young people and trade unionists forced home the severity of the abuse and put the Lustration concept into its proper human rights context. Face after face, afraid, contorted, shaped by the fears and hopes of the time.

“Did you know that Bartek Securities is still active? They undertake government contracts and work with some of their Eastern equivalents. They have their main office in Starowiślna in Kraków, but have holdings and property across Poland and the Ukraine." Krolas interjected with a different stream of thought, bringing minds back to the task at hand.

"What do they do exactly?" Gabreski needed to fill in the spaces in the company's history.

"Surveillance, personal protection, securing property and land. There are always land deals with these people. Exactly what you would think these former security personnel would do in the new world order." Krolas pointed repeatedly at her screen in a stabbing motion. A straight google search gave some information, but a clutter of emails from the ŻYCIA office in Kraków filled some of the gaps. Krolas continued to tap away.

"The big question is, who are the heads behind Bartek? What are the names? The TW? Who are these people who can be such a threat to the Lustration process?"

"Let's try to get the press release together." Lubeka wanted to get the system creaking to see what would transpire.

"Okay, okay. I have a draft, if it is not what we are looking for, we can change it." Krolas had been busy. The others gathered around her laptop as the short statement came up on screen.

"Conclusions from academics from a symposium on the Lustration process held in Kraków this week, have discovered concrete evidence that links a network of former security personnel from the late nineteen eighties to current commercial activities across Poland. Newly sourced Russian files from the Institute of National Remembrance have emerged which can place key business interests, currently at executive level in international security firms, in security services across the country in the autumn of 1988. The evidence which the academics from the UK, Poland and America are working on, prove that certain prominent business leaders' past histories have included working for the Russian and Bulgarian security services, torturing opposition members and the disappearance of members of the trade union movement and student organizations."

After reading the statement aloud, Krolas paused and then shouted, "How does that sound?" The silence showed a level of agreement. Gabreski reassured Krolas: "That's good, Beata." Wójcik chipped in: "It's good, but will it get us all killed?"

"We have waited long enough for this. We've got to make our move." Lubeka felt that with this press release it could break the collective amnesia on the whole subject. "We cannot make the mistakes of the past in getting this information into the public domain. Let's do it and see what happens."

"The sky might just cave in, Kasia. But isn't it exciting." The fight of the journalist came through in the enthusiasm of Krolas's voice. This was her life's blood, battling against the big men of the world. "Are we agreed to go with this?" The heads around the table nodded with approval. With one final read of the statement out loud, Krolas emailed it through to her desk in Kraków for immediate release.

They returned to the files to link up dates and names. The orders were specific, the instructions having obvious and horrific implications for those involved.

> Kraków 03.08.88. File 90938900. Solidarność gathering at the Barbican. Zomo to confront. Arrests made and live rounds used. Interrogated organizers.

> Kraków 03.08.88. File 90938901. Solidarność gathering at Nowa Huta. Zomo to confront. Arrests made and live rounds used. Interrogated organizers.

File after file, slim but detailed, the files had Stasi like efficiency, succinct and direct, they listed anticipated actions and results. A frontpiece to each gave the general detail, the subsequent material went into the brutal exercise of the law. The photographs that were taken as evidence of the actions were blurred at times, others were digital in clarity. The faces were mostly of the prisoners, some close-ups, others of groups, the garish eighties clothing, black and white harshness, suggesting a different, yet all too familiar world.

Occasionally, there were shots of the operations with commentaries jotted in pencil on the back. The black and white format of many of the photographs dated the events, yet they remained within the lifetime of most Poles. 'Bartek' as a name was mentioned twice in the files they froze. The details of arrests and instructions to interrogate resistance in Kraków were scrupulous and galling. Torture was the mainstay of the process, endured by young and old alike.

"This guy looks like he is giving the orders." Wójcik zoomed in on one of the photos in the files. There stood a thin man, perhaps in his late thirties, in Zomo fatigues, pointing towards a group of young protesters. Others were reacting, the movement could be seen to come from the manner in which his unit looked at him and the authority of his deportment. On his arm the small label 'Bartek' could be clearly seen, wrapped around the insignia of a lighthouse. "We have got one we can target."

"That could be a picture of anyone." Gabreski was cautious. What if it was just another puppet in the system, wary of pointing the finger at any functionary. "We need more than this, Marianna."

The energy of the press release going out dissipated as the scale of the search took its toll. The four worked towards lunch time. As the day went on, the scene of the snow starting to fall again – viewed from the thirteenth floor of the Palace – brought a general feeling of awe mixed with vulnerability. This was a place that, even given its confused history, was a powerful reminder of the potential of Warsaw as a European capital. They needed to move.

"We have to get to Toruń." Lubeka was impatient to get to the only definitive link they had been given on the issue, the only person named who could provide insight into the complex that had filtered its way across not only Poland, but also through the Eastern states. As they emerged from the Palace, the shutter of the winter hit the four of them collectively. Within steps, the conversation jumped from Lustration to the freeze.

"This is unbearable." Gabreski had been out of the country that long that his levels of endurance were weakened in comparison to the women. The cold burnt his lungs. His Oxford Street raincoat was more attuned to the weather fronts in Finchley than the biting wind chills of Warsaw. More secure in the standard Eastern European women's uniform of black padded feathered knee length coats and boots that were more military than fashion, the women were prepared for the worst.

"My car is in the Palace car park at the back." The walk was brisk. The exchange of cigarettes between Lubeka and Wójcik forced a stop and stall movement through the snow, with the smokers eventually taking up the rear.

Krolas felt obliged to let the Krakóweans and the outsider, in the guise of Gabreski, know of the continual struggle to keep Warsaw alive. "After we defeated the fascists, the Soviets wanted to leave the city levelled as a permanent reminder of what fascism could do. We, the good people of this city, had to rebuild it brick by brick. For me, that Palace is a part of that. Most people don't mind it. We survived the hell of Nazism and would certainly not be defeated by a few tourists from Moscow."

"Well done for you." Gabreski shouted to make sure Krolas heard a voice of empathy, but also recognizing the differences that exist between the north and south of the country, the regional divides that developed in the post-communist era. Moving towards the car, the black Mercedes re-emerged at the other side of the car park. Krolas circled her car. "I don't mind bugs." She shouted. "I do mind getting blown up in my own car." The stoicism was not lost on the others, and the resignation that this had been Krolas's life for a very long time.

The car slowly meandered its way out of the car park, followed by the tail, to enter the Warsaw traffic, trickling its way through the city to the hotel. Gabreski and Lubeka fought their way out and into the warm lobby. "Just get enough for a few days, Kasia, we will be back to get Marianna later." The division of labour meant the two women would be split up for the first time since Gabreski met them, but he was aware that the trip to Toruń would be a quick one. "We need to get back here to catch the fallout of the press release."

"Beata can handle it. She knows the media networks here better than anyone."

"Five minutes and we are out of here. Is that okay?"

"That's good for me."

Within minutes both had reappeared, simultaneously outside the bedrooms. Both had backpacks which were discrete enough to get them through a couple of days, but small enough to make travelling quick and effective. Both had an awareness of the need for efficiency and ease of movement. They had done this before and knew the drill. The lift was already opened, leaving the short journey automatic as they went down to the lobby. There remained a sense of compatibility between the two researchers, where silence was not uncomfortable, reflecting the trust that they had developed from their first meeting. Trust without trying was an unusual thing for both.

As the car pulled away, Lubeka was concerned that the separation may leave one duo or the other vulnerable to the TW.

"We need to track your work, Beata. We will need to have text updates regularly to ensure that you are safe, if that is okay. We know what these people are capable of doing. We don't know what they have planned when they have us separated."

"Sure. Marianna will text regularly to make sure you are happy." Krolas was responding to the worry, taking the concern with some light-heartedness by passing over the responsibility to Wójcik.

"Okay then, Marianna, you text me at every move. We have got to keep communicating. It is just about all we have against them."

"Text back, so that we know you are still alive." Wójcik appreciated what Lubeka was up to. This was a way of not only linking on safety, but also keeping a steady dialogue on progress.

The car bumped on, the snow piled high on the sides of the road, ashen grey from the discoloration that spewed out of the exhausts. One of the most congested cities in the world, Warsaw often looked as if it had just emerged from the phoney liberation of 1945. Krolas noticed in her mirror the Mercedes staying within eye-shot of them. At this point they were resigned to being followed. The Volkswagen ploughed through the slush, the smell of fumes and the residue of smoke lingering in the car.

Lubeka was engrossed in the detail of her notes, flickering through pages on her tablet as they moved. Gabreski strained to get a view of the city in all its severity. Krolas habitually hit the radio on at twelve p.m. to get an update on the news. Russo-Polish political tensions headed the bulletin as it had done for days. *Polskie Radio Parlament* gave the state line on most things, but it was minority listening. It was what the circle around the politicos listened to and presented stories that would be picked up across the elite and its media cliques.

Cross-border tensions were simmering since the end of the occupation. The various churches had even intervened to plea for a relaxation of tensions between the two countries. The Baltic countries feared invasion and a Ukraine style infiltration. The Poles feared they would be next in line. There was no love lost between the political hacks in both countries. It was, however, politically shrewd to hype up the tensions for anyone involved in politics in the country, because of the residual hostility that most Poles felt for the Russian establishment. Memories were long in Poland.

The second news story was more relevant to the occupants of the car.

> "A team of international researchers has located documents relating to former secret service personnel who are still working in the security industry across Eastern Europe. In a statement released through a media outlet, the researchers say that they have evidence on key figures within the SB and Zomo who are currently engaged with work to do with security contracts and international finance. Beata Krolas, a

> journalist representing the team, stated that this is the most crucial evidence yet to prove that members of the communist-era secret service were still operating in a clandestine manner within the Polish economy. She said that further evidence will be released that will be as explosive as the Wildstein case. While the government has not officially commented on the claims, an inside source said that the security services would be looking into the allegations."

A ripple of excitement went around the car. "We have made the big time. Well done, Beata. That statement will be carried by the papers." Krolas was notably chuffed with the level of exposure and Gabreski's comment. "We need to produce the goods now." Krolas pulled into *Warszawa Centralna* train station, crunching up onto the raised pathing at the side of the building. In a bullish manner she winked at Gabreski. "Here we are."

"Make sure you are moving in public areas and record as much material as possible when you get to the Institute. We have got to make the most of this." Lubeka's enthusiasm was obvious. "This is the furthest we have got in five years at least and we do not want to go down without taking a few of them with us." Lubeka was well aware of the significance of the news broadcast. Their work had made it to the core and was sure to cause ripples. Gabreski punched his backpack as if to finalise the trip and moved to get out. "We will leave you here, Beata. There is no point you coming in."

From the Mercedes, one of the surveillance team emerged to stand at the wall beside the station. Gabreski and Lubeka went into the vast hall of the station followed by their tag, joining the flow of people ploughing through the damp concrete concourse. The snow had taken its toll on the slippery interior as they fought to get through to the ticket booths. The history of the station made it all the more depressing, another imposed statement from Moscow. The roar of the trains and the clatter of the passengers echoed through the halls.

The platform for the one o'clock to Toruń was sparsely occupied, with a small gathering of students loudly competing with the trains pulling up at the various other platforms. The Toruń carriages were bunker-like, with a passageway lined with 1970s cabins. The grey and green carriages, still encrusted with ice and snow, were uninviting and industrially dated. Again, Gabreski lamented the speed of modernization in Poland, wishing that the three hour journey could be taken another way. They boarded and settled into a carriage with the same colour scheme as the train itself. Blow heaters blasted dry air into the sealed cabin and immediately there was a warmth that demanded the shedding of layers of clothes.

"No sign of our friend then, Kasia."

"He will be somewhere. If not him, I am sure he has a clone."

"Are you fine with this cabin?" Gabreski was concerned that Lubeka was wary of the exposure of the train and the fact that they would be caught in a single confined space for hours to come. He also saw it as space where he could get behind the political exterior that Lubeka had created.

As expected, and with characteristic efficiency, the *Warszawa Centralna* to *Toruń Glówny* left at exactly thirteen hundred hours. The shutter of the train was only disturbed by the students making their way through the carriage, the chatter matching the chug of the tracks. The view became bleaker when they moved away from the city. Snow drove across the windows, white field after white field, barren in lifelessness. Occasionally, a house would appear, with the look of abandonment, yet the snow-engulfed cars outside would suggest that these were living and working farms, bolted up for the winter, with families hibernating from the cold. This was where vodka and Polish resilience lived side by side. This was the toughness that won the war for them. The environment was uninhabitable, yet families and communities resided and waited for a release from the season, in the same way that the good people of the Warsaw Ghetto resisted, and the miners resisted, holding on until a break in circumstances provided an opportunity to rebuild.

"Do you have a lover, Łuka?"

The question from Lubeka was a shock.

"Love is for people who stay in one place."

"Anyone?" She was persistent and mischievous.

"It takes me too easy, so I stay away from it. I leave it up to the young these days." Gabreski felt vulnerable at the question. He knew of her world, yet she obviously did not know anything about him.

"I was living with my girlfriend for years and lost it. I moved on and have just kept moving. I went to London to the only woman in my life, my mother. I teach and write and that is about all that is left of a spark these days."

"Do you not mind being so free? I have known nothing but Andrzej. I cannot imagine the freedom."

"At times it is an imprisonment in its own right. Freedom can be a captive institution also. It just happens. We just walk into these lives and that's it." Lubeka sat for a while looking out of the window. She pulled a brightly coloured scarf from her bag and wrapped it around her neck, gesturing to Gabreski on the opposite seat. It was the first splash of colour he had seen from Lubeka's wardrobe.

"What about you, Kasia? How are you coping?"

"I have not had time to cope. This has been a hateful week, and it does not seem to be ending. Andrzej's death was just the start of it all. He would have loved all the excitement. You know, he was very caring. That was killed in him by the world we lived in. Feelings died and it was brutal at the end. I miss him, I miss the Andrzej from 2008. That is the man I love, to answer my own question." Lubeka struggled to avoid eye contact.

"And what now?" Gabreski needed some hope in her story. Both were staring out the window, talking indirectly. The snow drifted horizontally across the carriage window.

"A new life, if I survive this experience. When I buried Andrzej, I buried my old life. I will go where the journey takes me." The sense of fatalism was very raw, the starkness of the halogen lights in the cabin highlighting in a visual way the existential journey that Lubeka had been forced into. She moved around to put her feet up on the seat. Gabreski was hypnotized by the snow. The time went slowly as the train rattled through the small midland towns. Clusters of snow covered houses. Gabreski drifted into sleep.

His slumber was broken by Lubeka shuffling pages and hammering the screen of her tablet. Without looking up she continued the broken conversation, pointing at times to files that were saved.

"The fight here is between the old guard or what is left of it and the life that is left in Solidarność. We have Bartek located at the Zomo raids on students' protests on and around the twenty-second June 1988. He is there. We also have him at the interrogation of steelworkers from Nowa Huta after the seventh of February. The notations on the files provide just the code numbers and the name Bartek, then a list of names of the tortured and the information that they divulged. Some of these protesters resisted the torture for twenty hours. It must have been hell for them."

"Who else was there?"

“The files mention external secret service observers. This was an operation on a transnational scale. Obviously, at that time their world was collapsing, this was the endgame. The only way of fighting their way through it was by brutalization.”

“So we can assume that the others were there throughout the period and participated in the operations. This would mean that the old KGB was standing as a controlling mechanism for the whole Eastern system. The frightening thing is that they still run Russia.” Gabreski drew on his wider knowledge of the region to surmise an ongoing link between the old system and the new. The problem was that the connectedness could be wholesale or partial. Key sectors of economic and civil life were frozen in time. Lubeka drew down some of the Russian transcript of one torture session and fed it into Google translator. The translation was rough, but the message was clearly readable. Paraphrasing the transcript out loud, adjusting the translation at times, it brought home the urgency of the period.

“The students were separated into adjoining rooms, interrogation rooms eight and nine of the Kraków headquarters. Males and females were stripped and held under spotlight. The Zomo guard beat the woman first in room eight to ensure the screams could be heard by her colleague in nine. The body took little pressure. The bruising was severe and the prisoner collapsed within ten minutes. The questions were repeated and shouted. One: who is running the dissident cell in the university? Two: what is the connection to Western organizations? And three: who is printing the leaflets?”

Lubeka paused and glanced at Gabreski before summarizing another section.

“The girl was beaten unconscious. They made sure it was her naked body that took the blows. They left the face blows for her boyfriend. She did not seem to know any of the answers. Five men took part in this. Two were named Bartek, from the Zomo, mentioned by this name. The others were coded agents, one Russian the other Bulgarian. One SB commander was also present."

There was a silence and a moment of reflection as both Lubeka and Gabreski searched to envisage the context. The train was warm and the flickering light on the side of the cabin faltered occasionally as the power surges jolted the train onwards. The snow drove across the tracks. Lubeka cited other examples of torture. The patterns were the same, the round up, the targeting, the isolation and the beatings. This was routine and sanctioned by regimes across a number of countries. They were taking notes on how to deal with their own populations fighting for democracy. *This* was the day to day routine of oppression.

Lubeka thought of her father caught up in the middle of this chaos. For her, his patriotism was core to his life. He had suffered with asthma in the steelworks, with treatment that was medieval, and took the beatings from the Zomo with everyone else in his union as they marched for change through the 1980s. He also left his faith, something that she and most of the younger generation of Poles struggled with. It was part of the package. For most to be Polish is to be Catholic, and to go through the motions of both identities defined who you were, squashed between two countries who had brutally occupied their country for almost sixty years of the past one hundred. Lubeka fiddled with the small crucifix around her neck and looked to Gabreski in acknowledgement of where they were at in this point of their own small struggle.

"We will get there, Kasia. We have the future on our side."

"*Komu pora, temu czas* (When it's your time, you have to go)." Lubeka recited an old Polish proverb on death and the tragedy of trying to hold on to the old ways.

The train arrived in Toruń at 15.42 exactly. While the heavy snow had subsided somewhat, a light drift blew across the station as the train pulled up. The pair were quick and eager to alight and joined the haggle of students trying to push their sleepy colleagues into action. Stretching in unison, the line down the center of the carriage slowly disembarked, each trying to smother themselves in scarves and beanies, bubble jackets and replica mountain jackets. Toruń was bitterly cold. From the concourse of the station, they could see the roofs of the old town, the red tiles mostly snow covered and laden by a cloud that remained oppressively low. It offered the city two options, one being claustrophobia and the other the melodrama of being protected by the environment. Gabreski had never been to the old town before. Lubeka was familar with its social and educational life having taken groups from the university on the occasional field trip. It was invaluable knowledge in such inclement weather.

"What about a hotel, Kasia? We need to get a base here. Do you know of anywhere we can cold-call?"

"How much do we have?"

"Obviously your budget is nil, Kasia." Gabreski smiled. "I am taking that as a given. I cannot see your university funding a research venture while you are on leave." Lubeka gave Gabreski a wry smile and replied.

"What do you have, Łuka?"

"Give me a minute." Gabreski stepped to the side and under the canopy of the station began to dial on his mobile. He knew that he also was on a budget, but that his own department in London had an emergency fund in the event that their professors had worked themselves into situations while on trips away. Lubeka busied herself anticipating the sensitivities of a business call where Gabreski was negotiating money. Gabreski's English echoed along the platform.

"Three days max, Anne. The symposium is over... I know I have to teach... We are almost there... The Polish media." The sharp sentences were interspaced with silence as the negotiation moved and ebbed. "A research assistant... We need the support... The product will be certain." The last faded comments shifted the discussion onward, but the expression portrayed by Gabreski was one of relief and a result of sorts. He offered one thumb up to Lubeka.

"Well, Kasia. We have a budget for three days. The department will run with this as long as our partners are happy and the results are legal. They don't mess with governments. Anyway, we have the funding and you are included."

"So, a hotel?"

"Let's get a taxi." Freed from the worry of financial constraints for the time being, Gabreski felt that the department credit card would come in handy to keep the two of them warm at least. The two moved into the small taxi rank outside the station. Lubeka grabbed the first passenger door she could find.

"The hotel off Wola Zamkowa." The weather had obviously calmed the traffic of the town, but as with the rest of Poland, snow was not to be an obstacle for ordinary life to continue. The lines of school children plodding home after a day freezing in school was considered the norm. The cold was ever present. There was a general acceptance that nothing should interfere with the workings of family and jobs. The minus ten caught Gabreski more so than Lubeka. His self-imposed exile had tempered him to sunnier climates. The taxi was warm, the smell of the residues of the driver's smoke and body odour lingered.

"Do we try and find Mazur tonight or wait until light tomorrow?" Lubeka was obviously tired and with freedom from Warsaw she realised that this could provide respite for a while.

"My instinct is to search for him. But maybe he will find us. You need a rest, Kasia. Let's just take it easy tonight and that will give us the energy to track him around the city tomorrow."

There was relief on Lubeka's face. She sensed an opportunity where she had been given release to escape the pressure, even to take a moment from the speed of the events. The taxi ploughed through the slush along the riverbank and to the main Warszawska Road. The raw power of the Wisła River carried the panorama across to the other bank. The stream of the moving and groaning ice-flow was a humbling spectacle, its energy carrying anything unlucky to be caught in it rapidly through the city centre, too powerful for human intervention. The odd tree would struggle to survive among the ice and rushed violently down under the Piłsudski and Malinowski bridges. The contrast was enormous between the force of nature and the containment of the taxi.

"I have never seen a river so angry," Lubeka commented.

"It has been like this for days." The taxi driver assumed the comment was directed to him.

"Has it overflowed anywhere?"

"On down the country, but not here."

"It looks dangerous."

"There was a lot of lives lost in the last big flood around here in July 2010, if you can remember that." The power of the river brought both excitement and fear to the occupants of the car. Gabreski was taken aback at the force of the flow. The taxi driver acted as if it was a normal event, driving parallel to the raging flow.

"We will get through this one. We always do." The standard regional resilience sounded through.

The hotel was located just outside the centre of the old town. Its external and internal contrasts were extreme, with a 1980s frontage and an interior which tried hard to replicate what is perceived to be the grand interior designs of the renaissance buildings that survived the war and distinguish Polish architectural heritage. The hotel was just too new, missing the genre. Lubeka worked to get a packet of cigarettes out of her backpack before the taxi had even stopped. She left Gabreski to cover the fare, and stepped out into the freeze. The evening was closing in and darkness had already settled. The fridge-like conditions gave the street lighting an orange glow, flickering into a telling atmosphere which suggested that it would be like this until the next spring. Anticipating Toruń in the middle of winter, Lubeka had lit up by the time Gabreski had emerged from the other side of the taxi.

"Have you texted Marianna yet?"

"I will do, when we book in."

"It is bloody cold here. You'd better get me a room." Even Lubeka was taken by the plummeting temperatures.

"I will see what they have available. This is well out of season and the hotel is out of town. We should have no problem."

Gabreski went on ahead into the lobby where the grey marble of the reception provided a complementary image to the ice flow outside. "Two hundred and twenty zloty each, which is forty-three British pounds or fifty-five euros". He immediately thought that this would be appreciated in the accounts office of the university. He handed over his credit card to the receptionist.

"Two rooms, two nights." He repeated the arrangement. "Is that okay?" Gabreski called across the reception as Lubeka strolled in.

"Perfect."

The hotel seemed to be almost empty. No one was around and the usual sea of university people, who would at other times of the year have commuted through the town to the Nicolaus Copernicus

University, were not there. No one was hugging the bar. With forty thousand students it was the biggest thing happening in the whole region. The weather had obviously been having an effect on the commercial life of the city, even if the locals could endure the cold.

The rooms were on the fourth floor of the hotel. Gabreski's faced the river and Lubeka's the town. For him, the power of the ice-flow, the rush, was awe inspiring. It fixated him as soon as he went into the room. The windows had sealed the room in a dry heat, but the view over the river caused him to appreciate the raw life of the torrent. This was nature at its fearsome best. There was a knock as Lubeka pushed her way through the unlocked door. She also went straight to the window and watched as the last light of day shimmered on the heaving mass of broken ice.

"This is beautiful." The chill of the window and the vista of the river in twilight sent a rush of life through her.

"I have never seen anything like this, Kasia. This is just wonderful. I am sure the locals treat this as an inconvenience of winter. What a wonderful spectacle." Gabreski remained in his coat, the bag dropped by the door.

"What will we do?"

"What about Marianna and Beata?"

"They are okay. They worked in the archives until four and then went to Beata's apartment to sift through the files and videos. They have found similar material as before. Photos have turned up which show some of the establishment at the site of protests. Some are political, some military and some business. They seemed to be surveying the specific protests. We will need to clarify this with Beata when we get back. They have kept the search to Kraków." Lubeka walked over to leave the room. "And, they are still being followed by the same thugs."

"Okay. How about we take a walk through the old city and find a pub somewhere." Gabreski had heard about the city and felt that there was some time to explore, even briefly, the reasons why this one was a world heritage site.

"I have a friend here. I will call him to see if he is free. He can take us around." Lubeka saw the opportunity to rekindle a friendship from student days.

"Do you think he would mind?"

"I do not see why not. His name is Tomasz, Tom. He lectures in international law. He is a bookworm. He will be only too happy to take us on a walk around the town. He should also be able to tell us about Mazur and where we can locate him."

"Okay, go for it."

Gabreski offloaded some of his clothes to give the room a presence. Lubeka dialled Tom Spyra. Spyra was an enigma in Lubeka's life. Bespectacled and rotund, he had been a part of her circle of student friends. His passion was Africa, even though he had never been outside Poland. His research and teaching had brought him to a position where he was recognized as one of the most knowledgeable voices on Polish development policy in the country, yet he remained demure and autistic in his manner. In Western societies, the glamour and professionalism of Lubeka would not have connected with academics such as Spyra at any time in their careers, but through their unique circle they developed a bond that had lasted as their respective worlds progressed. Lubeka changed tone, her use of language softened as she spoke to him on the phone.

"Yes, Tom. I know, it was hateful. He was buried in the city cemetery. I am good though. It is done. I have to move on."

"Listen, are you free this evening? I have Professor Gabreski here from London. We are doing some work on the Lustration process. You may be able to help us out.... Yes... Yes... Okay... nineteen hours at the Copernicus statue in the town... Great... I will look forward to it. Goodbye."

Turing to Gabreski, she said: "We are on for tonight. Tom knows the city inside out and will be able to give us some directions to the Interior Ministry."

"Kasia, that's good. I would be interested to meet Tom. This place is as far as you can get from Kraków. I would think that they are either trying to keep Mazur out of the way or he is hiding from something. Anyway, have a rest and then we can get to business."

Lubeka stepped across the corridor and both doors closed simultaneously. She went straight to her tablet and with an hour of space, chopped and changed between her iPhone and her tablet, clicking it into its keypad. Emails had been building up, mostly condolences, but two were of particular relevance. One was from Nowak. They had not heard from him in days and this was an appearance in a manner that she was familiar with. On reading the email, annoyed, she pushed the machine onto the bed and stripped to take a shower. The heat of the train and the freeze of the evening had made her sweat then cool down a number of times since leaving Kraków. Her and her clothes were musty.

The shower was refreshing. Just what was needed to give her time to reflect on what they had actually come through over the past few days. It was a moment she had to herself. She knew her life scenario had changed immensely. This was a new fight, no longer hiding in historic archives that she did not know what to do with. Something had shifted, someone had been spooked. This is the message that she read from the attention she was getting. Something was starting to unravel. As she dried off, she built up the confidence to return to the email. Nowak's message was straightforward:

> "Dr Lubeka, it has been brought to our attention that you have been working on a different project while still employed by this department. This contravenes our contract from last year and while your work is considered important to the overall international profile of the department, I have been instructed by the university authorities to release you from the contract forthwith. Please call in to finalize the relevant documentation as soon as possible. Prof. Nowak."

"Bastard." It was the only word that Lubeka could muster. She realized that he had not even mentioned what had happened to her that week – just the sack. The one word "bastard" was hammered forcefully into the reply window and sent. She just accepted that they had got to him and that was that.

For her, he had sold his soul for a promotion and everyone knew that. Selling out his history was more serious than that. The next email was more intriguing. The name was not recognizable, but the banner was of immediate interest. 'Kraków Student 1988'. The email was from a woman living in Krosno. "Dear Dr. Lubeka, I read the statement in the newspapers about your research into the Soviet collaborators. I was a student in Kraków in 1988, and was arrested and beaten by the Zomo. I am afraid because they know who I am. But I have something to say. It may be of interest. Can we talk? Maria Braszak."

Lubeka hurriedly replied, with more courtesy than the previous email. This was exactly the type of person she had been struggling to find, and with care presented a rationale for her recent work, requesting a meeting anywhere at the nearest convenient time. She knew that Braszak would be in her fifties and, if living in a quiet southern town, would be out of the vortex of political intrigue in Warsaw or Kraków. This could be fresh, someone who was there and wanted to witness on behalf of the dissidents. Lubeka realized it was a brave move by the woman. She closed down her computer and buried it in the middle of her clothes. On opening her room door, Gabreski was there, opening his door at the same time, cleaned up and ready to go to the old town.

"We have some movement, Łuka. Nowak has sacked me. I could not work with him anymore. Also, we have a contact, from 1988, a woman has come forward after reading our press release."

Gabreski was still trying to take in the first snippet of information.

"Why would he sack you?"

"He is looking for a promotion, that's why!" Lubeka snapped. Gabreski put his arm to her back and gently moved her along towards the lift.

"I have known Piotr a lifetime. He is a bit bureaucratic, but not malicious."

"You only know him as a student. People change, particularly people who have become bitter."

Gabreski changed the subject, feeling that his sympathies should be with Nowak.

"What else?"

"A woman from Krosno wants to talk to us about the June 1988 protests. I have agreed to meet her. We can do that, okay?" The appeal was to Gabreski's credit card as much as to him. Without a budget or a wage, Lubeka was quickly calculating how vulnerable she had just become.

"Why not, the train is rolling on this and we have to find some closure." Gabreski knew that there would be no satisfactory result in the whole saga, but felt that they needed to push the case to the point where they were forcably or legally stopped. Nowak's intervention worried him in that he knew if the pressure was that close to them, it could get more intense as the evidence started to stack up. Coming out of the lift the breeze from the open door at the front of the hotel brought an urgent tussle to wrap up. The bite of the evening was fierce.

"Shall we walk?"

"Sure." Gabreski was convinced that he was not acclimatizing well to this minus ten or twenty degree environment, but felt sturdy enough to get on with the walk. Lubeka was obviously more familiar with this temperature, with her Eastern clothing to match, unperturbed and wanting to get on with it. Her pace and silence, interjected with the occasional cigarette, was a picture of struggle. For Gabreski, walking through the open space of Tumult Kino on the way to the old market square, he followed Lubeka pounding through the snow and thought of the calibre of the women who had been fighting on this land for half a century and more. Lubeka was one of them. First to question, first to punch and first to be put into the trucks to be taken away. He tried to think of any monuments to the fighting women of Poland, but none came to mind. The five minute walk trebled in time, as each laboured step needed to break a new footprint in the snow. Gabreski had got used to the luxuries of middle class life in London, viewing taxis as an extension of his living room. For Lubeka, walking saved money, that was it, it just was a part of life. Treks through the snow, be it at five forty-five a.m. to get the first tram from Nowa Huta, or to the supermarket with a backpack loaded with shopping. It was just life.

When they turned into Szeroka, the main pedestrianized thoroughfare in the old town, the breeze was bitter, but the snow had already been walked into the cobbled stones. The Lens Centre, selling sunglasses at the corner of the square, and the Egyptian bar, really seemed to be out of context in this environment. The irony was not lost on the life size brass donkey that the local government had installed outside the shop.

"There he is." Lubeka picked up pace again as they walked towards Spyra and immediately the two faces lit up with recognition. For Gabreski, Spyra had an uncanny resemblance to a young, but weightier, Lenin. His mannerisms were stiff but he was obviously someone who felt comfortable in his own skin.

"Łuka – Tom: Tom – Łuka." Lubeka in her gestures was insisting on friendship. Gabreski felt he was just about to confide in someone who looked like the founder of Eastern communism.

"Where shall we go, Tom?" Lubeka was eager to get talking. Gabreski wanted out of the cold.

Skyra had been going in and out of university archives in Toruń (*Archiwum Państwowe w Toruniu*) for a number of years now, and had a reasonable knowledge of the material that Lubeka was working on in Kraków.

"Let's find a bar." Spyra's sentiments were immediately well received.

"With dinner. We are not here to relive your student clubbing days." Lubeka felt she had to discipline the situation. She ushered her two colleagues back down the street and onto the platform of one the new Italian restaurants in the city that sat out proudly into the cobbled road. "This is good. It will keep Łuka happy also. It is one of the few places here that has good cheap Italian wine. Not a thing we take much of in Poland. It's only for the British!"

The establishment held the same gastronomic formula that could be seen throughout Europe. It was still a novelty of sorts in parts of

Poland, with regional conservative tastes and its resistance to wine drinking. It was ideal for visitors, and was also, first and foremost, warm. They settled in at the back of the restaurant, ordering an international mixture of drinks to match the personalities of the three colleagues, Polish vodka, Italian wine by the bottle, and local beer. Gabreski was first to break the niceties as they huddled around the table.

"Kasia has had a tough week of it, Tom. We need to get to some answers before we get back to Warsaw. Kasia has told me of your work and position. You know of the death of Officer Stanisław Kaszowski in Kraków?"

Gabreski waited for the nod from Spyra.

"We are convinced it was not suicide. We also think that Andrzej's death was not suicide. Now, Kaszowski told us to get to a senior officer in Toruń called Mazur. We need to get to him to see if we can get through to Bartek." Gabreski stared at Spyra moving to pour the wine that been unceremoniously placed in front of him.

"Mazur is here. He is at the Office of State Protection. I do not know much about him, he lives out of town somewhere. He is not front line and keeps himself to himself. I know him through the university training days, where these people are brought in to brief us on dealing with issues that are sensitive to state security."

"And what about Bartek?" Lubeka pushed on.

"That's the company. That's all I would know about it. That history and that link is something that you need to get Mazur to talk about."

"Do you know where we can find him?" Gabreski was keen to get on to the plans for the coming day.

"They have an office in the Pomeranian Provincial Office at Plac Teatralny, just up the street from here as you go away from the old town."

Spyra began to get unsettled as the questioning continued. The intensity of Lubeka around these questions revealed a side to her that was unfamiliar. She listened to every word, elbows on the table. Spyra's history with her had always been relaxed and casual. In this, he picked up on the experience that she had, and was, going through.

"Let's eat, Kasia, tell me about your plans."

The three returned to a more cordial discussion as they chatted carefully about everything and anything beyond what had happened over the past week. Gabreski came into his own as the wine flowed freely around the table and the perfectly made pasta arrived to disengage the topic of the day for a short period. The talk revolved around nightlife in Kraków and the changes that had taken place in Poland since joining the European Union. The roads came up, standard chatter across Poland when the EU is mentioned. The World Cup caught Spyra and Gabreski's minds. Lubeka wanted to know more about the Poles who emigrated.

"What was London like for the Polish diaspora? Is Polish Dublin any better?"

"Let's take this to The Lazer." Spyra was in his comfort zone, returning to the idea of a night out with Lubeka.

"What is it?" Gabreski liked the sound of the place.

"Jazz and blues with live bands. Two minutes' walk. Finish up, finish up and let's go." Spyra was out the door as Gabreski struggled to get the waitress to process the credit card.

"You not only look like Lenin, you run from the bills as quick as him." Lubeka laughed. She felt safe, something that she had not felt in Kraków and particularly not in Warsaw. She knew that they were being tracked, but obviously they saw them as out of harm's way in this part of the country.

"Kasia, text Marianna to see if they are okay before we go on."

Lubeka produced her phone from her pocket to flutter a sequence of letters into the window. "Sent. They can do without us for a few hours." Lubeka turned off the phone and stashed it away in the inside pocket of her coat.

They walked through the cobbles that had dried with the freeze, surrounded by lines of neatly shovelled snow, grey and crust-like at the side of the streets. The heat of the alcohol had taken the chill from the night. The old fashioned pub crawl made its way to the club.

Designed for a younger clientele, the club was sparsely occupied and darkly atmospheric. Groups of young people were dotted around the bar, huddling together to listen to each other in competition with a local blues band. At points in the singing of American classic blues songs, the Polish accent came through very strongly. For Gabreski, it only added to the authenticity of the band, with perfect riffs and a stage presence that was either Toruń or Woodstock. Occasionally, young people, presumably students, would break ranks to come over to Spyra to say hello. The popularity of the young academic was plain to see. Gabreski thought of himself when he was in his late twenties, lording it up in the pubs of Bloomsbury in London where his students would keep a steady flow of cheer. Lubeka listened to the music and was content in the noise of the night. By the time the band was beating out its final riffs, Spyra was holding court at the edge of the bar. Gabreski and Lubeka had sunk deeper into conversation, curtained by an ever-increasing throng of young people. By one thirty, they shouted across to each other on leaving the bar.

"We have a long day tomorrow. Let's get out while the going is good."

"I will hang on for another while, Kasia." Spyra was in no mind to leave. Gabreski and Lubeka bid their farewell to him and navigated their way towards the door. The neon guitar outside the club shone a red glow across the steps and with the snow almost luminous, the clear sky offered a fitting backdrop to a night that had, for a short moment, frozen time out of the turmoil of the day. The walk back to the hotel was slow and laboured, with both suffering the worst of mixing drinks and the 'dobra zabawa', the fun of the night.

Back at the hotel, they steadied themselves to get through the lobby and to the lift. Gabreski's arm instinctively shadowed Lubeka without touching, in a protective shield that he found natural and she found safe. On reaching the adjacent rooms, they paused and looked at each other. The night had softened the tragedy of the previous days, it was a time without anger and Lubeka appreciated that. This was a world away from the apartment in Nowa Huta or the aggression of work. It was a tender moment and this she was drawn to.

"Do you feel okay?" Gabreski sensed a change in Lubeka's mood and a silence that was vulnerable.

"Yes. Just sad."

"Things could have been better all along in both our lives. We walk into life and it has its own plan for us. With all things right, neither you nor I would be here."

"I suppose." They stared at each other knowing that the circumstances were so extreme for each of them.

"Well, we need sleep." Gabreski's voice lowered as he turned.

"Please don't leave me alone, Łuka."

Without talking, he opened his room door enough to let Lubeka through. She walked shakily to the window and looked towards the ice-flow. He sat on the bed and put his head in his hands. They both knew that they were in a whirlwind not of their making, but they felt sheltered in that room at that moment. This was as peaceful as Lubeka had been in her recent life. She pulled the curtains open to let the full splendour of the river be visible to Gabreski on the bed. She moved to the bed and sat down looking at him inquisitively. Their two worlds collapsed into the dry heat of the room, with a vista of the power of nature as the backdrop.

22rd November

In Warsaw, Krolas and Wójcik had taken the reading of files into the early morning. They had cross-referenced the original material with online released data from the Stasi files in Germany and what little the KGB had donated to the institute in Warsaw. Krolas stayed with Wójcik in the hotel to plough through the video-shots and online files. Eventually, they had been able to amass a core stock of four hundred files with relevance to Kraków in 1988, some with reference to Bartek, most with long gone figures of a violent and desperate past.

Their concern about Lubeka was manifested in a long list of texts, lined up, waiting for an answer. Their worry was lessened by the knowledge that Gabreski had a reputation for being able to handle himself in some very difficult situations. Also the last received text was of them meeting up with Spyra and going out to a student club. This was a positive sign.

For Krolas, the late nights did not get any easier. The coffee never seemed to get any sweeter and the pedantic need to accumulate precise details on stories led her to the occasional exhaustive collapse. She revelled in knowledge and the journalistic instinct that she had developed while trying to chip away at the old system in the 1980s. Her world had not changed that much. She still struggled with arthritis and cold, the inability to make enough as a journalist to break outside the world of Warsaw and the eccentricities that she had developed living in poverty for so long. She carefully snapped away with her battered digital camera, collecting the screen files in a manner that Wójcik thought weird and antiquated. "It's safe here. It's safe here." Krolas repeated the mantra through the night.

By the time the dawn was breaking through the two were barely awake, but remained at the task. The tens of thousands of files from the Stasi that had come online had given an added source to cross-reference. With fastidiousness in the last days of the old system in East Germany, the secret police attempted to rip up as many documents as possible, before the whole archive was left to the scrutiny of history. Only in late 2012 was the technology created to enable shredded and ripped pages to be electronically matched, to supply an unending bank of material on the German communist regime.

As Krolas and Wójcik were to find from this source, there was also Stasi influence in the Polish system. They were present for interrogations and were there throughout the eighties, to glean whatever information they could from the Polish dissent. Renowned for their efficient ruthlessness with prisoners, they shaped the manner in which the SB and Zomo went about their business.

Beyond the Stasi, the two worked through the regional Polish newspapers from the time, which would have been state sanctioned and short on security detail. The propaganda was so pervasive that even neutral statements on crashes and industrial accidents had to be tailored for the party faithful. International affairs at the time – the Soviet war in Afghanistan, the rise of the extreme right in Western Europe, the combustive Middle East – were easy distractions from the oppression at home. It all added up. The language and semantics were of that time. The blanket of distraction was all encompassing. Unless it rallied the party, Poland was not to be mentioned.

The cold awoke Krolas. She struggled to get from a fully made bed covered with A4 sheets, annotated with meticulous, handwritten notes, packed with dates and incidences. She was content. She felt that she had been able to break the back of the mountain of files that gathered over the previous couple of days in the Institute and online. All she had to do in the morning was print key files from the memory card of her digital camera; safe, offline and untouchable.

In Toruń, Lubeka turned to the bedside table and fumbled to turn on the iPhone. It shuttered and went alive with incoming messages. Gabreski had been awake since dawn, but had spent the time just looking at Lubeka sleeping. Without returning to the tenderness of the evening before, Lubeka went to the window while reading the mail. It was obvious to Gabreski that, irrespective of anything that was said or done previously, Lubeka was already back on the warpath.

"Eight from Marianna. There are some from Spyra and some from home. Everyone seems to have had a busy night of it."

"How about home, Kasia?"

"They think I am going mad. Why would I not want to be back in the tenement, acting the mourning wife? They should realize that that moment in my life is over. God, the community has its claws."

"You are a tough one, Kasia." Gabreski could see a woman who had just about had enough of it all and was set on fighting her way out of her past and the past of others.

He looked at Lubeka drying off from a shower and dressing in a manner that was efficiently graceful, flowing to and from the shower room, to eventually present, *Vogue*-like, to take on another day.

"Okay, Łuka, we have to take this show on the road again. I need a smoke. I will see you for breakfast. I am ready to move."

"Give me five minutes." Gabreski was impressed at the speed of Lubeka's readiness. The morning had come quicker than he would have liked. The task at hand was very much back with her mission. He felt that she was driving a train that may or may not come to grief. He packed up, ready to go. Leaving the backpack in the hotel room with Lubeka's, he ensured that his tablet was securely gripped within his inner coat pocket. With one last glimpse out to view the ice-flow, he felt caught in a world that was alien to him. His good nature again had led him on a path that was dangerous. At times it left him numb.

Lubeka stood at the front door of the hotel, solid in her black Iceguard padded jacket and surrounded by smoke. The still of the frozen atmosphere held the puffs of smoke lingering. The illusion of the moment was broken by Gabreski's arrival.

They settled for the ubiquitous continental hotel breakfast, in a ritual that Gabreski had come to consider normal through his feral lifestyle. Lubeka had never travelled outside Poland. Her lack of experience at the etiquette of hotel life showed. She was noticeably awkward going back and forward from the breakfast bar for each forgotten item. Occasionally, she would defer to Gabreski with the question "What's this?" He found it curious but dutifully responded with a sequence of one word answers. The hash brown and salami were eaten quickly, the coleslaw and cottage cheese carefully side-lined on Lubeka's plate.

"What's the agenda for the day, Kasia? How do you think we should handle Mazur?"

"We handle him with care. He could be working for anyone here. The old guard, the state, the president's office. Who knows? But he is the only lead we have, and Kaszowski gave his life to present us with his name. The least we can do is ask the questions that Kaszowski would have wanted us to ask."

"I have anguished over this, Kasia. What do we want from him?" Lubeka stirred another sugar into her cappuccino and paused to the point where Gabreski was feeling that she had elevated onto another planet.

"We need to get scalps to justify what we have been through and what others have suffered. Is Mazur the scalp we need? Or is he someone we can trust? I don't know. We have to sound this out with him and then take a judgement call on it." Lubeka was impatient with the lack of movement and the slow pace in getting results.

"Well let's go then, Kasia. There is only one way to find out where this will take us."

As the two moved to the door, Lubeka produced another new packet of cigarettes from her jacket pocket and proceeded to the habit that had started at school, one she was never able to shake off. As they walked out of the hotel to make their way to the provincial buildings at Aleja Solidarności, Gabreski quipped.

"Kasia, why do you do this to yourself? Those things are more lethal than the Zomo and Stasi put together."

"It's one of my few pleasures." Lubeka smiled in a knowing manner with a sub-reference to the night before.

"I live my life in London, rarely coming across anyone who smokes. It is the last refuge of the wretched of the earth."

"That refuge gives me time to think, wretched as it is. Have you no vice that will eventually kill you? Something you still need every now and again." The sardonic tone was a sensitive one for Gabreski.

"So we are indulging in a long term suicide pact, Kasia, eh."

"Would you like a cigarette?" Lubeka gestured with the box. Gabreski smiled and retreated from the debate.

"Maybe later."

The snow had crusted overnight and glistened under a crystal clear blue sky. As they walked, the pathway was still slippery. It crunched under foot. The red bricks of the old church and townhouses that lined the route were camouflaged white. The buildings gave evidence to a history that had survived the last century, some of the few in the country. The contrast between the antique gothic and the monolithic Soviet style of the provincial building starkly reasserted a contorted past, a place occupied continually with bureaucratic imprints running architectural marks through the region. The regional, state and EU flags flew over the provincial building, profiling the only significant statement of ownership by the Polish residents in the city of government buildings. Otherwise the history of this type of landscape belonged to others, those who had come and gone, but who had left their statement of intent in stone.

The intersection was surprisingly clear for a working day. Lubeka and Gabreski briskly made their way across and onto the steps of the imposing concrete, pillared entrance. As expected, the security was imposingly official. The two security personnel, dressed in a uniform that predated the Fall, dominated by overly large peeked caps, requested identification, signatures and details of why they were at the building. This was followed by a brief formalized spell of questioning about the visit.

"We are here to speak to Colonel Mazur in regard to Officer Kaszowski." Without removing his glare from Gabreski, the security officer lifted the phone and spoke in a hushed voice. The other guard stood menacingly behind Lubeka. They were well armed and had a demeanour that suggested a past in military service of some sort.

"Okay, Professor Gabreski, Doctor Lubeka, could you please go to room 124 on floor three. Colonel Mazur will meet you there."

The stairwell was dark and unlit, presumably with the intention of saving on lighting. The building was warm and solid, the echoes and dusty smells leaving hints of a not too distant alternative use, a remnant of a world still struggling to change. The stairs led through on each floor to a network of corridors. On the third there was a glint of light coming out of a number of the offices with some of the doors left ajar. As they walked through the hallway, the opened doors gave a view of officials hunched over desks, fighting with dated computers and card indexes that had become a lost figment of bureaucracy. 124 had a solidly closed door, lacking name or character. Just the number. Lubeka knocked. The door opened.

"Come in. I have been expecting you." The voice from inside was precise. Lubeka and Gabreski froze. This was one of the figures from the pictures they had been looking at in Warsaw. The pictures may have been grainy, but it was definitely him. Older and greyer, but nevertheless the same man as they had seen from 1988, coordinating Zomo operations against students and miners. In his late fifties he had chiselled features and cropped hair, recognizable from the old photos. He was politely spoken and official in his mannerism.

"Bartek." Lubeka was taken aback at the sudden revelation of this person.

"Please come in and take a seat. I have been informed of your work. I have been expecting you. You met Officer Kaszowski, I believe." For Gabreski, he sensed a resistance to even engage.

"Who is Mazur?" The desk was piled high with what looked like invoices and receipts from municipal offices.

"I am Mazur. I am also from Bartek."

"What did you and your thugs do to my husband?" Lubeka stood up suddenly, putting her fists on his table, leaning over to confront Mazur.

"Kasia, please, we are here for an explanation, not a fight. What do you mean?" Gabreski directed his question to Mazur.

"I can understand your frustration, but you must understand that you are both out of your depth in this and in danger." Mazur's monotone voice reflected his demeanour.

"What do you mean?" Lubeka, seated again, held to her combative disposition.

"I am Colonel Mazur and I work for the Office of State Protection. I am coming near retirement and have been sent to Toruń to sit out my final few years in service. I am not your enemy. Get that clear Ms Lubeka. I have been tracking rogue collaborators in Kraków since the early 2000s. We have had a team working on the Lustration process there for years. We have a problem with Kraków in particular. That was why Officer Kaszowski was sent to investigate. He was one of our best. He will be a sad loss, and get this straight. He died in the service of the new Poland. The police idea of suicide was convenient. We know what happened."

“What about my husband?” Lubeka was needing answers and felt that there was some movement with this man. She settled back into her chair.

“He may have been collateral damage. You were a target after giving away your findings from the Warsaw Institute. The TW, the old Zomo and SB personnel who are all still out there, do not like your kind. Mr Lubeka must have fought back. They were there to wait for you. From our sources, you were uncharacteristically late back that night, presumably due to the university function. No one was meant to get hurt. People were there to search your house. That was it. The Kraków TW have been sent into turmoil over this and they are seeking to close files on their mistakes as quickly as possible. It is bringing undue attention from Warsaw to their existence. Someone followed our people to your house. Your husband must have startled them. He must have come in between our people being there and the TW.”

Gabreski and Lubeka were suspicious of his frankness. The older man sat as if undertaking an interrogation; still, threatening and focused, shifting stares from Gabreski to Lubeka, distancing himself from the events and the history.

“This is Kaszowski’s last text to me.” Mazur raised his phone and held it up for the other two to read.

“CM. TW split. Bartek panicking. Coup talk. Urgent. Act. K”

“Do you know what that means?” Mazur pulled the phone back, and sat back to hear a response.

“We now know that Kaszowski was murdered at Bernatka Bridge. What does the rest of this mean?” Gabreski absorbed what was being said. Lubeka worked to get her tablet live.

“This is one of the most dangerous periods since the breakup of the Soviet Union for Poland. The last of the cabal of the old regime are restless. They see the Ukraine as the start of the fight back. Some want action against the state, they see it as having moved too far to the West. Internally, they are in turmoil. The shuffle for control within the TW organizations is coming to a head. And you just happened to stumble upon files that could reveal identities and activities. They are talking about a coup and have split down the middle."

Lubeka pushed the tablet in front of Mazur, with a picture of him at the interrogation of students in 1988.

"We all have histories, Ms Lubeka. Believe me, I am on your side. I was a junior officer in the state security in the late eighties. We were given our orders and we were told the US was orchestrating the dissent. We did not know any different from others working for the state. In those days, it was all that there was."

"You tortured our people."

"Every police force on earth tortures its own people in some way. Torture continues to this day, Ms Lubeka. Your beloved West is no different. Have you ever heard of water-boarding? Have you heard of extraordinary rendition? We all do it. But I chose to work for our new democracy. We had to learn what democracy actually meant, and we are still learning."

"Bartek? What did Kaszowski's text mean?"

"Bartek was a Zomo unit in Kraków in the 1980s. I was Bartek in the same way that eighteen others were Bartek. Some were too senior to be exposed to the cameras and files of the day. Others, such as myself, wore the badge and played to the piper's tune. We were told that we were suppressing the Western insurgency. The unit was tough, they prided themselves on the fear they could instil in the population."

"So there is infighting in Bartek?" Gabreski pushed the point.

"Bartek's lack of discipline was a revelation to me, that the remnants of the old unit were now fractionized. I was one of the few who broke away, but they were my former comrades. That has meaning to soldiers. The agreement from the 1990s to settle into business and disappear has been broken. The hard core, who found it difficult to accept the passing of the Soviet world, seemed to be wanting to stage some sort of return. We do not know what. We just know that your symposium frightened them, and frightened them enough to kill."

The picture of Mazur lay on the desk in front of them. The tension of the meeting was dissolved, as the points being presented made sense to both Gabreski and Lubeka. Why else would he confide? He was in Toruń to hide. The room darkened briefly as Mazur closed a set of red curtains, the only expression of personality in the whole structure. This was the two generations meeting, the perpetrator and the victims of the past. Mazur lifted a brown, newish looking folder, pushing it towards Gabreski. It was similar to the file covers from the Institute.

"We try to get out what we can. You got to some of the more sensitive material before the state researchers, or the TW, could. Here is one you may find interesting."

Gabreski opened the file to see a clipped picture of his mother. She would have been in her twenties. Her home details and domestic circumstances were listed in detail on the front.

"The Stasi had more on her. This was all we could locate on you and your family."

As Gabreski opened the document further, he saw a picture of himself as a child and one of him as a student activist in London in the 1980s. It detailed his activities, his companions, even his girlfriend at the time. He flicked back to see that his mother had been pulled in by the SB prior to her leaving the state. It explained her hatred for the old system. She was tortured.

"What about me?"

"Ms Lubeka, you have only recently come on the radar. May I also point out that you are no longer living in a Soviet security vacuum? You have freedoms that Mrs Gabreski could only have prayed for in her day."

"What about my father?"

"There is no current record of him. I assume that he was too small a fish to fry. Records are sure to be there somewhere, but when I called these out, our team could not locate him. I'm sorry."

Lubeka was eager to look at the file on the Gabreskis also. It was meticulous in its characterization and provided information that even Gabreski could barely remember or had not heard his mother talking about. The make of carpet in their apartment, providing evidence of additional finances coming through to the house, the list of neighbours and their work details, the music the family liked to listen to, a list of his mother's Western music albums, the style of clothes they were wearing, the number of times his mother went to get her hair done. The file gave the names of the neighbours who were informing on them, which shocked Gabreski because some were still in the family circle.

His immediate thought was that the state seemed to have nothing better to do than spy on a young family who were simply trying to get on with being young. Gabreski recalled one statistic from the former Democratic Republic of Germany, which, with a population of sixteen million in 1980, had a security service with a network of three hundred thousand operatives. That was one state security operative for every fifty three people. Everyone was spying on everyone else.

"What do we do now?" Lubeka was at a loss to find a way through the weight of this problem.

"I do nothing. I am here to retire. I am just waiting for a modest state pension, a townhouse well out of a sniper's range and a medal from the President. Your options are different. You can follow Professor Gabreski back to London or you can work as a waitress in the bars of Kraków. With the information you have, you need to get it circulated in a form that will bring the Bartek rebels into the open. Link them to a conspiracy and they are finished."

"What influence do they have?" Gabreski was thinking of the impact of the old regime on the formation of the Russian Federation.

"They are small, but have money and access to power. This gives them some weight. But it is being monitored. I would also suspect that we are all in the lens of them as well as the state. Just like the bad old days. Just watch your step. Play this game in the public gaze and know that if there is a clear threat the Office of State Protection will react."

"So we are bait?" Lubeka was suspicious of a state office that had as its role tracking down disgruntled former security personnel.

"If you want to look at it that way." Mazur leaned over and closed the Gabreski file, lifting it and returning it to a locked cabinet behind his desk.

"Does the Bartek network have files also?"

"They were the first in to extract what they could from the SB and Zomo stock. The additional material that came from Moscow. We have some of that here. You have located some, from what I have been told."

"Can we see what you have?" Lubeka was impatient.

"I will have to check with Warsaw. I will have to get authorization for the viewing of any sensitive material."

“Can it be done?” Mazur seemed to be moving out of his comfort zone. He shifted in his leather swivelling desk chair and tapped his pen on the side of the desk. It was the first time since the two walked into his office he appeared not to want to engage. The time ticked towards midday as they sat and pondered the extremities of the situation. Lubeka looked at the figure on the other side of the desk and could not help thinking of an aging civil servant who felt he had served his country no matter what was asked of him. He was just sitting out his last days of work stamping forms and signing invoices. This was where they ended up, the ones who did not step sideways into the business world.

“It will have to be first thing tomorrow. It will take the rest of the day to clear this and verify your security clearance to get access to any material.”

At this, Mazur stood up and moved towards the door. The signal was enough. They were both thankful of the clarity that he had brought to the issue, but still felt that there was more to gain from talking to him.

“Thank you for calling in. I look forward to seeing you tomorrow.” Mazur was back to his official self and a persona that obviously ensured his continued employment through the transition and into the new Poland. His lapel contained a pin of the eagle, caught in the glint of the light. Lubeka and Gabreski rose to go into the darkened corridor.

The questions remained unanswered from the moment they left Mazur. Was he a patriot who had served his country and participated in its eventual liberation? Was he merely a bureaucrat serving whoever could offer him favour or give him status? The latter was a concern that Gabreski was particularly aware of. These people were the cabal who had silted up progress throughout the nineties and still obstructed transparency in Poland. Age had taken most of them, but there were obviously some still entrenched within the system, sitting out time.

Lubeka was satisfied with the conversation. She had gained some detail of the world in which her father fought and was able to confront someone who was there, and on the other side. Previously there was a cloak of denial covering any of the direct questions that she had to ask.

"Do you think that was sanctioned?" Lubeka sought to get an answer as to why Mazur was so candid.

"It seemed to be, Kasia. But he was a bit nervous at the end of that discussion. That worries me." The two remained silent as they made their way out into the street. The snow had stayed crystallized, the brightness of the sun felt warm in the purity of the winter.

"We have the rest of the day to get back to the files, Kasia. What if we visit the state archives [Archiwum Państwowe w Toruniu] at Fosa Staromiejska. There is bound to be something there."

Lubeka took the first steps onto the road and out of the provincial buildings. The security guards followed them out, offering a similar amount of menace as they had on the way in. Lubeka walked without looking back, while Gabreski strode alongside her, directing the way.

"I want to go by the church on the way. I want to light a candle for my father." Gabreski did not answer, holding dutifully beside her.

***

Lubeka trudged quickly through the snow. Gabreski tread carefully, afraid of slipping. The Church of the Holy Virgin Mary was on the way to the archives and stood prominently above that end of the old town. The church looked more like a silo, decorated with stained glass windows that shot up skyward. Simple in its understated Franciscan façade, its red brick solidness told a story of another world – one of protection, patricianly. They went down Piekary and past the old prison tower, turning right into the dark wooden side entrance of the church. Lubeka took a lead and went into the nave of the illuminated church, genuflecting and blessing herself as she went towards the candles glittering at the back of the aisle.

Gabreski followed, uncomfortable with the rituals and the need for compliance. This was not his space. He humoured his mother on her devotion to the faith, but his sense of self was more absolute. He envied Lubeka in a way, for holding on to something that his world had been struggling to give up. Hers was obviously different. She had faith hardwired into her from the streets of Kraków, her family, her community. This was natural to her. This is what holding on to hope entailed for those with faith, going through the rituals and serving out the machinations of church and legacy.

Gabreski felt awkward. He was a tourist. He moved from the paintings to the series of altars along the sides of the aisle as if in a museum. All he could do was marvel at the gold leaf spread and sun blasts around the heads of the saints. The remains of incense made him cough, its smell disconcerting. He watched the slow moving figures of the elderly, seeking favour from something he believed could not exist. It took him beyond his understanding. He signalled to Lubeka and pushed his way to the exit.

For Lubeka, this was a deeply personal moment, somewhere she could connect with her own. This was the world of her childhood, her parents still with her in this sanguine discipline. And what was more, she knew the suspicion others would have of her, in her late twenties, a professional woman, kneeling to invoke hope from long dead saints. It worked for her and it was her culture, with all its contradictions. It was how she was made up. She caught up with Gabreski at the front door, putting another cigarette onto her lips.

"We have been doing this forever. Why should I stop just because everyone else has taken up shopping instead?" Lubeka was aware of Gabreski walking out of the church and felt that she had no reason to justify her faith in any way to him.

"I don't care, Kasia, I just do not understand. My mother goes and plays the game, but I cannot understand. I do not feel I want to either."

"If that is it, then leave it up to us who do to go about our ways. I would never question what gets you through the day, although I have a good idea. Everyone has their own spin." Lubeka was obviously irritated by the speed of Gabreski's departure and his dismissive manner.

"Okay, Kasia, let's call a truce on this one. We have things to do without fighting an internal battle about who doesn't believe in what." Lubeka subtly raised her eyebrows to acknowledge Gabreski's appeal for a truce on the issue, and proceeded to text Wójcik. "All fine. U OK."

The moment represented a different type of conflict within Poland, one which had not as yet come to a head, but was bubbling under the surface and anticipated a future battle between cultures, between the generations, the cities and rural communities. They walked down the cobbled side streets, the sound of Lubeka's boots echoing off the walls. The town was still, distinctly quiet for the time of the day. The weather had been keeping the day trippers away and the town's people indoors. It was a short walk to the state archive building. They had not booked in, but were assured that, with the opportunity for researchers making use of the facility, they would be able to get some form of access. The building was less imposing than the provincial building, secured by solid wooden doors in a concrete corner spot. Lubeka went straight to the little vendor located outside the front door to get a coffee to warm up, holding the cup in a chalice-like grip. As she did, Gabreski went to the door and pushed the intercom.

"Hi, I am Professor Gabreski from London and this is Doctor Lubeka from Kraków. We are in the city doing research into the Lustration process and would like to know if we could spend some time in your archives."

"Please, push the door." The voice was inviting and casual. Holding the door open, Gabreski waited until Lubeka had joined him to go into the building.

An elderly administrator appeared from upstairs and gestured for them to go on into the building.

"Please, come in. We do not get too many from outside the city. I am sure you are kept busy these days. It has been on the news and everything. I recognize you." They assumed that this was Krolas's interviews that were being referred to. Together the three went into a side room with box files and a number of what looked like old school desks.

"Please, feel free to look around. We have some material that is relevant to the region, but it is not as good as the Institute in Warsaw."

The lack of security immediately gave the impression that this stock of files was very vulnerable, or could have been raided.

"Does Inspector Mazur come here?" Lubeka decided to enquire as to other interested parties.

"Oh yes. The inspector and other police colleagues have been in. Not recently though. They were present when the files were initially cleared for public use. When interest died away so did the police interest. No one really visits here anymore."

As they settled down at the table and opened the cabinets, they realized that the material was just too freely available. Gabreski and Lubeka proceded to lift boxes down, again catalogued by dates. The dust and smell of the brittle browned paper was overwhelming. They were thinner than the files in Warsaw, but reflected the extent of activity in the Toruń area in the 1980s. It was not known to be a hub of revolutionary activity. The administrator left them to their own devices and the two set about going from box to box. The silence was only broken by a flutter of paper. As the time went by, there was a realization that the whole stash of material had been systematically stripped of anything sensitive.

"They really went through this building." Gabreski was, by now, familiar with what was tampered with and what was not. The lack of photographs, selected pages missing and periods with gaps. The omissions were glaring.

"What is left here is useless. Everything is sanitized for a dead public's consumption. It looks as if the secret police did not exist in the 1980s."

"It is the remnants we are looking at here. Empty and doctored files telling us that this city had nothing going on during the period from Martial Law."

"This is why the Warsaw archives are so important to them. It is why they need to watch us closely in that part of the country, whereas here, there is nothing left to hide." Lubeka threw a batch of files from the table to the floor, frustrated with the lack of information. They had produced nothing of significance.

"Let's get out of here."

The evening was closing in and the darkness of the night was only disturbed by the fluttering of the snow. Lubeka felt that she had come up against the obstruction that she had felt through most of her adult life. Systems were continually frustrating her way. One system had halted her continually in her university career – that one was gilded with nepotism and sexism. Another system held back her progress in her passion for Poland's freedom from the past. Her marriage brought her to her knees continually, and her poverty meant that she could not escape from any of it. This was not a world of her making. It was not her life, but her context only. She had to fight on, there was nothing left to do but struggle on.

They shuffled again out and through the chill of the night, moving down the main street and past the town hall towards the hotel. Gabreski sensed an uncharacteristic darkness descending onto Lubeka as they moved silently through the empty streets.

"Kasia, don't let this get to you. I know it drains the soul, but there are people like us working on this everywhere. We are just one team of many trying to get to the truth." Lubeka stopped and there was a silence. The sound of the snow softly falling emphasized the growing pain.

"You do not know what it has been like here. You are a foreigner. Year after year, knowing that everything is controlled. Your childhood monitored, your hopes stillborn, everyone and everything beaten down. You were safely out of it. Here it continued long after that wall came down. They watched and watched, year after year. They held back the good people who stood up to them. Look at me, a generation on. As my father's daughter, I am still being held in their open prison. They delivered us into poverty as a lesson that we should know our place. And now they steal our truth. You know nothing."

For Gabreski this was it. The silted up emotional reality of the moment had finally spilled over for Lubeka. He had nothing to say. She was absolutely right. The silence returned as they stood like two bickering teens in the middle of the road. The tears broke one by one onto Lubeka's left cheek. The beads rolled down without a flinch or change of expression. The fortitude was a sign that she knew emotion would get her fight nowhere, but she was caught with human frailty and the desolation that sometimes comes with it.

"They killed Andrzej." Lubeka forced the final defiant statement out before Gabreski could intervene.

"I know, Kasia, I know." Time held as the chill of the evening worked its way through to the bone. She was visibly broken. He stood there motionless for what seemed hours. There was not a sound or a word from Lubeka. He moved to comfort her and as he leaned to hold her, she seemed as fragile as he had seen her yet.

"Would you like to catch some dinner? It will take your mind off things."

"I need a cigarette." She pulled free and walked to the side of the street, fumbling in the bag as she moved. "Let's get drunk, Łuka." It was the last thing he felt like doing.

"Food, Kasia. We need food."

"Okay. Then we get drunk."

The old town of Toruń had a magical glitter of the medieval in winter. The snow had been refreshed and the soft yellow lighting of the streetlamps provided a glow which reflected in circles on the snow. They moved without talking to the nearest restaurant in Piekary, just meters from the archive building. Lubeka was first to the door and on stepping through asked if there was a bar. Gabreski held back and gave her space to regain her confidence.

“What do you want to eat, Łuka? Pierogi?” Gabreski was in no position to go more European than that. This obviously was going to be Lubeka’s night and in turn, he would serve as the insignificant other.

“Pierogi and Tyskie. That sounds like a night out.”

“Good. It will go with the vodka.” Gabreski at this point did not resist the schedule.

As with most Polish restaurants, the lighting was brighter than in Western Europe and the bar staff overly vigilant to the signs of customers being eccentric. All the signs were present with the new customers as the matriarch of the premises came over to bring the couple to their table. Lubeka’s accent was regional and business-like, giving an impression of her being tougher than she was. Gabreski tried, where possible, to break the direct manner in which Lubeka addressed the staff. The exchange was uncomfortable, but the result was as desired and plate loads of pierogi were delivered along with a difficult concoction of beer and vodka. Even before the meal was finished, the libation was taking its toll. Gabreski had a physiology to cope with the mix; he had a lifetime of practice. Lubeka was more susceptible.

“Should we not check in with Beata and Marianna, before the night is out.” Lubeka fumbled under the table to retrieve her phone.

“Hey, hey. Marianna, how are you?” The muffled voice could be heard above the hum of the almost empty restaurant.

“We got what we wanted from the inspector, but nothing from the archives. They have been stripped. It was similar to the Kraków archives, photos removed, names displaced, everything.”

On responding, “I would say yes, the same people, as clean as ever.” The reference was to the effectiveness of the censoring of the files.

"And you, Marianna. How are you doing? How is Beata?" On this question Lubeka gestured to the bar staff for another mix of beer and vodka.

"Okay, okay. Take care and I will see you both tomorrow." Lubeka picked up on speaking to Wójcik. The day had been long and emotional and this was contact with what she considered to be the familiar and the trustworthy. Gabreski was obviously a surrogate.

"Beata has been on TV and has taken some interviews for the radio and newspapers. The threat of exposure is making a bit of a splash in Warsaw. Beata has dug out some more Russian files and has a link though to Moscow. WikiLeaks has also been in touch, wanting to post as much as they can."

"Will this not cause more complications for us all, Kasia? The more discrete we are, the more damage we will be able to do, remember." Gabreski drew from his knowledge of lobbying and conspiracy, arts that ran counter to her politicized and journalistic instincts.

"Let's see where this goes first. People obviously have an appetite for this. Also..." An index finger arose jabbing at Gabreski accusingly, "...how are you going to hold back Beata? This is her life's mission and it has been given one big boost in the arm." He held on, not wishing to confront his increasingly drunk colleague.

"Has Toruń been a shock to you?" Gabreski decided to go to the point.

"The contradictions here are a shock. The inspector was full of contradictions, but he did not seem to hide anything from us. As with the archives: what did we expect? Did we really think we would come all this way and get confessions? We have got more than I hoped for and more tomorrow, then back to the 'war' in Warsaw." Lubeka used the English word 'war' to give a sense of urgency to what they were at. Gabreski sat back and finished off another litre of beer. Lubeka again waved to the bar staff, who were, at this point, amused at the dedication of the young woman to getting drunk.

"So, Łuka, who is she?" Lubeka's topic shifted as quickly as the shots.

"Who?"

"There is bound to be a she, or is it a he?" She shuffled in her seat as the depth of the question seemed more dramatic to her than it did to him.

"There is no her or him. I have given that all up."

"I don't believe you."

"Why in God's name, after coming out of a painful separation, would I pick up exactly where I left off?"

"I don't believe you. Who is she?"

"I told you. The only one left in my life is my beloved mother, who shaped my world and gave me everything I know about Poland and your revolution." Gabreski smiled and eulogized.

"No. Who else?" Lubeka's index finger stabbed him this time on the shoulder. "I think there is someone else. Is it Nowak?" Lubeka waved backwards and forwards between the two of them with a dismissive glint. "I am going to tell everyone you are gay. And being gay in Poland is twenty years behind being gay in England."

"I don't care. I will be able to go to the pride marches in Warsaw then."

"Ha, ha, I knew it."

"Suit yourself, Kasia. If that's the best you can come up with."

The conversation held to the subject without either giving up on current affections or past flirtations. The time seemed to drift, the strength of the spirits was hitting Lubeka, quicker than the sturdier constitution of Gabreski. He acted at eleven thirty p.m. to call for the bill and some coffee. Her last demand for vodka for her coffee was begrudgingly accepted by the waitress. Gabreski took on the role of guardian, politely thanking the staff of the restaurant and helping Lubeka with her coat. The whispers from the staff of the establishment were targeted largely at Lubeka, as she bumped off the door frame on the way out.

The cold nip of the air caught them both, still struggling to fix their coats for the short walk back to the hotel. The streets were empty, the fresh mist emerging from the river hanging in the atmosphere. When they made it to the Copernicus statue in the middle of the town, Lubeka insisted on mounting the bronze donkey at the side of the street. As if a berated father at the beach, with a child awkwardly perched on the real thing, Gabreski stood beside Lubeka, waiting for her inglorious collapse.. She muffled a refrain from the nursery ryhme *Wio Koniku*, with each line growing louder and with confidence:

"Wio koniku, a jak się postarasz, na kolację zajedziemy akurat. Tobie owsa nasypiemy zaraz, a ja smaczna zupkę będę sobie jadł ." ["Go, go horsey! And if you do well, we will be home right on time for supper. You will get a bunch of oats right away, and I will eat a yummy soup."]

On that, Lubeka rolled from the donkey taking Gabreski down into the snow. Their laughter echoed through the street as they tried to compose themselves and stay dry at the same time. "We will get arrested." Gabreski held on to the few sober thoughts that the couple could muster. "Good." The defiance of Lubeka held out to the last.

They made their way on down Szeroka and navigated their way slowly across the narrow streets to the hotel. Gabreski and Lubeka managed to regain composure enough for the staff at the reception to pick up that they were the worse for wear. Lubeka's pace to her room picked up somewhat as they got closer. Gabreski opened her door and she fell straight through to the bathroom. Before he could close the door he could hear her retching. The sink taps were all on as she tried to recover from the excess. "I am sorry. I am so sorry." Lubeka shouted from behind the closed door. He sat on the bed and waited until the taps were turned off and Lubeka emerged looking totally defeated by the intoxication. For him, it was a normal enough intake for an evening, for her this was unusual, and a release from the experiences of the week. "Are you okay?"

"Yes, I had too much." She fell onto the bed.

"Kasia, take plenty of water." She was out cold. Gabreski lifted the blanket that was over the wardrobe. He lifted her as if a child and carefully laid her onto the bed, removing her boots and gently folding the blanket around her. He held the hair from her eyes and watched for a moment before being satisfied that she was safely asleep. He watched and smiled, then crossed the corridor to his own bedroom.

Gabreski went straight to the mini bar. The room was dark and the hum of the river flow brought him, glass in hand, to the window to marvel again at the natural spectacle. He was enthralled by the complexity of the evening's company and felt as though the bureaucratic process of chasing down files had become an all-encompassing life and death chase for everyone concerned. Unlike the drab monotony of other previous commissions and trips, this one was alive for him. The automat of research had been released to feel the vitality and vulnerability of life for those around him. He put his half empty glass of whiskey down, undressed and went to bed.

23rd November

Lubeka awoke first. The cold atmosphere was sobering and the polyester smell of the room's carpet was heightened by the staleness of her hangover. She glimpsed at her phone to check the time. 6.43

a.m. Her mind was still ticking over with the previous night's exploits and she took comfort in that sense of freedom it gave her. As with other explosions on the social scene, she saw the wildness as a necessary evil, a release from the other things that burdened her way. She checked to see if Wójcik had texted yet, and then hit the handset to turn on the TV. The dehydration and the taste of alcohol compelled Lubeka to struggle her way into the shower. The first cold blast of water shuttered her into the day, the fragrance of the shampoo worked to refresh her from the night before. As she dried off, the issues of the day caught up with her immediately. *TVP1 Telewizja Polska* relayed the seven a.m. news.

> "The former Italian Prime Minister has been released from prison after serving four months of a four year prison sentence for tax fraud. The health of the media mogul turned politician had deteriorated in recent weeks and he has been moved to hospital closer to his political heartland in the north. Regional news now. The recent revelations that Polish security interests were being run by members of the old regime's secret police has provoked comments from the president's office on recent progress within the Lustration process. A spokesman for the president stated that this was a serious issue that reflected on state security and needed to be scrutinized and dealt with comprehensively. One of the journalists who discovered the evidence of a breach of Lustration protocol, Beata Krolas, had this to say..."

Lubeka dived for the phone and quickly dialled Grabreski. "Answer, answer, answer." On a response coming through, without any formalities, she shouted: "Turn on the TV. Beata is on the news."

She then sat down on the bed hearing the echo of the other TV from across the hall.

"We are working on the basis that those involved had cleared their own files from the archives, but had not been able to locate the Russian and Bulgarian documents. We are currently at a stage where we are building a case for the Office of State Protection. To date we have had a number of former prisoners contact us to provide evidence of where they think the communist state security operatives are still engaged in state sponsored activities."

Krolas was composed and highly disciplined throughout the interview, not exposing the general chaos of the research or the lack of detail. Gabreski knew the pressure was doing exactly what they had intended.It was drawing out the enemy. He joined Lubeka.

"She is very visible in this, Kasia. We have to be more discrete." Gabreski was aware of the growing interest, and not only by the media but in governmental circles.

"We are in a conflict with them, Łuka, and we need to break cover sometimes." Lubeka was emboldened by the bravery of Krolas. The natural cautiousness of Gabreski was protective, but he had no say in the assertiveness of the others, and found himself caught between his security consciousness and an eagerness to engage.

"Okay, we need to go. We can grab a quick breakfast on the way out and get to Mazur before we head back to Warsaw. Apart from sightseeing, there is nothing left here for us." Lubeka and Gabreski rushed to get their bags packed and in unison met at the doors of the corridor, ready to move on as effectively as possible. Both were of a mind to get back to Wójcik and Krolas as quickly as possible. The view from the breakfast suite of the hotel was again of the brightness of the winter sun over the full splendour of a snow covered town.

The last scattering had been heavy enough to recoat the streets and paint the trees with a white layering. There were no signs of a hangover in either, and the etiquette of breakfasting in the hotel was such that both had to slow to the generic anonymous pace expected across Europe.

"What do we want to get from Mazur this morning?" Lubeka set her coffee down with a slight tremor. Self-aware, she followed up with an apology of sorts, smiling at the incapacity.

"We need to see if he can give us solid detail. We need names, even to pin people to the files and the prison interrogations. This is a chance to get to the core. Mazur has more to give, even though he is obviously too damaged by his own history to show any remorse."

The sense of progress was starting to encourage Lubeka as she grabbed her bag and drank the last of her coffee in one interconnected sweeping action. Without a word she left the table. Gabreski followed. Lubeka went out of the front door as Gabreski went to the reception to finalize the bill. He threw the expenses card from the university across the desk and watched as Lubeka blew smoke rings at the front door of the hotel. In perfect English the receptionist responded: "Thank you, sir. I hope you enjoyed your stay. That will be eight hundred and eighty zloty." The receptionist smiled in an inquisitive and suggestive manner. "Yes, thank you. It was excellent." Gabreski was as sincere and dignified as he could be, given the antics of the previous evenings.

Outside, they prepared themselves for the short walk around the edge of the old town to the regional offices. They retraced their steps from the previous day, following tracks already made in the snow, and aware of the traffic as it picked up for the morning rush of the town's people. With a cigarette still in hand, Lubeka struggled to keep her backpack secured and steady for the walk ahead. As they moved along Prosta, a wail of sirens broke the humdrum of the morning. Their pace quickened as they arrived into the open concourse of the Pomeranian Provincial Office at Plac Teatralny. Five police cars with lights flickering surrounded the opening to the building. The time had just turned eight a.m. and the normality for people gathering at the front door to start work was frustrated by a flurry of activity by the local police. An ambulance pulled up as Lubeka and Gabreski joined the huddle of people on the pathment at the front of the building.

"What's going on?" Gabreski enquired of one of the workers standing beside him.

"I don't really know. The police said that there had been a security breach. A cleaner said there were shots."

They pushed to the front of the group of bystanders. One of the men standing on the steps watching the crowd made a move towards them. The police stood to the side and saluted as he made his way across the concourse.

"Professor Gabreski, Doctor Lubeka. I am Commander Browarczyk. I am the head of operations for the provincial Office of State Protection. We have had an incident. Would you care to follow me?"

Lubeka, uncomfortable, looked around her, checking out the viewing public. She showed signs of panic. Gabreski picked up on this and grabbing her hand, whispered.

"It's okay. We need to see what has happened. We will be okay. This is too public."

Browarczyk, waiting, could see the nervousness between the two. He turned to walk towards the building. Lubeka and Gabreski followed in discomfort, bemused at the deference that the local police had to the suited official. When they entered the doors, he turned to them:

"I believe you had a meeting scheduled with Inspector Mazur this morning."

"Yes. At eight a.m."

"I am afraid to have to tell you that Inspector Mazur died this morning at approximately seven fifteen a.m. We know you were both at the hotel. You are not suspected of anything."

Browarczyk indicated that he was going up the flight of stairs towards Mazur's office and proceeded taking two steps at a time, followed by Lubeka, Gabreski and two uniformed police officers. Medics were at the front of the office door. They entered. Mazur was sitting back in his seat, head tilted to the left with a small puncture wound to the side of the temple. Lubeka walked around and stared, fascinated by the neatness of the wound. A small hand gun lay on the floor beside him.

"Was anything taken?" Gabreski looked to Browarczyk.

"Interesting that you ask. The only thing that we have seen to be disturbed is the file case on the right. It was not fully closed. We can check it for finger prints, but, if this was not suicide, I would think those who did this would be experienced enough to clear up after them."

"Will it go down as suicide?" Lubeka sounded cynical.

"Maybe so." Browarczyk was matter of fact.

"That would be two of your officers committing suicide within the week."

"That is our problem and we will deal with it our way." Browarczyk looked at Mazur and voiced his resolve. Agitated, Lubeka came back. "Can we go?"

"Give the officer your contact details on the way out. We will need to get in touch. As you note, Doctor, that is two deaths within the week in our office and you were in contact with both prior to them being discovered."

"Can we go?" Lubeka was persistent.

"Yes." Browarczyk gestured for the two to be released and went back to the body, standing over it while the medics went through the procedure of surveying the scene. Flashes lit the darkened room as the police photographer catalogued the site. Lubeka and Gabreski hurried down the stairs towards the fresh air of the morning, to be halted by a young uniformed policeman with an urgent demeanour.

"Commander Browarczyk asked me to take you to the train station if you want." The two hesitated before Lubeka nodded. For her, it would give them the quickest way back to Warsaw. They pushed through the growing band of onlookers and curious workers who could not get into their building to start for the day, and stepped into the blue and white stripped Ford with the familiar *Policja* in large letters across the bonnet, sides, back; a flickering red, white and blue light on the top. The quiet of the car was broken only by the policeman talking to himself about other drivers on the road.

Gabreski and Lubeka sat with bags in hand, still stunned by the sight of the corpse, a man who had provided them with as much as he patiently could, and suffered the consequences. The car rattled to a halt at the front door of Toruńs train station and with a brief acknowledgement from Gabreski both passengers got out of car and went into the seats located on the inside of the entrance.

"What do you think, Łuka?"

"Contact Marianna and let her know. Mazur was executed."

"How are you so sure?"

"No one organizes a meeting to divulge sensitive information and takes their own life before the event. As I understand the psychology of suicide, victims almost always would complete what they believe they have to do before they die."

"Another one?" Lubeka worked with her phone and began tapping away, feeding the details through to Wójcik and Krolas. As if it was a natural extension of human communication, when she completed the text and sent it, she returned seamlessly to the conversation.

"We need to get back as quickly as possible." She stood up and stepped forward to look at the timetable above them. "10.02 a.m. It will arrive at 13.09. That's good for two hundred and thirty seven kilometers. We will be able to meet Marianna and Beata for lunch."

"I think we can manage that, Kasia. Don't be worrying." Gabreski was aware that Lubeka was painfully conscious of the costs, given that she had lost her husband, her job and was struggling not to be dependent on him to get to the answers. He went over to the ticket booth to buy the tickets. They both went out to await the arrival of the train. The few others who dotted the platform were similarly occupied, standing like smoking statuettes against the white of the snow that cut up the rail lines out of the city. As ten a.m. arrived, the numbers waiting to travel to Warsaw were not what would have been expected from an intercity train. The rumble of the train livened up the platform as the heave of passengers prepared for boarding.

Gabreski and Lubeka got a carriage close to the back of the train. They were hit with the dryness of the blow heaters that lined the walls and caught by the dampness of the seats. For them, simply moving had become important, getting back to the security of the others. They faced each other across the carriage. Within minutes of leaving Toruń, Lubeka was on her tablet again, ploughing through files that been videoed, freezing the frames periodically and noting anything relevant in a packed bullet-pointed window at the side of the screen. Gabreski stared out the train, occasionally getting a glimpse of the river as they travelled inland through the rural belt that feeds Warsaw, desolate at this point of the year, covered and isolated. He reflected on the casualness of the death. The clouds poured over the land as the sky got darker and darker, the brightness of the morning giving way to the weight of winter.

To find a distraction, Gabreski flicked through notes that he had been carrying in his bag since leaving London, notes on the rationale behind the process of Lustration, working to the sensitivity of the revelations. Time rattled with the train. En route Lubeka found a small window just outside the carriage where she could carefully poke a cigarette with the option of losing it quickly if the conductor made an appearance. Then back to the tablet and the files. On occasion, Gabreski broke the peace with interested soundings on what Lubeka was up to: "Did you find anything?" Only to receive the curt response: "No, nothing."

By the time the train arrived in Warsaw, the snow was fluttering across the tracks and the chill was penetrating the windows, in absolute contrast from the blow heaters on the train. Lubeka and Gabreski waited until the train pulled right up to the platform before shuffling papers, the packing increasingly urgent. Lubeka texted Wójcik: "13.15. Arrived. Meet Hotel 14. Lunch. K." The skill and use of the tablet had become habitual to Lubeka, as with most of her generation, that the means of communication was now faster that talking directly. It was an automated world in its own, its users eschewing direct contact. Almost immediately, the familiar buzz of her phone returned the confirmation from Wójcik: "K. OK. M." The conversation was complete. Gabreski stood behind Lubeka as she reengaged with him and put the phone away.

"Right, we are going to the hotel. It will be great to see those two again."

***

Warsaw station throngs with people during the day, the flow unrelenting, the noise of a thousand conversations competing with the announcers and the rhythm of machinery. Coming out into the concourse of the station, in the bump of people, Gabreski noticed two middle aged men making themselves visible to them by walking towards them and shifting in the direction they moved, without actually making contact.

"Our friends are back, Kasia." Lubeka looked around and caught one of the men's eyes. He did not distract from the glance. The intention was to let them know that this was their domain and that Lubeka and Gabreski were intruding again.

"Back to the 1980s." Lubeka was enthused by the interest and, after the death of Mazur, the energy of the danger gave her the anger of an embattled fighter. Toruń had been a respite for her, death and all. Gabreski rushed her into the lead as they marched to the taxi rank at the side of the station. A silver Nissan hatchback was already revving up, the 'five 1s' transferred onto the side marked a familiar firm in the city. The snow around the streets at the side of the station was foot-beaten and grey. An unmarked Mercedes pulled up behind the taxi. The two who were following them slumped into the back seats.

"Chmielna, please." The taxi driver pulled out without speaking a word. The accompanying Mercedes awkwardly forced its way into the traffic and followed closely behind. "Do you want me to lose them?" The taxi driver was instantly aware of what was happening and livened up when he realized that there was more to the couple in the back seat than the fare. "No, they know where we are going. It is better to live in the open. Keep them in view." Gabreski was concerned that the driver would take it as a mission to escape the Mercedes, simply for something to do, and was not prepared to be the entertainment for the day for a bored driver. "Okay, your life."

The driver slipped back into the stream of traffic, navigating by the Congress Hall and Galeria Centrum and cruising down towards the hotel. The traffic was heavy enough for that time of day and the slowness left the uncomfortable disposition of the Mercedes sitting behind the taxi every time there was a jam. This was obviously their form and a trick learned from the old days – intimidate without directly confronting – waiting until orders tell them to act.

Wójcik and Krolas were standing under the cover at the entrance to the hotel when the taxi pulled up. There was a rush of smiles as the women regrouped after the seperation of the past couple of days. Gabreski paid the driver and joined them. They made their way through to the seats in the lounge of the residence. Wójcik proceeded to unload wraps from her bag. To the rustle of the packaging, the four settled into the leather seats. Wójcik ordered drinks and took it as her task to 'keep house'. Lubeka was, as always, first to get to the politics of the situation and distract from the small-talk.

"Beata, you have hit the big time. We saw you on TV in Toruń."

"Yes, I have been doing interviews since you left. There has been a lot of interest. Even the BBC has been in touch. Our friends are definitely not liking the attention." Krolas pointed towards the door, assuming that everyone knew the target of the comment.

"And what about you two? That was horrendous this morning."

“Mazur was dead when we arrived. He was about to give us more detail. We were hoping that he would name names... but they got to him first. It was plain for everyone to see. Thinking it through, this has exposed an open wound between State Protection and the TW’s people.”

“That is where we are as well, Łuka.” Wójcik spoke over Gabreski to get a cross reference on the point. “We have been followed continually and with the media interest they have become more intimidating. What we have found is interesting though. Bartek is a team of operatives in the Zomo from the late 1980s. The Russian material shows this very clearly, but, and here is where it gets suspicious. All references to the unit have been stripped out, file by file, picture by picture, from the Polish archives.”

“The same in Toruń and Kraków.” Lubeka gestured loosely to Wójcik. “The security companies and the lucrative deals are all linked into a two decade long plan to position these people close to the Polish government and business world. We suspect it is being driven through Moscow or Bulgaria, or Hungary, but not here. My guess is that they operate across all these places and are fluid in their management, wherever the profits move.”

“This would confirm our suspicion that the Polish security services are under pressure to manage these people, and are struggling to do so. They can act at will, but how far are they willing to go.” Gabreski pushed the hypothesis to its logical conclusion.

“They have murdered three people linked to us alone. How many more have they killed?” Lubeka went straight to the life and death of the situation.

“We have more files, and have been able to narrow them down. Each with detail and photographs from 1988, and the Kraków crack down.”

Krolas changed the subject forcefully.

"Look, we have them scared and it is working its way out. The momentum is growing. We will have our material on WikiLeaks tomorrow. It will be broadcast around the world. There will have to be government action then, or it will look complacent and ineffective in enforcing its own policies on former state security operatives. It is happening, folks. We just have to keep this momentum ticking over. Now... you have something more urgent to get to." Pointing at Gabreski and Lubeka. "Warsaw's NGOs want you to talk tonight on the Lustration process at the Neon Przyszłość."

Lubeka looked to Gabreski with a hint of sarcasm. "Do you know what you want to talk about?"

"I will think of something. I suppose it's an opportunity to get some genuine public feedback on the process. We will at least get a friendly reception there."

"What about Mazur." Krolas cut over the whole conversation. Gabreski continued.

"He went too far. He gave us, and I assume others, information that he should not have passed on. It is leading us back to Kraków and that unit that operated across the city in the late 1980s."

"We have some names and profiles from the unit at the interrogations of 1988. There is no point releasing them until we get a tipping point on this and some backing from the state." Krolas was conveying the vulnerability of their position, which received nods of approval around the table. She went to her bag and pulled out her phone.

"I have something for you, Łuka." She played with the screen of the phone and scrolled through the dozens of files that had accumulated over the past couple of days from the archives. They waited patiently as the dabbing of the screen slowed and then stopped. “Here...” Krolas pushed the phone towards Gabreski. “Is this the same Piotr Nowak that you know?” Gabreski held the screen and zoomed. What was visible was the faint picture of a young security operative with details from October 1989. He held it and remained passive while trying to collect his thoughts. Lubeka leaned over and redirected the phone so that she could get a better look.

“I knew it. I knew it. Bastard. He has been after me since he arrived at that university. He was always working for them.” Lubeka was almost gleeful at the exposure. Gabreski was contrite.

“He would have only been in his late teens at that point. He never ever said that he had been involved. I wonder if he had made the biggest mistake of his life and spent the rest of his career trying to compensate. As long as I have known him, he has always been against the regime. That is the Piotr that I know, no question. It was his idea for the symposium. I am not sure if this is him. It kills him to look back to his own circumstances.” Gabreski knew that there was a national bi-polarity around Lustration and what it meant, but for a generation that lived through those last years of the regime, the contradictions of the liberation meant that many were caught building lives in one reality, only to have it quickly replaced by another. One year a state police officer would be defending a certain type of status quo, the next, he or she would be working in another. When the world turned upside down in Poland in 1990, many of its people were caught on the other side of the fence.

“He was in the Freedom Union since its foundation. He never had anything other than condemnation for the old system. This is a shock to me. I have known Piotr a lifetime.” Gabreski awaited the judgement. Lubeka was quick and ready to judge.

“Łuka, someone has got to him. He has been evasive since the whole question of stolen files came up and with the symposium, well, he scared me with his attitude. Maybe he was afraid that I would discover something about him."

"Maybe so." Gabreski struggled to accept the revelation.

"His old friends must have returned to haunt him. His past has caught up with him."

"Kasia. He would have only been a teenager when that photo was taken. We all make mistakes."

"Some more than others." Lubeka was quick to intervene. Wójcik moved to halt the conversation.

"Okay, okay. We need to move on. Nowak has a history, big deal. We now know that. Someone is maybe on his case, but we may need him for support at some point. Let's leave this one. Łuka, I would think that you may have a few words to say to him. We have bigger fish to fry, don't get caught with finding minnows."

"I would appreciate it if I could deal with this one personally. We are close friends and I would like the space to talk to him first." Gabreski was taking the embarrassment for Nowak.

"I will be having a word also." Lubeka could not help taking the opportunity to attack. After starting the discussion, Krolas moved in to close it, shutting the file and bagging the notes and equipment she had assembled on the table. "That's it. Marianna is right. We have something substantial here, and need to stay on the game or we will get lost in the paperwork. That's not my way. And, Kasia, I know it is not your way either. Let's go for it. We have an opportunity." Reluctantly, Lubeka agreed and the movement around the coffee table brought the conversation in other directions, with the two who stayed in Warsaw wanting to know what Toruń was like and the other two asking about the menace that had been tracking them over the past couple of days. Krolas characteristically suggested that there was one man she would like to follow her back to her apartment, but thought it would cause a conflict of interests. As the four reengaged, the energy of this small community became immediate.

The rooms in the hotel were untouched, unmade, and as with every hotel room across the continent, comfortable but homeless. Gabreski went to the mini bar. His ritual of shoes off, whiskey, water and flick on the television news before finding a comfortable spot on the bed, brought a familiar routine back to him. This was snug. Lubeka, Wójcik and Krolas went to the adjoining room and went into a dizzy exchange of files and events. Krolas amassed the printouts from her camera, taking pride at the security of the old methods.

There were a few hours pending before they had to make their way around to the venue for the talk. Gabreski tried to mentally recall Nowak, to see if detail in their correspondence would suggest that he was anything other than genuine in his sentiments about Lustration and the symposium, and all that that meant. Nothing. Gabreski could only surmise that he had wiped this episode from his youth and from his personal history. Gabreski knew that the Nowaks, as a family, were split between those who were involved and supportive of the regime, and those who were adamantly opposed. This was the case for many families. Maybe Nowak stepped over the line before crossing back to join the resistance. He hoped this was the case and feared that their whole friendship had been a lie. He texted Nowak to request a meeting in Kraków when they returned.

The night closed in quickly with the lowering cloud line, and while insulated from the freeze and the wind-chill across Warsaw, the mist of the evening and the grey tracks of snow on the roads created a sullen atmosphere.

Neon Przyszłość, Neon Future, was a venue that they were familiar enough with. It had a reputation across Poland as a venue for progressive discussion, art and culture. It hosted the liveliest debates and the most distinctive jazz in the city and attracted an audience that delighted in the alternative. Often frowned upon by the more conservative elements of the political elite, and suffering periodic bouts of closure, it nevertheless resounded of '68 in Paris and '56 in Hungary. Essentially it opened space for ideas.

Gabreski's phone went. It was Krolas.

"Do you have a tie?"

"Unfortunately, yes. I usually carry one around just in case someone organizes an event where I can't wear jeans and a tee-shirt."

"Stick it on and we will collect you on the way down to the car." Krolas had kindly volunteered her two colleagues for the discussion and set about managing the event. As the women emerged from the room Krolas continued to nervously finalize the evening. "Mention WikiLeaks, Snowden and State Protection. Keep focusing on the snowball effect of information." Lubeka listened but remained detached. Her black dress, boots and tights heightened the severity of the event for her. These were her mourning clothes and this was her moment in public to tell it all. Gabreski heard the movement in the hall and emerged from his room.

The shower had woken him up and dressing up a bit gave him the look of a civil servant who had gone somewhat astray. Meeting the others en route out of the hotel with the refinery and justification of the cause, gave the event a formality that they had not encountered before. This was an opportunity to outline the process to date and get some willing participants, hopefully inspired, to widen the battle lines. Lubeka was particularly caught in the adrenaline rush of the evening and focused on the audience as much as the presentation of research.

"Will there be anyone representing the government at this?"

"I presume so, but I am sure they will not be making themselves known. We expect a couple of hundred people, some from the media. This evening is basically the civil society organizations in Warsaw picking up on an issue. They can then take it away and do what they will with it. It is a first for the Lustration process here." Krolas sounded proud of her arrangements and the opportunity to show off to her Warsaw community.

Her Polo was cramped as the four of them squeezed in with bags and notes. The familiar black Mercedes' lights went on as the engine of Krolas's car ticked over. The drive was only a few minutes through the back streets of the city center. Krolas pulled into a parking place a few minutes' walk from Neon Przyszłość.

This area of Warsaw was witness to the impressive military processions of 11th November to celebrate Independence Day. The rebuilt post war baroque buildings looked older and were it not for the destruction of the war, would have been as splendid as the boulevards of Paris or Prague. But this was Warsaw, loaded with its history and its laboured recovery. As the group approached Neon Przyszłość, the Mercedes drove by without the occupants acknowledging their 'marks', their duty for the day complete. The cold of the evening and the proximity to the entrance gave the group distraction enough not to entertain the departing trail. A small group were huddled outside the pillars of the entrance, some smoking. Laughter and chat was the general noise emanating from the venue.

"Let's get a quick bite to eat. We have thirty minutes or so." Krolas had the evening planned as if it was her own wedding, perfectly timed and with a guest list that she had personally selected. The others agreed, loosened their coats and scarfs, and made their way through to the bar and restaurant. "This is a lovely place, Beata. It could almost be Kraków." Wójcik jested with Krolas and helped to release the nerves that both Lubeka and Gabreski had generated between them on the journey. "Marianna, we are keeping this one for ourselves. You have enough places to go to down there. And, anyway, this is big city stuff." Krolas teased.

As they worked their way to a spare table in the corner of the bar, friendly patrons in the place would break ranks from various groups to come over to hug Krolas or kiss her on the cheek. This was her natural environment. One man shouted across from another table: "Beata, well done, you are a real celeb now", in an obvious reference to the television appearance. Krolas lit up with the recognition, waving and smiling as if she had just arrived home. The echo of conversation mixed with soft background music to highlight the buzz of the place, dark and moody, but atmospheric to the point of friendliness.

They all felt comfortable and safe in the place. It was something that Lubeka recognized and warmed to, reminding her of big nights out with friends at home. Krolas seemed somewhat dizzy with the attention. She was usually caught in the isolated eccentricity that came with living alone and fixating over a raft of human rights issues. Gabreski celebrated with her in the sense of solidarity that places such as this could bring to like-minded colleagues. This was the Left Bank of Warsaw, crushed into one exciting building. Despite temporary closure, the recent reopening of the facility seemed to give new life to the NGO community around the city.

By the time the waitress had found her way to the table, Lubeka was worrying about getting into the hall in time to set up for the debate. Tapas was the agreed option for something quick, and the round of drinks comprised of wine for the table, hurriedly poured by Gabreski, fighting around the conversations that Krolas was engaged in on a rotational basis.

"Do you have enough material with you to handle this audience? It is not what we are used to." Gabreski sensed the growing anxiety of Lubeka and moved to assure her.

"I am going to shoot from the hip this evening. The research material and files are now only a part of what has happened. We can make a few feathers ruffle here." Lubeka shouted into Gabreski's left ear causing him to jump back. With the patrons beginning to drift into the restaurant and bar, the noise levels rose correspondingly. The buzz of the room built the anticipation of what was expected of the speakers. "This is where life is at in Warsaw. There must be hundreds here."

"I wonder where they all come from?" Lubeka enquired.

"I would presume the universities, but there also seem to be some journalist friends of Beata." Gabreski lifted the wine and poured the last of the bottle around the table. Krolas was the first to jump when Wójcik shouted the time to each of them around the table. "Eighteen forty-five. Eighteen forty-five. Eighteen forty-five. We must get moving." The chaos of leaving the table and paying the waitress heightened the dynamic, with Krolas taking the role of a manager more than a player in the choreography of the evening. The group squeezed through the throng of the crowd to the stairwell, which opened up into a haphazardly renovated baroque ballroom with lines of chairs down each side and a set of speakers chairs elevated at the front. The room was two thirds full and filling up rapidly as the bar emptied. With a gender mix that was noticeably equal, most were in their twenties and thirties.

The lights trained on the front seats carried with them a heat that Gabreski found distinctly uncomfortable. A burdensome television cameraman cluttered the center of the aisle, straining to get shots of the arriving speakers. The entourage fanned out across the front of the aisles, and the chatter of the audience gave a level of anticipation that the group had not expected. The room had more of the feel of a press conference than a university type talk. Gabreski tried to get his cues from Krolas, who had accompanied them to the front. They were greeted by a distinguished linen-suited man, whom Lubeka recognised instantly from the national news broadcasts. She introduced herself, offering a firm handshake and directed him across to Krolas and Gabreski.

"Łuka Gabreski from London. This is Adam Dinan, a friend of mine with years of experience in investigative journalism. He worked with the *Guardian* for a while."

"It's a pleasure to meet you, Adam. Thanks for organizing this discussion. We have a few things to say that may update those interested."

"Łuka. Before we start. We have had some interest in this evening from the State Protection Office and others who may not be as welcome." Dinan was politely offering a warning.

"We need to be sensitive enough to the legal issues and keep it as formal as possible. Do you hear that? We need to keep our comments within the law." Lubeka moved over to join the other three and shrugged, giving hesitant approval. Dinan arranged the seats and fixed the microphones in a manner that would pick up all three of them speaking. The back of the hall was more packed than the seated areas. Behind the glare of the spotlights, the shadowy figures of solemn middle aged men lined the back. They were noticeably different from the rest of the audience and brought a menace to the room. They seemed to appear from nowhere, eight or ten in number, overcoats on and each silent to the other. A couple of them had phones which lit up the corner, held by their sides. Gabreski presumed that they were recording the proceedings.

The room had a used feel about it, with the reflection of dust across the two spotlights at the side of the aisles. The smells from the restaurant below were still present and the darkness at the back of the hall presented the speakers with an antiquarian context within which to deliver ideas.

When Dinan stood and looked knowingly across the audience, the chatter settled. Showing a familiarity with this kind of forum, he set about explaining the background to the evening and the agenda for the discussion. The silence in the room was borne out of respect for the personality and anticipation over what was about to be said. The introductions were straight from the university staff profiles. Lubeka fidgeted, awaiting her intervention and correction. Sitting in the front row of seats, Krolas was visibly the most enthusiastic person in the hall, clapping without cause before they had a chance to speak, but setting the tone for the audience's response.

Gabreski was up first, taking the position of a television chat-show host, steady on the chair but gazing between Dinan, Lubeka and whoever was at the back of the hall. He had notes with him and his tablet sitting to the side. When it came to engagement with the issues in this unusual venue, he took the judgement call to go for a more populist approach. The silence before he spoke seemed like hours, as he composed himself to get impact with an opening comment. He could see in the back corner, the lights of phones, elevated to record what he had to say.

"The silent witness of the state has continued to fear the legacy of the past. Victims' voices from not so long ago are still with us and are demanding justice. We, as activists, academics and journalists have not done the injured from the past any favours by avoiding the issues. Many of you are not old enough to remember Gruba kreska, the thick line policy from Mazowiecki's Poland in the late 1980s.

Gruba kreska was the start of a process which we hopefully called Lustration, but which has come to mean complacency. National reconciliation is as necessary today as it was in those painful days of the 1990s, and the ghosts of the past will only be exorcised if we take them through the light of truth."

Gabreski built up the philosophical layers of his argument, carrying his years of lecturing experience to an audience who were increasingly receptive to the points being made. He knew he was playing the tune that they wanted to hear, but it was hammering home a mission statement, carrying voices from the past.

"We, as Polish people, are tired of our oppressed history. We need relief from it in order to build a positive, assertive, European community who are living for the future with all the prosperity it can bring. We are tired of those who still block this aspiration at every point. We are tired of those who come from our darkest past and attempt to strangle our future."

The conclusion of Gabreski's talk was intended to stir emotions. He fixated on his mother's plight and that generation who were never released from the angst of the Second World War and its aftermath. Lubeka saw another side to him, beyond the bourgeois façade. His political instinct had come out when he put the university papers to the side. Lubeka took a different lens on the forcefulness of the oratory, and thought it was powerful to have him on side. This was what Poland had lost and is losing to emigration. The Poland outside its borders could hold an answer in its struggle to be released from history.

The spotlight moved to Lubeka, as Dinan shifted his chair to redirect the gaze of the audience towards her. Uncomfortable as she was in this arena, the street fighter in her was more aware than ever that people were listening and someone out there, even the suits at the back, could be in a position to influence change. Her target was the grey shadows at the back of the hall, her positioning calm and personal. Dinan's introduction had not been tampered with by Krolas as he rolled out the academic credits and citations for the young woman: 'excellence', 'passionate', 'specialist', 'dedicated' – the words did not fit with the person Lubeka knew. She was embarrassed by the limelight.

"Thank you, Adam, for that kind introduction. One correction though." Gabreski held his breath and waited for it. "The university you just mentioned has just sacked me for researching the Lustration process." After a brief retorting apology from Dinan, she continued. Gabreski saw her academic career well and truly ended at that point.

"I have been working on this subject for most of my adult life. For me, it has been straightforward. People from a horrible past still affect my life. They tortured my father for standing up to them in his day, as did a lot of young men and women. They took over from the Nazis when they were beaten, and oppressed the Polish people from the comfort of their offices and bars. They killed my husband and they continue to punish the good people of this country for standing up to them." Immediately, Krolas led a chorus of applause which encouraged Lubeka to take a more combative seated position on the edge, her pointed finger stabbing at the air as she went further and further into the issues. Her language was forceful and the points were succinct and accusative. On occasion she hit high notes of a political pitch, which inspired the instant ripple of approval from the audience.

"We need the Russian files to be translated and released to our public by the Institute. Where is the president's office on this issue? The good people who went through those years, and who continue to suffer, demand justice."

Thirty minutes spun by on the catalogue of governmental and social failings. Sensing the time constraints, Dinan interjected to return the atmosphere of the hall to a more ordered adjournment. He declared that time constraints were catching up with them, thanked the two speakers and then directed the discussion towards questions. Gabreski sat patiently as Lubeka fielded the vast bulk of the questions, covering a raft of concerns on files and third country involvement in Poland. Before the hour, one of the men from the back of the room stepped forward and clearly, authoritatively, relayed two questions. He seemed to be reading one from his phone.

"Doctor Lubeka, I am from the State Protection Office. I have two questions for you. Are you saying that members of the former regime's security services murdered your husband? And second, are you willing to name anyone involved in that crime, or the others that you have cited, in public?" It was a legal minefield. Gabreski leaned over as Lubeka sat searching for an answer.

"No, Kasia, I will take this." Dinan gestured to Gabreski to answer the question in the hope of taking the sting out of the end of the event. Lubeka conceded. At the back of the hall, four of the men who had been present during the discussion discretely made their way out of the back door.

"Sir, I am pleased that your office is present here this evening and taking notes on the evidence that we have gathered on the limitations of the Lustration process. May I also pass on my condolences on the loss of your colleague, Commander Mazur. As you can appreciate, we are in the final stages of our research, and while Doctor Lubeka's views are based on her personal experiences of the involvement of former senior members of the state security services, we remain at a stage where we are finalizing our judgements for legal consideration. I am sure you appreciate the complexities of the legal case."

Lubeka stared at Gabreski. He was aware that Lubeka was not happy with his interjection. Dinan cut in to close the proceedings. On that, a media pack emerged out of the dark, directed by Krolas, towards the two speakers. As they jostled to respond to the questions, Gabreski was aware that Lubeka was still fighting to send, what was at this stage, a glare in his direction. The heat of the bodies and the intensity of the lights made the crush of people uncomfortable. Lubeka's eye shadow had smudged, giving her the image of a Goth. The back of the room cleared quickly. The discussion for the younger part of the audience was shifting to the bar. The posse at the back of the hall had left as soon as Gabreski intervened with his disclaimer.

As the questions came through, there was a clear consensus on what the media in the capital was looking for; a rogue element within the former state security forces who were breaking rank. It was the revelation of a flawed path that had agitated them since the 1990s. Something different was happening and the group of researchers were stumbling their way into it.

The evidence was mounting up. There had been an attempt to assassinate the Polish cabinet and the president in November 2012. Court cases were ongoing against the group involved, with many calling for the execution of the perpetrators for trying to overthrow the government and democracy of the country. Many questioned who had set them up. It had heightened the public's awareness of conspiracies to destabilize the government, but had also brought into focus the fact that, from different angles of left and right, there were individuals and groups out there who wanted to plunge Poland into the same chaos that other former Soviet states were forced into post liberation.

"A steady pace wins the race." Krolas shouted in English across to Gabreski and Lubeka, with the inference that they needed to take each step of the journey slowly. Gabreski smiled, taking it as an acknowledgement of him cutting across Lubeka. Lubeka caught Gabreski's eye, but offered no compromise on her desire to fight that last question herself. As the media scrum dissolved and each journalist was dealt with in turn, the room was left with a core of a dozen people at the front. The spotlights being turned off brought an instant relief from the heat and a reminder that there was an outside to go into, which had not taken a break from the snow. When he could take a breath from the questioning, Gabreski went over to join Lubeka, who was still in the middle of an interview with Wójcik. Gabreski stood in the queue. When the camera trained at Lubeka lowered, she turned her attention to Gabreski.

"I am my own woman and I can answer my own questions."

"Kasia, we need to keep aware of the legalities of what we are doing. We cannot name names without evidence. We are leaving ourselves open."

"I am already open. How about you, Łuka?" Lubeka rebuked.

"I am sorry if I cut you off. We need more space to get to the end of this. They were wanting you to compromise yourself in a public environment. What do you think that was about?"

Wójcik stepped between the two, fearing it was moving to a full blooded argument. "We are in this together, like it or not. This has been hell for everyone. We cannot break up now, as soon as they start to hit us with the hard questions." Lubeka stepped back and grabbed one of the unopened bottles of water that had been set on a side table for the speakers. She returned to stand face to face with Gabreski and whispered. "You are just too much of a man." Gabreski could only but accept that as criticism. "I am sorry, but we need to tread carefully." Lubeka packed up her bag and retrieved her coat, putting it and her scarf on as if donning a uniform. She shouted over to Gabreski, including Krolas and Wójcik: "Well, let's go. We have done what we came to do." Gabreski went over to thank Dinan and tried to pull Krolas away from the huddle of local journalists who had remained to compare notes from the evening.

The walk down the baroque facade of a staircase was accompanied with a frosty silence. Well-wishers commented in small groups as the four, in twos, meandered their way through the growing numbers of revellers at Neon Przyszłość. By the time they made it to the front door, the freeze between them had thawed.

It was nine o'clock and the street lighting outside was buzzing with a brownish yellow glow. Surprising for an evening with so many people, the streets seemed eerily quiet. The weather had forced the outside in. Even the smokers, a hardy movement in Polish life, had been driven in by the minus ten degree wind chill. Their breath blew out pipes of frozen air as they struggled to get over the Świętokrzyska, Nowy Świat crossroads, the zebra crossing, to get to the car. At the corner of Staszic Palace, beside the imposing archways of the Instytut Badań Literackich PAN, Gabreski noticed a dark non-descript saloon taking off towards them from the bank not fifty meters away. The darkness of the car, the driver and passenger were in stark contrast to the light grey surroundings and snow. The two figures were caught as a silhouetted image against the light grey walls.

"Who are these lunatics?" Gabreski was the first to register concern at the erratic driving. As they drew closer, both occupants of the car could be seen to pull ski masks over their heads. For once, he missed the presence of the Mercedes and its old school approach to surveillance. The exhaust from the back of the car coughed out black smoke as it skidded violently to a halt at the roadside in front of them. A passenger athletically alighted. Wójcik was the first to react by running behind some pillars, effectively disappearing from sight. Krolas was still talking, oblivious to the events that were occurring around her, only becoming silent when a hooded figure in a grey boiler suit was standing not three meters away.

Gabreski had been trained to respond to this type of assault. He had been there before, in Libya in the early summer. Run, on instinct, get to cover and keep moving. He knew this was what he had to do to get out of this situation, but loyalty to his two remaining colleagues held him to the spot. The man raised a handgun. Gabreski recognised it as a Makarov pistol, favoured by the Stasi and the Russian services. Gabreski looked to Lubeka and held his place. The gun moved around the three of them. The snow fell gently and the silence of the street was emphasized by the murmur of the traffic in the distance. Gabreski absorbed as much information as possible – the details of the car, the build of the driver and the mannerisms of the gunman.

Lubeka was fixed to the concrete, her reaction more to do with personality than fear. She didn't flinch and stared through the gun. This was the culmination of all her work. She had got to them, if this was where they ended up. Gabreski was afraid that Lubeka would spook the hooded assailant. "Kasia, please do as he says." The stand-off remained silent for the seconds the gun was pointed at them, the gunman seemed to have a job to do. He said one word, authoritatively answering an unheard question. "Affirmative."

Two sharp shots rang out, both into the body of Krolas. The snow muffled the echo leaving a thud, thud noise. As she went down, Gabreski, who was at her side, moved to catch her. She slumped to the ground, her knees breaking first. The gunman responded again to his silent order. "Affirmative." He moved the muzzle of the gun towards Lubeka's head. She stared and braced herself.

"Kraków bitch. You are next." The gunman shouted loudly in Lubeka's face and on that turned and jumped into the waiting car. The smoke spewed from the exhaust, the dirt of the machine extinguishing any signs or evidence. Lubeka stood for a while watching as they drove off, before breaking her trance to hear Krolas's moan and Gabreski shouting: "Get an ambulance, Kasia, get an ambulance." The brightness of the blood seeping onto the snow covered pavement was all the more shocking with its speed. Gabreski ripped to get to the wound, two puncture marks to the torso. "Stay with us, Beata," he shouted loudly. Wójcik reappeared from the pillars. The screams of the emergency services could be heard pacing towards the scene. Gabreski pressed on the wound with his scarf and spoke continually to Krolas. Lubeka watched silently and detached. Wójcik was shaking, half crying and half singing: "Hurry up, hurry up."

The whoop of the ambulance was as aggressive as the shooting. The blue lights of the police cars that came through from two directions illuminated the walls of the buildings around the site, giving a surreal hue over the vicinity. The broken silence of the past minutes sped up, into a clutter of unconnected noises and people. The paramedics unfolded the legs of the bed from the back of the ambulance, its doors wide open and flickering in the blue lights. Gabreski struggled to get up from Krolas, only relenting when the two paramedics took control of the bleeding. "We will take over from here." One of them surveyed Gabreski for any wounds and then, on one knee, worked with Krolas to get the oxygen mask secured and a pressure gauze in place.

A policewoman held Lubeka as she swayed slightly in shock. "What did you see? Did you get a car registration?" Lubeka remained stunned by what had happened. Gabreski shouted the names of the four of them, repeating Krolas's name to the paramedics as they pushed the trolley into the back of the ambulance. He presented immediately what he had observed, with one of the policemen taking notes on a touch-screen pad. "Two men in black jumpsuits; black ski masks. The gunman was communicating with someone through a concealed mic. A regulation handgun. He fired two shots. The car was unmarked and they sped towards the river. That is it." A paramedic was standing with Lubeka. "We need you to go to the hospital also." Lubeka stepped weakly into the ambulance and sat beside Krolas, caressing her hair. "It would be an idea if all of you come along." One of the police officers stepped forward and intervened, a voice providing instructions from a hand held set.

"Take them all to the Medical University off Stefana Banacha, they are still vulnerable to attack. We need to get them somewhere secure. Is that clear?"

The paramedic responded in the most authorative way possible: "Tak, tak, tak [yes, yes, yes]", and then instructed the driver. Within minutes the ambulance, with the full complement of passengers, left the scene. Wójcik was still sobbing. Krolas's breathing was laboured and loud.

***

Gabreski had been here before. In July 2005, coming from work in London, he had got caught up in the Al Qaeda bombings. He had ended up in an ambulance comforting people who had been wounded in Tavistock Square. The flashbacks were vivid, the feelings the same. Adrenaline helped to focus every action; waiting to act where needed, watching intently, comforting where possible. It was a very human response to violence. "How bad are the wounds?" One of the paramedics looked up and across Lubeka with the clinical appraisal. "From what I can tell, there is one puncture to the right below the lower left ribcage, still lodged, with a liver puncture, and one higher to the left going through the third rib up. We need to get this one checked immediately. The lung is punctured. The heart, I don't know. She's still alive at this point."

The cabin went silent. Krolas lay struggling to get air. The rhythm of the ambulance and police sirens synchronized as the convoy cruised through the streets towards the university hospital. As they drove to the entrance, there was a huddle of medical staff already waiting. The four casualties were helped from the back of the vehicle, Lubeka still stroking Krolas's hair. On entering the front door, she was whisked away into the emergency zone. The officer from the scene joined the remaining three. Lubeka held Wójcik.

"A black Honda saloon has been set on fire in the Gocław area of the city. It has no markings whatsoever, and therefore totally anonymous. Probably brought in from Belarus. From there they are on the ring road and they could go anywhere."

"So, they have got away with it again." Lubeka could not help herself, quietly but soundly responding to the policeman. "No one has got away with anything. This is the start of an attempted murder investigation." Lubeka moved towards him. Gabreski cut across them both. "We will need to stay here tonight. We are all part of the same team working with Beata. We are all in danger here."

"Okay, that can be arranged. I will get some guards. Wait for orders." The policeman seemed to be used to this type of event and they obviously had protocol in place. "Get checked out and then we will have you relocated to one of the upper floors, just in case." He gave directions to the security at the hospital, moving around in sequence in a managerial role. On returning to the group, he made one comment before departing. "What this looks like is a professional or military assassination attempt. Whatever you have been up to, he meant to kill Beata. He left the rest of you for a reason. He knew what you were doing and who you are. They needed Beata dead." On that, he left.

They knew Krolas's life was in the balance. The hit was direct and forceful. It was meant to kill. The three of them sat quietly in an anteroom in the ground floor of the hospital. Lubeka was visibly traumatized by the violence of the attack. A nurse entered with a tray of coffee. "Please take some. It will help to put some sugar back into your system." As she turned, she also informed the trio. "There are press people at the reception wanting to talk to someone. Do you want the hospital to deal with it, or do you want to make a statement yourselves?"

Gabreski responded. "I think it would be better if the hospital dealt with it at this point. Or maybe the police want to make a comment." The room returned to silence with the buzz of the halogen light and the smell of antiseptic providing a sickly morgue-like environment. Every five minutes or so, a nurse or hospital representative entered to check up on the survivors of the attack. Wójcik remained traumatically silent. Lubeka was regaining her colour and Gabreski had returned to his phone to hammer in assurances to his family and colleagues. After one hour of waiting, a young man suddenly pushed his way into the room. He was urgent and scanned the room quickly. "I am Dan, Beata's son."

The others stood up. "She never said." Lubeka adopted a compassionate tone moving to comfort the man. "How is she?" It was as if the young man was familiar with a group he had just met. He was aware of them as friends. Krolas was obviously giving him an update on their activities, but had never mentioned him to anyone. Lubeka shrugged her shoulders. "They are working on her now, Dan. We will see soon enough." Wójcik's tone filled the starkness of the room.

"She has always been a trouble maker. That is who she is." Krolas's son tried to make light, while struggling to hold back tears.

"She will be all right. She will be okay. We are in the best place."

The circle of seats in the room filled up as each returned to the silence. The buzz of the light continued and the bareness of the room became all too apparent as the severity of the situation heightened awareness of the surroundings.

"We will just have to wait and see." With the lack of daylight and the constant chatter outside the room, time was not perceivable. This was a vacuum that could only be found in institutions, be they prison cells or hospital waiting rooms. Time did not exist. For something to do, Lubeka retrieved her tablet and began surveying files again, a habit which had become compulsive for the four of them. Scan and freeze, scan and freeze, picture after picture, statement after statement. The search seemed to be never ending. It took her mind off the events of the evening. Occasionally, she would read out a piece of a statement, a date or name. The others were relieved by the distraction. The translations from the Russian were more stunted as she struggled to grasp some of the terms. This went on for what seemed like hours, and seemed to be getting nowhere.

"Where is Beata's netbook?" Gabreski enquired.

"I have it. It was in her briefcase with her papers." Wójcik replied.

"Can I see it?" Wójcik handed the machine over and, on opening the welcome, Gabreski tried to get past the password, shouting: "Does anyone know Beata's password?"

"Give it here and I will have a go. We have a family pass that may help." Gabreski gave the machine to Dan, who set about hammering in a number of options. "We usually use children's names from the family for passwords. Dorota, Bogdan, Kacpar – one of them, with their birthday." He hammered away at the various options eventually to get to: "'Kasiarine2008'. That'ss it."

"Well done, Dan." He handed it to Wójcik, who proceeded to search the files for something different from what the rest of them had been looking at. Gabreski, sitting beside her, watched on. The material that came up most often was to do with Kraków in the 1980s, but there were hundreds of files on Warsaw, listed by date and place, the names were endless. The Russian and Bulgarian files were clustered together, more refined and extensive. "There must be something in here that gave Beata the edge or she would not have been singled out. I was with her for two full days in the archives and she did not mention anything exceptional. She must have something though." Wójcik struggled to find anything definitive.

"The files have been catalogued in an odd manner here." Gabreski noticed a break in the standard system. "There is a gender categorization in the Russian files. I have never seen this before. Have you, Kasia?" Gabreski passed the tablet to Lubeka to view the sequence of files from 1988 in Kraków, listed by number, then the name of the person being interrogated. "No. Beata has selected mostly the women. They must have interrogated the women differently. I wonder, was this Bartek's role? I do not remember anyone talking about this. The women. Why the women?"

"Why did Beata consider this so important? It was mostly men at the forefront of all the protests in the day." Searching the flagged priorities in Krolas's files, there were a dozen interrogations selected, all documented in Russian, all in Kraków in May 1988, all to do with young women.

"Beata even went as far as to print some of these out. Where's her camera?" On flicking through the pictures taken of the files, the information was the same. Almost all the photographs were from the files of women prisoners.

"Look, Kasia, for most the men's files and interrogations are days after the women's and the codes collate." Gabreski started moving Krolas's pictures of the files around like a deck of cards on a coffee table in the centre of the room.

"These women must have been the partners of the men. They interrogated partners first." Lubeka stood over the pictures, looking at the young faces, and the fear. She lined up the faces in pairs, coded through the last numbers of the action code and the dates. Some of those being brought in were young men, obviously boyfriends or relations of the women who went through the grilling days earlier. Most were women lifted first and tortured to get information on those, she assumed, to be their partners. For Lubeka, it was diabolically cynical, callous in its routine.

As the night struggled on, one by one, the group closed their work and drifted into an exhausted slumber. Any movement was met with the opening of weary eyes and a return to sleep. Wójcik and Lubeka were linked on the plastic-cushioned, institutionally-blue seats, Wójcik's head resting on Lubeka's shoulder, her legs curled up on what was left of the plastic. In the artificial light of the room, there was no evidence of night or day.

24th November

The hospital room chilled in the depths of the night. In the morning the door of the waiting room rattled open and in came two policemen with two representatives from the hospital. The figures towered over the slouching exhausted visitors. Gabreski was first to straighten himself up, followed by Dan, who stood up and waited for whatever was to come from the officials. The two women emerged from the discomfort of the seats.

"Good morning. I am the chief consultant at the university hospital." The authoritative looking older man taking the lead had obviously had to do this before. His matter of fact approach belying the severity of the situation or the emotional stress that they had all been through. "I presume that everyone here has been checked and that you are sufficiently recovered to leave the hospital." The nods of agreement prompted him to continue.

"Before the police brief you, we have issued a statement to the media, which in no uncertain terms, specifies the severity of the wounds received by Ms Krolas. There is still a threat hanging over her, so no visitors apart from immediate family. Is that clear? This was an attempt to kill. She is still with us due to the angle of the second shot missing her heart. She remains unconscious, has lost a lot of blood and has suffered systemic shock. So she is alive, but critical." The group remained fixed to the consultant's words. "We will need to keep her here in intensive care for the foreseeable future, until secondary damage can be assessed and we have safely removed the bullets. This in itself is life threatening. Do you understand?" His experience came through with the bluntness of his manner.

"Are you clear on this, Dan?" Lubeka redirected the question.

"Yes." Dan had turned a greyish colour and was visibly unsure on his feet. Lubeka put her right arm securely around him.

"What next?" Gabreski looked towards the police to see if any action had been taken. The consultant and his colleague took this as an excuse to leave the room. No other words were exchanged. The science was brief and blunt, and was all that was required for the moment. The professionalism of the hospital staff did not leave any room for doubt.

"Okay." One of the policemen released the pressure of the situation. "We have cleared the media for the time being. They will probably try to get statements later. If you want to talk to them, that is up to you, but remember that there is an investigation going on here and you are witnesses. So please, try to be cautious in how much information you give to the journalists. You know..." He looked towards Wójcik. "... They will always take fact number one and fact number two and get ten. Be wary."

"What is the official view of what has happened?" Gabreski looked to the room for consensus.

"Contrary to one report, it was not a robbery. From our perspective, from the evidence we have at this point, the attack was planned and targeted. That is our line. As for connections to other incidents, at this point, we do not see any."

"What do you mean?" Lubeka jumped in.

"We are not working on the theory that a number of deaths are linked. We have been instructed to take this as a specific, isolated incident."

"And what 'specifically' does that mean?" Lubeka highlighted the one word and stood eyeball to eyeball with the capped officer.

"We can work with this. He is just working the official line." Gabreski softened the tone.

"The police in Warsaw have seen similar murder attempts over the years, and indeed murders. That is where we are going to start our investigation. Beyond that, it is up to State Protection. They will be in touch about other aspects of this case. I am doing what I have been instructed to do and that is it." Closing the conversation, the two police officers moved towards the door.

"And what do we do?" Lubeka let fear replace anger.

"May I suggest that you get out of Warsaw as soon as possible? It will be safer for you in Kraków. You know your own city. We do not have the resources to give you protection here and you seem to have annoyed some very dangerous people." The policeman moved to the open door. Lubeka could not help but quip.

"Some things never change."

"What do you mean by that?" The policeman spun around to engage Lubeka.

"It's okay, officer. We're okay. It has just been a long night." Wójcik raised her hands as if to surrender. On that the police left, leaving a threatening atmosphere in the room.

"What do we do now?" Wójcik introduced the lingering question.

"I have to stay with my mom." Dan, being outside the exchange, had a more emotional duty to take.

"It's okay, Dan, you have to stay here. You are not a part of the investigation. We will make our way back to Kraków. I think from the policeman's attitude and what has happened to Beata, we cannot pretend to be safe here." The others nodded in agreement.

"I need a smoke." Wójcik sounded urgent and was first to pack up the equipment and papers to get moving. "Please, pass on our love to Beata, will you, Dan?" Dan flinched quickly in acknowledgement.

"No statements to the press. Right. We are in trouble enough, Kasia. Okay?" Wójcik pointed to Lubeka and then set about clearing up the room, fixing chairs back in the order they were in when the party arrived. The three, in turn, went to hug Dan and offer support. Dan stood as he had done for most of his life, the single child of an eccentric mother, a role that had come to an ultimate conclusion. "We should be able to get a taxi from here and clear out our rooms for the next train out of the city." Gabreski stood with the door open.

As if they were jumping from a plane, the four left the room. Dan made his way for the stairs upwards to the emergency unit and the other three discretely navigated their path through the trolleys and changing staff from the morning shift. Finally, they could see out to the glowing morning light. It was bright and illuminated by snow. The coats and scarfs became lifesavers again, as the bite from the protection of the plate glass dissolved through the opening automatic doors, taking breath away. Lubeka led the three of them out, heads down, disciplined and forceful. The hospital door closed behind them. The media were light in number, presumably satisfied with the statements from the police and consultant.

Gabreski scanned the car park for a taxi. Something caught his eye. Waving from the corner of the car park, with one hand on the roof of a car, was Browarczyk from Toruń. Double checking and working from memory, Gabreski asked Lubeka. "Kasia, is that Browarczyk from the State Protection Office? Remember. From Toruń."

Kasia's response was predictable, but confirmed it for Gabreski. "Shit – not another one." Gabreski took the lead and was gingerly followed by the others as he made his way towards the car.

"Please. I hope you were not injured last night. I had been informed of the shooting. I have been reassigned to look into this.

Please. I will give you a lift to your hotel." Browarczyk gestured in a conciliatory manner, inviting them into his car. "What have we got to lose?" Lubeka whispered loud enough for Wójcik and Gabreski to hear. She bent over and stubbed her newly lit cigarette into the snow, first to get into the car. Browarczyk seemed genuinely pleased that he had caught them before they left the hospital.

"Call me Aron. I have been reassigned to check up on a number of incidents to do with the TW in the south of the country. What are your plans? I hope you are not going to give up on what Beata Krolas has achieved." The comfort of the car, the exhaustion and the heat induced a sense of submission. Browarczyk struggled to drive and look at the passengers at the same time.

"What has she achieved?" Lubeka took the opportunity.

"International human rights organizations have already been reporting on the attempt on her life. She was powerful in the media interviews over the past few days and the suddenness of the attack is making our country look incapable of dealing with this threat. The president's office is not happy. State Protection are not happy. And you three are perceived to be in need of protection."

"You expect me to believe that this government is going to do anything about these issues. Where's the evidence so far?" Lubeka needed reassurance.

"Have you not seen the jailing of General Wojciech Jaruzelski and Czesław Kiszczak, and a dozen others recently, for communist era murders and criminal activities after that time? Believe me, things have been moving. This is an issue of national security, not just a journalistic or university adventure. It is a painful process and you all know it." Browarczyk alluded to the imprisonment of senior members of the old regime for leading criminal gangs in the years after the regime fell, and of the trial of police officers who had killed miners in Warsaw during a protest in 1981.

"You give those men ten years each. They will be out in four. And anyway, that is a handful out of the tens of thousands who, day and daily, tortured our people." Lubeka stared in the car mirror at Browarczyk.

"You are a tough one, Dr Lubeka. The Cold War is over for most." He responded.

"It's not for Beata." With Lubeka's quip a pause set into the car for a moment, broken by Gabreski returning to the practicalities of the trip. "We are going back to Kraków. We don't feel safe in Warsaw. Can we go straight to the station from the hotel?"

"Okay, that's probably a good idea. There is someone here intent on killing one or all of you and that's a good reason to get out I suppose." Browarczyk looked in the mirror to catch the eyes of Lubeka and Wójcik in the back. The lack of a response was taken as approval. The roads were starting to fill up with the early morning traffic.

They rounded the city centre pulling into the driveway of the hotel. There was an awareness of the silence as the three went into the lobby. It was as if this was Krolas's space and her absence was registered through the sobriety of the movement. The rooms were as they were left the day before. Lubeka and Wójcik carefully and slowly packed the material that was still scattered on the floor, scanning pictures that Krolas had printed out for further investigation.

"Kasia, most of Beata's prints are of the women also." They spread the pictures out on the table, oblivious to the car waiting at the hotel door and intent on finding what Krolas had been looking for. "Just faces, codes, some names and what they suffered. But who are they?" Wójcik interrupted. "More importantly, where are they?" This was a realization. The faces in the pictures must either be dead, in another state, or alive and living in fear in Poland. Gabreski joined them with his grip bag. "What is it?" "The pictures that Beata printed were mostly of the women. But why were the interrogators and Bartek so concerned with questioning the women?" Lubeka repeated her concern. "Where are they now?"

"Kasia, we need to get out of here. Can I suggest we gather all we have from Beata and take it to Kraków with us?" Lubeka, without acknowledging the suggestion, began lifting the notes and photographs and pushing them into her own bag. Wójcik went around the room cleaning and making the bed. "Leave it as we found it." Her actions seemed more like habit than intent. Lubeka was more interested in forcing the additional material into her backpack for travelling.

"Okay, we're done here. Let's move on." Gabreski held the room door open, insistent that the other two move quickly. "Let's go. Let's go." Obligingly, the two women rushed by him as the pace changed to the speed of a prison escape.

Gabreski broke ranks to sign out at the reception. Cards were exchanged in a polite official manner. As he moved to join his colleagues just outside the front door, the receptionist walked towards him and addressed him. "I am sorry to hear about your friend. She was very brave to do what she was doing." Gabreski stopped to acknowledge the sentiment. "Thanks. Yes, she is very brave." The use of the past tense was alarming to him. Gabreski joined the women at the door.

"Do you think Mister Secret Service will mind us taking time to smoke at his expense?" Lubeka returned to her hobby horse. Browarczyk sat in his gun barrel silver Audi at the entrance to the hotel, his elbow resting on the window, occasionally glancing over at the group standing at the door.

"I have seen worse. He is not that bad." Wójcik stubbed out her cigarette. It was a habit Gabreski still found alien, feeling sympathy, oddly, for the spoliation of the snow. He led the walk over to the car, followed by the other two. Browarczyk emerged from the driver's seat to open the boot of the car, then helping Wójcik into the back seat. "Do only men sit in the front?" Lubeka continued to tease Browarczyk. "It's a government car. What do you think?" The retort broke the ice as the four settled in. The crunch of the wheels on the ice was loud and drowned out the chug of the engine. The smell of diesel lingered as they merged into the congestion of the city center's roads.

"We should be able to make the 7.50 to Kraków." Browarczyk had checked the times and had the schedule already planned for the group.

"Good, we will be back home just before eleven." Wójcik could not help trying to bring some closure to the events of the past few days. The Audi moved slowly around to Aleje Jerozolimskie, the thoroughfare which runs alongside Warszawa Centralna, and into the car park. Browarczyk pulled up in one of the spaces at the front. He reached around to get a glimpse of all three passengers.

"Before you go, you need to know that Beata is not doing so well. The hospital sent her to the critical care unit. She is not responding to the treatment. Her son Dan is with her and other members of her family have been arriving. She is one of ours in Warsaw and we will do our best for her. Now, I have been assigned to investigate this case, so I will be down later to Kraków. We know that you are being followed by a number of private security firms. Stay wary of them and be cautious when confronted by the media.

They are attempting to sensationalize the whole issue and this does not help anyone. Stay clear of the populars. Have you anything to ask me before you go?"

His severity returned the car to the tenseness of the morning. "So, what you are saying is that you are willing to help us. How can we trust you, working for the state?" Lubeka dismissed any conciliatory mood.

"I am here to represent the president's office, not the police or the security services. My interest is to get to the bottom of this. It is my country as well." Browarczyk's voice became stressed. "You either take the support, little as it is, or you are on your own. It is up to you. And where are you going to go on your own? Łuka. Will the university help you with this?" Gabreski shook his head. "Kasia, will the Nowa Huta community stand with you now?" She stayed silent, knowing that she was expected to stay at home and mourn as every good black draped widow of conservative Poland is destined to do. "Marianna, do what you can with the journal in Kraków, but know that if you put a foot wrong, they will have you cleaning their ashtrays for the rest of your career. Your choice!" Lubeka got out of the car knowing there was no option but to trust him. Gabreski shook his hand. "Thanks, we could do with backup." Wójcik tapped Browarczyk's shoulder in approval and then got out.

The station was wet and cold. They made their way through the morning crowds to the platform. Bags bumped uncomfortably and bodies shuffled. The clatter of the crowd was notable, all moving in sequence, all avoiding eye contact, searching for a break in the next approaching group to move forward. Intermittent tanoy announcements automated the times and platforms. Gabreski joined the queue for tickets while the two women stood to the side. Lubeka scanned the concourse for tags. For the moment they seemed to have been left alone. It crossed her mind that they had given up. Gabreski pushed his card through to the cashier and fumbled numbers into a panel. Without uttering a word, he rejoined the women and they forced a cut through the crowd to take their position on the platform. The wind drove across the station with a bite that forced passengers to cluster together for protection. The train, and its staff, stood oblivious to the discomfort of the customers.

"Freezing." Wójcik let it be known, with even the other passengers moaning in agreement.

"Here we go." The train doors glided open and the huddled mass of people sieved through to the warmth of the carriages. The occupation was spontaneous. In the carriage the three settled into a cabin with some foreign students. The young people energized the cabin as the bags, coats and scarfs were loaded onto the rails above the seats.

"Where you from?" Gabreski stepped in to make the journey more entertaining, utilizing his perfect Middlesex accent.

"Dublin." A young man proudly responded with the two adjacent students beaming smiles in support of the confidence of the response.

"Where are youse from?" His accent was pronounced, and while Gabreski picked it up, the two women stretched to get a grasp of the words.

"We are from Kraków."

"Not with that accent, you're not. Ever been to Dublin?" The young man's friends laughed at the audacity of their friend. Lubeka and Wójcik caught the sentence and smiled.

"I have been to your Trinity College. It's a great city." Gabreski broke into the colloquial rhyme to match the students. "What are youse three doing here?"

"We are exchange students. We are at the university in Kraków for the term. We have been in Warsaw to see the sights, but have to be in class next week, so need to get down. Sure we love it here." The young man had an infectious laugh for the others.

"What is Dublin like?" Lubeka was getting the ear of the accent and found it interesting and colonial.

"Sure it's mad." The Irish roared with laughter as one of the girls answered. The Poles sat in bemusement.

"The ponies run up and down the city on Saturday mornings. It's packed with students and the crack is ninety everywhere." The girl had lost the Poles altogether with this. The young man intervened in the form of an interpreter, as the others continued with the early morning laughter therapy.

"We have a horse market on Saturdays in the city. They are only for riding, mind, we try to keep them off the plate. And it's a university city with scores of colleges and bars. Loads of bars. It is a great place to be young. Even our old hold out at being young."

"Kasia, Marianna and Łuka." Gabreski went around the names pointing to his colleagues and then himself.

"Sean, Orla and Sinead. It's nice to meet youse."

"I thought Ireland was a religious country." Wójcik was curious as to where this socialite culture came from.

"Sure, it's Irish Catholic and we have a lot of good solid Protestants as well in the north. We make it all up as we go along. We drink, we fight, we travel a lot, but most of all we like a good laugh." The young man's pictorial was drawing the three Poles into a culture that seemed to be outside the usual stereotype.

"You could almost be Poles." Lubeka smiled at the portrayal of a different type of society. It was one which she recognised, but struggled to put a place to it. Possibly this was the new European

Poland that was emerging. The appeal was to the young and of the young.

The conversation criss-crossed as they moved through the countryside towards Kraków. The cabin became a microcosm of the changing nature of Poland and the openness that was forcing its way into the society and life. It was also a place where some would feel the need to resist. It was not controlled or authoritarian, and levelled its experiences towards the fresh air of the young. Lubeka sat at the window looking out periodically, being continually interrupted by light hearted questions from the Irish students about Kraków and being Polish.

The exchange relieved their minds of the burden of the previous day's events, the issue at hand and the uncertainty of what would happen when they arrived at the station in Kraków. The crystal clear blue sky lit up the city as the train pulled in, rattling and pushing into the station precisely on time. They bid farewell to the students. The backpacks and cases on wheels filled the corridor in a scramble to get from the train.

Gabreski, Lubeka and Wójcik alighted to the brightness of the morning. Shaking off the journey, they began the conversation that had been postponed by the students' enthusiastic intervention.

"What will we do now?" Gabreski opened the question as they stood on the platform. Lubeka looked around disorientated, grabbing her own backpack as if to realize that she had lost something.

"Are you okay, Kasia?" Wójcik sensed some distress.

"I need to get home." In the distance of Warsaw, Lubeka had lost her place. A moment of reflection brought back the experience of the past week and the need to face the starkness of a community who viewed her as leaving a grieving family. She knew that was what she had to face, and their perceptions of what she should be doing, her duty, for her husband.

"I will go with you, Kasia. I just have to phone my mom to let her know I am okay and then get to the office to check in. We can take a taxi."

"That's probably a good idea, Marianna. I have someone to visit." Gabreski approved of the home visit and presented his excuses. Lubeka nodded to Gabreski in acknowledgement that he was going to challenge Nowak. They moved their way across the square outside the station towards Pawia where taxis were lined up. Gabreski kissed Lubeka on the forehead and she hugged him. Wójcik, more formally, kissed and shook his hand. Gabreski hurried across the road to avoid a tram. Lubeka and Wójcik walked quickly through the track which had been made between a small trench of snow at the side of the Galeria and into a taxi parked at the corner of the shopping mall.

"Nowa Huta, please." It was the first time Lubeka had mentioned the name since she left. The events of the past few days had been a lifetime away and gave her an surreal distance from her home life. This had changed absolutely. She had become a different, more assertive person, forced without the comfort zones of marriage and a job, with a mission that was, at this stage, about struggle without any foreseeable end.

"Are you going to go to your mom or the flat?" Wójcik was concerned about where Lubeka may get the best reception.

"We'll go to the flat." The car pulled away from the traffic of the city and towards Nowa Huta.

"Our Lady's Church, Andrzeja Struga. We can walk from there." The driver said nothing. Lubeka sat and watched as the life that she had lived drifted by her. For her, it had been lost in the sequence of events. They drove through the cleared roads towards her past. The movement of the roadside was increasingly traumatizing, the markers of the recent days highlighting a sharpness to the memories. As they drove up to the church, the scattering of people revealed the last of the Mass goers. Wójcik paid the driver and, as it pulled off, Lubeka started walking towards the monument to Solidarność at the side garden of the church. Red lanterns were set all around the bottom of the rock, a witness to those who still remembered the struggle this community had went through. The congregation in the church could be heard to respond to the final acts of the service. Followed by Wójcik, Lubeka moved over. She blessed herself, touched the rock and went to the doors.

Lubeka walked through what the architects called the 'house of glass', drawn in by the final hymn of the Mass, Henryk Górecki's 'A Symphony of Sorrowful Songs'. Wójcik entered behind Lubeka and they stood fixated by the haunting melody and the trance of the congregation. "No, Mother, do not weep, Most Chaste Queen of Heaven Support me always. Ave Maria." A hymn from the grave, inscribed by a child on the wall of a torture chamber in the death camp, a testimony of another struggle and another broken Polish generation.

They stood at the back of the church, while the people exiting flowed slowly by them. One older woman with a head scarf, together with similarly reverent associates, made her way towards Lubeka. She hugged her mother, with tears running as small beads down her face. Lubeka knew her mother would be at the church at that time. It was a place where she knew it would be possible to see her without any preconditions or impositions from the rest of the family or community. They spoke briefly. "I am fine, Mom, I am fine."

Her mother's questions were soft but direct. "When will you come home, Katarzyna? We have missed you, we have been so worried." Lubeka's mother ran her hand through her hair.

"I have some work to finish." Lubeka's mother conveyed resilience with a knowledge of loss. She had been there before many times. This was her world and that of her neighbours, and she showed the resignation of a person who had lived a tough life, using faith as a measure of hope. Lubeka gently pulled away and went to rejoin Wójcik.

"Let's go to the apartment. I want to check something."

Wójcik looked back at the gathering of elderly women, recognizing Lubeka in the features of her mother. She could have come from nowhere else, this was in her makeup. Crossing the road and towards the apartment, Lubeka had returned to herself. Occasionally neighbours would call to her as they walked and she waved in reassurance that things were fine with her. The sense of community with all its strengths came through and Wójcik, with her middle class foibles, found this familiarity with personal space disconcerting. The stairs leading to the apartment echoed with their footsteps through to the hallway. Lubeka stopped at the front door and paused. The last time she had been there, it was to remove the body of her husband. She steadied herself and put the key into the lock.

They walked in. It was as it was left the previous week. It seemed damp and empty. It reconfirmed to Lubeka that she had now left for good. This was not her home and had not been for years, even with the trauma of married life. It was dead, as if it had been crystallized in time for someone else's life story. She moved around, quietly taking in whatever final sentiments she could.

"There is nothing here for me. Not even the glass wedding presents." She stood looking at the kitchen cabinet and the coloured glass vases that were lined up in a chronological row, now with no purpose, meaning or need.

"Your family will clear this up and we can all move on." Wójcik tried to assert the change that had been forced on Lubeka.

Lubeka sat on the sofa. It was cold to touch. She ran her hands over it as Wójcik surveyed the room. Lubeka saw something shimmering from the back of the sofa. She did not remember it being there the last time she cleaned and vacuumed. "What's that, Kasia?" Wójcik acknowledged Lubeka trying to locate some item from beneath the seat. As it came out, there was a hint of puzzlement. "It is a bit of a button with 'icja' left on it."

"Policja. How did it get there?"

"Andrzej had a broken finger. He must have been able to hide it before they hung him."

"He must have fought back. He fought them, Marianna."

"That coroner said there were no signs of a struggle." Lubeka rehearsed the story from the previous week.

"Then why would he need to rip a button from a policeman?"

"I don't know. They must have killed him just to get to those stupid files. God forgive them." Rubbing the button like a charm, Lubeka took some satisfaction in the idea that Andrzej fought back. She sat on the sofa, detached, looking at and pressing hard on the remnants.

"We need to go, Kasia. We can't stay here. They will be watching this place."

"Yes. I know." Lubeka put the button in her coat and went over to the fireplace. She thought that the dust had settled heavily there. On the fireplace, there was a small box with a mother of pearl top.

She opened it and lifted out two rings, looked at them briefly and then slowly put them into her jean's pocket. Wójcik watched, moving over to put her hand on Lubeka's shoulder. "We need to go."

They quickly exited the block. Lubeka looked back, taking it as a final visit. Clearing the place would have to be left to someone else. No one in the family network would reside in a house where someone had died under such suspicious circumstances.

The stairs at the entrance to the flat had dried off. The cold had become cleansing, and with the snow evaporating into the chill of the day, the streets were slowly clearing without the mush that comes with slightly warmer weather. Lubeka and Wójcik emerged out into the brightness of the afternoon.

***

Gabreski checked into the hotel overlooking Planty Park again. It was his hotel in Kraków and because of its proximity to the station and access to the airport, it would always offer him a psychological out clause. The antiquarian mustiness of the interior was homely for him. His new room overlooked the tramlines and gardens surrounding the old town. He stood for a moment in the room to gather his thoughts. It seemed like a lifetime since he last looked out over the tree lined mote. He had breadth to contemplate his own estranged circumstances. He gathered his bags and laid out his clothes on the bed, plugged in his smartphone and turned on the small TV in the corner of the room. He then went into the bathroom to shave and clean up, staring in the mirror at the grey that had caught up with him in recent years.

> "The Unmanned Aerial Vehicle's (UAV) Usage Act that was passed yesterday has come into force today. The vote was close and controversial, but advocates for the extension of the use of drones were able to swing the vote in their favour. As of today, the production of, sale of, and use of, these drones can be for commercial purposes in Poland. It is one of the few European Union countries that has introduced such liberal laws on this highly controversial high-tech spying equipment. In a statement from the Confederation of Polish Security Industries, Bolek Janowski, its director, said that this was a good day for Polish business. We can now compete with the Americans and Israelis for the global market."

The voice over of the TV announcer belied the images from the use of drones in the Afghan war before switching to the use of drones in crowd control at football riots, where they had been piloted in Poland. The whole approach was matter of fact.

Gabreski put his tie on and brushed his coat down, as if cleaning it for an interview. Before departing, he opened his tablet to check in with his office in London, an update and assurances, checking on any developments at home and registering his need to continue his research for the foreseeable future. His head of department had always given him the benefit of the doubt, with financial support to match. So there was confidence that he would be getting what he needed. Asking for a budget for Lubeka, he thought, would be pushing it, but the flexibility of his colleagues towards his freedom could only come with a busy department which was fixated with the research needs of the academics. It was, from their perspective, work after all.

He pocketed his tablet and phone, and set off to try and find Nowak. The path was well worn. The bright day had brought the tourists out from the city's clutter of hotels, moving in packs. He fought his way through the couples that were lingering at the menus placed along the length of Floriańska. The walk was refreshing after the journey. He collected his thoughts, occasionally being distracted by the flutter of hungry pigeons or the eccentric street artist plying a lucrative trade. Nowak's office was behind the Collegium Novum in Bracka, one of the oldest streets in the city leading to the square. Odd for a senior academic, his office was two stories above a milk bar, and seemed like a rental rather than university property. It was dusty and had the aroma of the breads from the shop below. Gabreski took two steps at once to beat the stairwell, using the end of his walk as a rare opportunity to exercise.

The door of the office was solid and dark, protected. Gabreski knocked the door and waited.

"Come in." It was Nowak's distinctive, cultured regional voice. Gabreski opened the door and entered.

"Well, Łuka, it has been a tough few days. Please, take a seat."

"Piotr, I hope that the worst of this is over. How are you?" The civilities of the moment belied the suspicion on both sides of the book covered desk.

"I am good. I have been reflecting a lot. The symposium went really well. We got a lot out of it."

"Why did you never say?" Gabreski moved bluntly to the point, staring at Nowak.

"Say what?"

"You know, Piotr. In all those years you could have at least given me some idea of what you were up to when you were a student."

"Łuka, my friend, I was eighteen. It was a communist state in the 1980s. The system was everywhere. Your family had left. We were stuck in the middle of it all. We just wanted to do the right thing. Those of us who stayed – or who could not leave. My family were convinced that we were under attack. We had no protection other than the state. Remember 'this is it, this is war'. Do you remember the fear? Our world was collapsing." Nowak strained to make the point.

"Were you there in eighty-eight? Did you get involved?"

"We were like boy scouts. We took our orders and served our kings."

"I know you as a dissident, nothing else. I believed you. If I was here looking for a future, I may have joined as well. You know the regime had its ways of keeping the young in line and promising careers was one of them. Did you leave or are you still there Piotr... that's what I need to know."

"I left a lifetime ago, but this is a small town. The older ones still know my history. They hold it over me to this day, and they are everywhere." Nowak got up and looked out the window. "Do you think I want to be shackled all my life by actions that I took when I was no more than a child? For many, the regime did not end, it just transformed into something else. It is the same across the East. For God's sake, look at Putin in Russia. They have not gone away."

"And why expel Kasia?"

"That's something different. I was instructed to get rid of her. She was getting too close."

"Did the instruction come from within the university?" Gabreski looked intensely at Nowak, knowing that if it was in-house, then the whole series of events was staged to expose the research to date.

Without saying a word, Gabreski knew Nowak's answer was "yes".

"We were set up from the start and those who came out of the woodwork in good faith were exposed."

"It looks like it. Łuka, I was not part of this. I'm as much a victim in this as you and the others." Nowak moved back to his chair and slumped into it.

"Mazur, Beata, Kasia, Marianna, Kaszowski. All of us caught in the line of fire." Gabreski was despondent.

"It looks like it." Nowak paused. "Include me in that list, Łuka. I have conceded on everything I have lived for over the past twenty years."

"And what of Kasia now? We can go back to our desks and hide. Where does she go?"

"We can arrange for another post somewhere else. She is one of the sharpest academics we have ever produced from this place. She will go far wherever she ends up." Nowak sounded as if he was trying to save grace from his imposition.

"But not in Poland. What I am hearing, Piotr, is that you have given in. You are with them, if not by your stupid actions, or your lack of conscience, then by your complicity. You had your hand on the trigger, Piotr, along with the rest of them." Gabreski stood up.

"I have to stay here. Your world is somewhere else. I stayed and it was bloody hard. I have to build a life out of this and playing the game is a part of that." Nowak's voice, raised for the first time, exposed his helplessness.

"The word 'no' is the same in every language. You could have kept your head down, the way those who were not beaten off the streets did. You became the worst part of the machine, the ones who watched and informed, but knew in their hearts that they were doing something wrong. Good day, Professor." Gabreski left the room and closed the door. He stopped at the top of the stairs and took a deep breath, breaking a lifetime friendship.

This was at the heart of the whole issue. Thc regime, its shadow world in the nineties and after, were supported by a web of deceit and suspicion. The 'others' were still there, still active. People were the stuff of oppression, not the system, the thousands of individuals chipping in to build a mechanism that was self-evolving, self-perpetuating. It was individuals watching families and individuals that maintained the fear. Everyone being made to fear everyone else. That was oppression.

Gabreski made it to the street, annoyed and flustered. Moving quickly he took out his phone and dialled Lubeka. He walked towards the main square, keeping an eye on the uneven pathments, cautious of his unsteady treads, dodging the tourists who poured into the streets with no business in hand, no urgency to speak of, except leisure.

"Kasia… well. What are you up to?"

"We are good. We have just left Nowa Huta. What are you up to?"

"I have just left Nowak. He is not very apologetic. As suspected, he admitted being a lackey of the regime back in the day."

"I hope you hit him." Lubeka communicated her feelings, tongue in cheek.

"Forget about him. He is out of the equation. He is not to be trusted."

"I could have told you that, Łuka. He is a snake. We need to get this pushed into a court. We need heads." She paused for a moment and then said: "Have you seen any drones yet?"

"What do you mean?" Gabreski was perplexed.

“They were releasing the drones today. It is the talk of the town. You can see one in the sky sitting above the city. It looks like a weird flying beatle with green and red lights.” Gabreski looked up and around to see if he could spot anything. The huge swaying tourist balloon hung over the river. Beyond that, nothing. He knew that if it was true, it was a serious development and would change the way the private sector surveillance network would operate for good.

“No, Kasia. Maybe when it gets dark. Where are you now?”

“We are on our way back to the town. We can meet you at the lobby of the hotel at Lubicz, and then plan from there. It is just across from your hotel. Do you know it? We also have to let Marianna contact her office before we do anything.”

“Okay. I will see you in the bar in, say, twenty minutes.”

As he tapped his way out of the conversation, he looked around him to get a sense of the normality of the situation. The list of the dead, the legacy, the loss of his friend, the speed of life at the minute. It was all beyond his grasp in a wave of events. Crossing the square he dipped into the underground tavern of Szara, hidden beneath the hustle of the world of architecture and tourism. It was the old Kraków, the work of people who served and lived underground. He liked that space between subterranean life and the business of the topsoil. It also got him back on track with his habits, denying that Lubeka had freed him from the respectability of sobriety. The women could wait.

Lubeka and Wójcik arrived at the hotel on time. The carpeted splendour of the neo-renaissance was not Lubeka’s usual choice for anything. Her world was the bland cafés that could hide the vodka intake and house music. Wójcik thought that the hotel would be somewhere that Gabreski would appreciate. It gave away his age and her perception of an older generation, particularly when he was perceived to be English by his hosts, and academically peculiar as a person.

As they walked into the hotel, Lubeka's phone sounded and shuttered.

"Hello, this is Colonel Browarczyk of the Office of State Protection."

"I know who you are. What is it?" Lubeka was sharp. It shocked Browarczyk.

"Kasia, I have some bad news." The silence belied the next sentence. Lubeka immediately knew what was coming.

"Beata passed away this afternoon. The internal bleeding could not be stopped. They did their best to save her. I am so sorry." Lubeka stared at Wójcik intensely, one tear dropping to her coat and, while speaking, drew her into the discussion.

"How is Dan?"

"He is holding up well. Other members of Beata's family have arrived. They have been here for a while. Look, Kasia, this is an important development for you. This is now a murder case, and you are witnesses to a murder. We have also been instructed to widen the investigation. The Warsaw police are looking into this from their area, but we have to scale the process outward and look at where this attack really came from."

"What does that mean?" Lubeka put the phone on loudspeaker to let Wójcik hear Browarczyk talk. She moved over closer. Lubeka could see tears welling up in her eyes and put her arm around her.

"It means that we are officially linking the cases of Beata, Mazur and Kaszowski. Possibly your husband. We estimate a dozen or so other cases that have been sitting on our desks with loose links to the security industry. This comes from the top, Kasia, so we have the authority to step on as many toes as we like." The break from this comment left space to hear Wójcik sobbing.

"Are you okay, Kasia?"

"Yes. Marianna is with me. What can we do from here?"

"Hold the Russian files and keep yourselves safe until myself and a team from Warsaw get down. We will be there tomorrow morning. We just need to clear up some paperwork here and then we will get to you. Where are you staying?"

"I don't know. I'm not going back home. Marianna has a flat over the river. We can stay there." Wójcik nodded in approval at the suggestion. At that point, Gabreski arrived into the lobby. He had had his customary double whiskey in Szara and had made his way through the cobbled streets parallel to the square at the hotel. He could see that Wójcik had been crying. He went over and looked towards the upturned phone.

"One more thing, Kasia. A woman from Krosno kept phoning Beata in the hospital, her message was that she wanted to meet her. Can I give you her number and could you arrange to meet up with her? She seemed to know something about the files and was urgently trying to talk to Beata."

"Yes, Aron. Please give me her number if you have it. I will get in touch as soon as you go."

"Okay, give me a second." Paper could be heard to rustle through the connection. "Her name is Maria Braszak. She lives in Krosno, but says she will travel to meet the women who have files. Her number is 53 43 73371. Is that clear?"

"Yes, I have got it."

"Okay, be careful with this and I will see you tomorrow at Marianna's flat."

"Do you need the address?"

"No, Kasia, we have that."

"Yes, of course you have." Lubeka had said it before thinking. The sentiment lingered. "Sorry, Aron. We will be there."

As the phone clinked out, without a word, Wójcik brought it back to Krolas, tears popping from her eyes, her breathing laboured, showing a spontaneous burst of grief. "Poor Beata. We led her into this... she paid for it with her life."

"Marianna, Beata is one of many martyrs. It must give us the reason to go on, not to let her or the rest down." Lubeka steadied Wójcik, holding her shoulders, fixing her gaze. Gabreski acted to release them from the growing sense of grief, putting his arms around both women.

"We need to contact this woman, Maria. She seems to have been trying for days to get in touch. She could hold something for us." Lubeka handed Gabreski the phone in which she had saved the contact. Hammering in the numbers as he walked, Gabreski settled, more comfortable in a chair by the window. He was followed by the other two, helping each other to pull chairs around in a huddle.

"Hello, this is Professor Gabreski. Is that Maria?" There was a short pause and then he continued. "I was asked to contact you in relation to our research on files from the national archives. I believe that you have some information for us regarding this research… Yes, of course. That would be very convenient. We are in Kraków at the minute... Yes, we can meet you there." Lubeka and Wójcik became more intrigued as the tone of Gabreski's voice turned more positive and interested. He dabbed the phone off.

"Maria does not want to talk over the phone because she fears it is being tapped. She wants us to meet with her tonight at the old Garison Club, just around the corner. She said it is safe there. She wants to drive up immediately from Krosno."

"Did she say anything else?" Lubeka sought to get more on a lead that came from Krolas's deathbed.

"I really think she was frightened of giving too much away over the phone. If anything, it goes to show that we are not the only ones paranoid about shadows in this place."

"Okay, let Marianna check into the office and then we can leave these bags off in her flat. We can get a taxi from here and stop off at the office in Kościuszki as we go." Lubeka looked at Wójcik.

"It will only take me minutes to let my boss know I am okay and still on the story."

Wójcik got up from the seats. She had an order to follow. The others struggled out. Gabreski went to the bar in the corner of the room. His first attempt at securing libation earlier had given him the taste for it and he was of the opinion that he could follow through with another before they left.

"Łuka. No." Lubeka countered him. Gabreski was shocked.

"Please, Łuka, we need to be clear headed to meet with this woman." The bar staff stepped back in deference to what they perceived to be a domestic tiff. Embarrassed, Gabreski withdrew from the bar and followed the two women out to a group of three taxis that were parked outside the hotel's main door. Wójcik was first in.

"Kościuszki. Across from the red apartment block and then if you could wait for a few minutes. We then want to end up in Piwna, which is behind the jazz club at Bernatka Bridge." By the time she was finished giving the driver directions, the others were in the taxi with bags on their laps, Gabreski solemn after his chastisement.

The car drove quickly through the city centre, circumnavigating the old town to reach the river. The chill was still alive in the drafts that were being carried through gaps at the top of the windows. The blow heater from the front of the taxi dried up the air, leaving a mixture of the driver's smoke, dust, oil and the smell of the city seeping through the window. The snow was clearing rapidly, as the sun continued to shine brightly in the late afternoon. The crisp residue of the remaining snow seemed to evaporate without melting, the atmosphere freezing and clean. They reached the river. The reflection of the sun shimmered across the waves. Couples and tourists steadily diminished as the car moved away from the old town into one of the many areas that had yet to be touched by the hand of Brussels funded developments. The vacant streets, littered by second hand hatchbacks from Italy and France, looked quaint.

"Here we are." Wójcik shouted, before the driver could act to stop the taxi himself. Wójcik jumped out taking her bag with her. "I will just leave the tablet in to get any files I have secured into the Cloud. That should take care of any hackers." She disappeared behind a solid wooden door, with a cautious young man quickly looking up and down the street before closing the door behind them. Gabreski and Lubeka sat silently and patiently. Gabreski watched the driver's clock, the minutes corresponding perfectly to the zloty count. Lubeka broke the silence and spoke to Gabreski in English.

"Łuka, you need to get hold of that. That was embarrassing. You remind me of my husband."

Gabreski sat and looked out the window at the row of small shops and apartments that framed the broad concrete street. The roads were drying up with clumps of snow around the sides, leaving the glint of the tramway tracks, steel and cold. The old buildings mixed with the new uneven structures, every one different, a site of previous prosperity now long gone. He turned to Lubeka. "Okay, you are right. It will not happen again. You know what it is like with the cigarettes. We all have something that has left us hard-wired to habits."

"I know, Łuka, but try to get a hold of it. We need you sober. I will give you a Marlboro if you want." Lubeka smiled. The time dragged on watching the price of the taxi ride rise. At exactly eight minutes and forty seconds after Wójcik jumped out of the taxi and when Gabreski started watching the counter, Wójcik reappeared from behind the wooden security door of the offices of the old building. She hugged the young man who had originally let her in and proceeded to get into the passenger side of the taxi.

"Is everything okay?" Lubeka sprung the question.

"Yes. They wanted an update and were concerned for my safety. They have also been watched over the past few days. The editor has been followed. They seem to be intimidating anyone connected to the files. The journal material is ready to release. I have been able to submit some of the work. Others will write it up."

"It is good that they are feeling the pinch. I am sorry, Marianna, but the more we draw into this, the more pressure we can put on the Zomo."

"Kasia, it is okay. They are good with this. They are journalists. They know the score. This is our field and we stick together. They are working with Warsaw to help out with Beata's funeral." Wójcik frantically waved to her colleague at the door.

"Good." Lubeka was satisfied with that as a response. As the conversation closed, the taxi moved into a 365 degree turn to get back to the ring road of the old town. The traffic picked up as they sped along the riverbank. The two sides of the city social opposities, the glitz of the old town illuminated by the castle with the hucksters selling tin jewellery and trips to an ever increasing flow of tourists. The footbridge was lit up in a splash of colours, silhouetted by the fading blue sky. The taxi crossed the Wisła and sped, looping around the jazz club to pull up at Wójcik's apartment. Gabreski leant over to thrust a begrudged note into the hand of the driver. He took the change, feeling a bit hard done by with the journey. The occupants worked their backpacks and bags out first, before standing on the pathment to watch the taxi speed off.

"Look." Lubeka pointed to the sky above the river. In the distance there was a ring of small green lights hanging over Kazimierz. It was as still as a helicopter, totally silent and the size of a small coffee table.

"That's a surveillance drone. I have never seen one of those before. They are banned in other parts of Europe." Gabreski knew exactly what it was and was intrigued by its sophistication.

"What is it doing?" Lubeka assumed that Gabreski had an answer.

"They are weird. It is like a spaceship. Basically, they are there to watch you, me and everyone else in the city. They can pick up conversations, read letters, gather evidence. In a word, Kasia, they do everything the secret police used to do, except they do not need the middle-aged men in anoraks. If armed, they can also attack."

"This is one day into the privatization of these things and we are in their lens already." Wójcik pinpointed the possibilities of this new bureaucracy. Lubeka perched on the edge of the pathment, almost tipping over onto the road trying to get a glimpse.

"We are not the only ones to spy on. I am sure half that city has a story to tell. Where are we?" Gabreski started to walk down the street at the back of the jazz club.

"We are down here, Łuka." Wójcik pointed down the parallel road of Józefińska and proceeded to lead the three of them towards new apartments with neat balconies and a row of shops. She fumbled with a set of keys and then proceeded to the stairwell. The whole building still smelt of concrete and drying paint.

The apartment was sparsely decorated.

"This is lovely, Marianna. When did you move in?" Gabreski was impressed, shifting over to the window to look out over the row of cottages that seemed to predate this side of the city. Lubeka was more familiar with the surroundings, and, after dropping her bag at the side of the sofa, to claim it for the night, made straight to the balcony.

"I moved here about a year ago. I was with my mom on the other side of the city and needed to be closer to work. I think she needed the space as well. I lived with her right through university to save money. As soon as I was bringing in a wage, I moved out. It was as selfish as that."

"After her bringing you into the world!" Lubeka shouted in from the balcony.

"I know; she was glad to get rid of me. She could finally get on with her own life." Wójcik sounded out in retaliation.

"This is a great part of town. Walking distance from the square and with all the benefits of being out of the hustle and bustle. Well done. This is the place to be." Gabreski liked Wójcik's pioneering spirit to come and settle on the south side of the river. Wójcik set out three cups and worked on an expresso machine that fitted perfectly between a microwave and an oven. The lights of the machine flickered and the three stood in waiting. Wójcik poured the coffee, mimicking the best of baristas.

"Here we go."

"We will need to get back on the road soon. I am sure that woman Maria will not wait for us." Gabreski was impatient, twitchy.

"I need to get a quick wash." Lubeka pitched first for a shower before the others could interrupt.

"Me next." Wójcik joined what sounded like a queue.

"Okay. I will sort out the files and bring the paper copies that Beata had, in case Maria knows anything we have failed to pick up." Wójcik unpacked the paperwork and handed it to Gabreski, who proceeded to shuffle the files and photos for a better inspection. Lubeka rushed to shower, occasionally sticking her head out of the door to check if there was anything she was missing in the other room. Gabreski ordered the files chronologically and Wójcik, out of habit, held her smart phone over each page as it passed by her, cataloguing each image in sequence.

"The answer is in here, Marianna. We just cannot see it."

"What is worth killing for here, Łuka?" Wójcik came straight to the point.

"Power, money. I don't know. Because they feel threatened by this and by us. A handful of files and a couple of suspicions. We can show them to Maria later, if we make it on time, and let's see what she has to say."

Lubeka brushed past and into the bedroom with a large white bath towel wrapped industrially and securely around her.

"Kasia, I will get Jason from our office to take us to the club. He is keen to help out, even if it is just driving. You have met him before... at the symposium. I will text him and he will be here in thirty minutes."

"Sure, great, we need to get around." Lubeka responded immediately and Wójcik started texting frantically on the acknowledgement, her movement and dexterity on the surface of the screen almost performance art.

“These files are as presentable as they can be.” Gabreski looked proudly at the little pile of papers ready for presentation, scanned and secured. Wójcik went into the shower room and Lubeka took up the seat she had occupied next to Gabreski. Instinctively, Lubeka lifted the pages and checked each one again as if not to trust Gabreski. “Łuka, do we have these secured?”

“Yes, Kasia, twice over. They are scanned, with Marianna’s office and my department. They are absolutely secure.”

“Good, Beata would not have selected these to print out for nothing.” They sat and sipped the last of the coffee as Wójcik emerged from the shower room in a white blanket of a towel. As she shuffled around her bedroom dressing, the doorbell sounded in an ever increasing tone. “Someone get that, it’s probably Jason.” Gabreski went to the balcony to get a view out the window, and sure enough, it was the young man who was at the office door earlier in the evening. Wójcik, still buttoning her shirt, hurried to the door before Gabreski could make it, letting in the young man.

“Jason Moss. Boston.” In a cultured American accent, the confidence and politeness of the man was striking.

“It is really nice to meet you. I am Kasia and this is Łuka. We met at the university.” Wójcik hugged him uncomfortably as the other two struggled to get shaking his hand.

“Where are we for?” His English was strange in comparison to the English accent that the others had picked up along with their education, the Englishness of their tones suddenly sounding old world.

“We are for the Garison Club restaurant, across from Planty Park, just down from the station.” Lubeka was narrowing the location down, but seemed to be confusing Moss further through the directions.

"We will show you, Jason." Wójcik jumped in. "He is an intern here for the year and is still getting to know the place." Turning to Moss, she clarified the direction. "From here it is over the river and to the right of the square. I will tell you when we arrive."

As they went down the stairwell, Moss felt obliged to explain who he was.

"I am working on a PhD with Boston and have been here for a few months. I was lucky enough to have relatives here who let me borrow a car for the time." Before he went on, Gabreski's interest picked up. "What are you working on?"

"The Polish diaspora in the US. I needed a year here to pick up on the language and get to the communities most affected by migration." He opened the car and proceeded to shout over the roof as the rest got in. "Chicago is the biggest Polish city outside Warsaw. Did you know that?"

"London is catching up, I hear." Lubeka was thinking of the recent drain of the population after the opening up of the European Union.

"Sure, it's becoming a Polish world these days. All we need is another Pope." The passengers smiled as the car took off over the bridge and into the old town.

The flicker of the street lights and the glow of the neon in the closed shops made the thoroughfare of Krakowske a contradiction of activity and shadows. The trip lasted all of five minutes to the Officer's Club. The layers of the city stripped away with each street corner; the underdeveloped south of the river, the still haunted Jewish quarter, the tourist mecca of the old town, the church towers protruding and illuminated against a star speckled black sky, and the transience of the railway area.

The Peugeot pulled up in front of a closed newspaper kiosk. Lubeka was first to get out and moved swiftly towards the door of the renaissance building. Another drone hovered over this end of the city, silent but visible with its ring of green lights. The others, including Moss, picked up pace to catch up with her. At the top of the stairs, there was a concierge. He stopped Lubeka and asked if they had a reservation. On hearing the name-check of Maria Braszak, the concierge directed Lubeka to the room on the left of a grand staircase. The others had followed Lubeka up the stairs and caught up with her as she made her way towards the open space of a dining room.

A woman appeared who was in her late fifties, looking fresh for her age and disarmingly formal in her approach.

"Good evening. You are Katarzyna. I recognize you from the television. I am Maria Braszak. I am so sorry at the loss of Beata. She was a real soldier of truth. Thank you all for meeting with us." Braszak went around each of the group shaking hands and welcoming them to the place. When she got to Gabreski, she enquired: "Do you have the Russian files?" Gabreski looked to Wójcik, who produced the files from her bag. It was a confessional moment with the four reacting responsively to the grace of a woman they had just met.

On receipt of the bundle of files, she made her way to the edge of the security desk positioned outside the dining room and slowly proceeded to open each page. She had claimed an immediate authoritative ownership over the files and the three who had brought the documents from Warsaw felt obliged to let her sift through their work. There was a solid sense of release. Her silence and studiousness enhanced her presence as a woman who was familiar with the fine detail of the evidence before her.

"Do you know something about these people?" Lubeka moved closer to Braszak and could see her hand shaking as she slowly turned the pages. Braszak looked up with beads of tears in each eye, waiting to overflow down her cheeks. "I know most of them. They look so young and frightened." She flicked through the pages and stopped at one grey page with a photo in one corner and a statement running the length of the page. "That is me. My name changed when I got married." Lubeka looked in disbelief. This was one of the missing. One of those who were interrogated by the Zomo in the summer of 1988. Looking up at her the resemblance was there, the grainy photograph was not able to hide the calm beauty of the woman. The others came over to look. On this, Braszak used a small silk handkerchief to wipe her eyes as she continued to flick through the files.

"You were there. You were one of those lifted."

"Yes." Braszak closed the last page of the document and lifting it said, "Can I?" The question was implicit; could she keep the files. The others looked at each other. Lubeka was first to reply. "Of course, Maria, it was you we got these for. It is a part of you." Braszak clutched Lubeka's hands and stared, motherly and direct, the others watched on. "Thank you, God bless you, Kasia." Braszak turned to the group and, regaining her composure with a business-like demeanour, stated: "I have someone I want you to meet." With the document at her side, she led them through the mirrored doors of the lobby and into an exquisitely furnished dining room with the draped curtains of a classical 1930s deco interior. The tables throughout were set for a formal dinner. It was totally empty on one side of the restaurant, but on the other side – a cordoned off section with a deco separation – there were a number of older women, all standing, statuesque, ghost-like, in a dimly lit corner. The women moved slowly, collectively, towards the approaching group.

Braszak stood between the two groups and announced. "Ladies, may I introduce Katarzyna Lubeka, Łuka Gabreski, Marianna Wójcik and Jason Moss. They have brought our files back from Moscow." Some of the women whispered to each other when the files were mentioned. By the deportment and presence of Braszak, she was obviously the spokesperson for this discrete gathering.

Looking to the researchers she redirected attention to the women in front of her, pointing to each, with each in turn nodding and nervously smiling as courtesy. "May I introduce you to some people you may know of. Magda, Karina, Julita, Berta, Edyta, Ewa, Ania, Ewa, Hanna, Izabela, Anna, and Bogna." As the names were spoken aloud the files came alive. These were the women in the lists, the people who had been through the interrogation by the Zomo. Not all were present, but the first names were recognizable as the sequence of names that Krolas had selected from the Russian files to copy. They were Bartek's victims. Some were reserved, some held to the back, afraid, vulnerable as exposed living witnesses. Others held hands, standing, waiting for revelations from the conversation. Braszak addressed Lubeka directly.

"We are the students they interrogated in that spring of 1988. Some of us they tortured. Some of us were taken. Some of us never came back. We have held together for most of our lives, never knowing the detail of what happened. The files can at least give us some release from this nightmare of our youth." Braszak spoke as if she had been rehearsing the speech for thirty years.

"We were all at the university here. We come from all over Poland. We were so excited about the idea of getting rid of the Soviets. Everything was possible back then. So we went on the marches, we made the posters for the miners, we played Western rock music and danced our way into the future. They first brought Hanna to Sofia to interrogate, then to abuse. I ended up in Chop in the Ukraine. They used us and threw us back when they got bored. We were away from our families and loved ones. Some of us were lost for months. They told us we were being brought to Warsaw for questioning. We all went through hell, and they have always denied it. Now we have proof." Braszak waved the files in the air.

One woman, Hanna, stepped forward and said: "Let us see." Braszek passed the files around the women. They huddled in groups of two or three, sifting through the names. Russian could be heard, as those who could remember it from school stuttered their way through the text. Lubeka and Gabreski watched. As the time went by, the scrutiny of the documents brought back recollections and reminiscences of those who were not in the room. The chatter rose in volume.

Braszak waved to two waitresses who were silently standing at the entrance. "Please, let us have a meal together." The waitresses disappeared as the women and their guests found seats in an enclosed area of the restaurant. Plates appeared in an overly formal manner, as the integrity and dignity of the group of women came resolutely through as time passed. Gabreski was intrigued, fixated on the stories of the resistance movement of the eighties. He felt as though he should be recording the testimonies, building the case further. This was the core of the movement of the eighties; the activists, the partners of activists. The memories were alive and visceral.

Lubeka was very much at home with this company and was received as one of the women in every respect. More so, the mannerisms were the same, the etiquette of Catholic Poland very much in evidence. Napkins were used almost like orchestral batons.

Hands were raised to emphasize points, the terminology opaque to the young, highlighted the sophistication of the educated language and a variety of regional accents. The courses were neverending, yet all in manageable proportions: kartoflanka, pierogi, surówka, kotlet mielony. The pitch of the conversation was hypnotic. At the close of the evening, Braszak stood up. On this, the cluster of tables went silent.

"Please, I would just like to take a moment to thank you all for coming here to share our experiences. This is a new beginning where, with the lead of these young people, we have not been afraid to meet and express our sad histories. Thank you for your courage in standing up to the shadows of this country's past and God bless you in your work." On this, the women spontaneously and lightly started to clap. Lubeka smiled in awe. She was fixed to the chair, looking straight at Braszak.

When the researchers returned to the car they sat silent in the moment. "That is what it has been all about." Gabreski tried to distil the evening down to a few thoughts. "These are the brave young faces in the photos. God. How we have kept our distance from them for all these years."

"One of the women said they tortured her for a week solid trying to get information on her father and brother. She showed me the whip marks on her legs. The scars are still there, after all these years." Wójcik was dazed at the experience.

"The thing is that throughout this time they have still been afraid. They know the secret state still haunts the streets of Eastern cities. It still has power to terrorize people." Gabreski stopped the conversation. "We need to get focused for tomorrow. Browarczyk will be at your flat tomorrow morning at nine. I will make my way there. Jason, if you wish, you are very welcome to join us to see what the State Protection people have to say. Now, I will bid you all goodnight."

"I will probably go to Warsaw for the funeral of Beata. That will be in a couple of days. I can bring flowers from all of us." Wójcik flagged up her obligation to her dead colleague and friend. "That would be nice, Marianna, I am sure the family would love to see you. Jason should go with you." They all sat for a moment and, again, Gabreski rounded back to the practicalities of the evening. "Right, I am away. Safe home." Gabreski stepped out of the car and began walking towards the hotel. The car reversed abruptly, bumping off the roadside before speeding off towards the other side of the river.

Gabreski's eyes were drawn to the sky, catching a brief view of piercing green lights, before rushing across the strip of trees and snow covered grass that is Planty Park. The lazer lights in the sky reminded him of conflict zones he had been to, where the constant rattle of helicopters alerted populations of their surveillance, that they were being watched. The reminder was always present and the drones played a similar role in this post-modern sky. The noise was not there, but the ring of lights discretely registered their presence. He knew that there was a Belgian pub en route to the hotel and this was a good target from where he could gather his thoughts.

"Could I have a large Tyskie and a double whiskey." The tender was used to lone drinkers colonizing the corners of the bar. They were a distraction from the marauding stag parties that drifted through the town at the weekends. The small talk struck up the simple acknowledgements of bar society. "Were you out this evening?"

"Yes, we had a work dinner."

"Very nice."

“Have you been busy here this evening?” Gabreski sounded disinterested.

“No. We are waiting for a few stag groups to come through. They phoned ahead, but no sign of them as yet.” Gabreski thought that he was not in the mood, just being polite. His lack of commitment carried the barman to another customer. Retrieving his phone from his coat, Gabreski proceeded to go through the daily ritual of texting his colleagues in London to give them an update. Also to ensure that his account was still live.

After meeting the women from the student movement, his mother came to mind. Unusual for him when away, he found himself tapping in good wishes to his mother in London, thinking carefully of the exact thoughts that she would respond to when mentioning the meeting with the women. Careful and concise he finished his whiskey to the promise that he would spend more time with his mom on going back. *... they reminded me of you, brave and Polish. Love Łuka.*

In the apartment, Lubeka and Wójcik settled in quickly. They too had opted for something stronger to get them to sleep. Wójcik always had some wine stashed away for this type of occasion. News of Krolas’s murder was headlined on the national stations. They watched the television until Lubeka’s head tilted into a deep sleep.

26th November

The nip was still in the air as Lubeka and Wójcik emerged from their beds. Lubeka, in a habitual round, set about cleaning the apartment in anticipation of Browarczyk’s arrival. Wójcik was an aspiring journalist to her core; order and tidiness were not virtues that came with the craft. Lubeka had them as instincts. With the patio windows being forced open to let the freshness of the day into the apartment, the anaesthesia of the chill immediately cleansed the rooms. The bell went at 8.40. Lubeka could see down from the patio towards Gabreski, who was standing at the intercom outside the bloc. As he entered the building Moss coincidentally drove up to the front of the building. Gabreski let him through the door along with himself. Within the minute, the living room of the apartment was a hive of activity. Wójcik had the coffee brewing continually. Lubeka strained in a rote of cleaning and the two men stood exchanging stories about the mid-west of the United States and their problems with the nuances of US foreign policy.

The news on the television registered nine a.m. The stories from yesterday – Krolas's death and drones – had been replaced by a new day, made up of Polish troops in EU wars and austerity measures from the government. The fickleness of the business of news shifted relentlessly. Two black Audi saloons drove up to the pathment across the street.

"This looks like Aron and his people." Wójcik went to the patio and waved down. The cars were filled with men all sitting quietly, the engines continuing to tick over. Browarczyk came through to the lounge. The four inside moved to greet him.

"We need to get out quickly. We have a tip off from our people in Warsaw that Bartek is moving equipment today. We need to get to them before they dismantle whatever they are working on. You met with Maria and her companions last night. We will need to get a report on that. This is the first time that this group has emerged. They would not trust any of the state forces. Thanks for giving them the space and a place to meet. Let's go."

Browarczyk was dressed casually, out of the styled suit they had seen him in previously. This was more of a uniform for the street, leather jacket, jeans and trainers. When they got to the cars, a similarly dressed man in his thirties saluted Browarczyk and opened the door for Lubeka and Gabreski.

"Jason. Take two of my men and Marianna and follow us. We are going to the office of Bartek Security in Kazimierz." The dryness of the morning air gave the orders an echo around the street, the brightness of the sky providing a blue cover for the events of the day. Gabreski noticed that for once there seemed to be no surveillance whatsoever. There was safety in numbers and he could tell by the silence of Browarczyk's colleagues, they were disciplined and there for business.

The three cars pulled away together, Moss's car struggling to keep up with the performance of the others. They moved by the Square of Ghetto's Heros and towards the new Schindler Factory museum, swinging left over the bridge and onto Starowiślna. The traffic was flowing well for the time of the morning and brought them out to the main thoroughfare cutting through the center of the city from Kazimierz to the old town. The cars pulled up in a sequence outside an understated hostel, bumping up onto the pavement and cutting through the remaining tracks of snow to hold up outside an in-stepped door.

Browarczyk turned and stated concisely: "Kasia and Łuka, you stay to the back of the team. Our men will go in first and then we can get to see what this place has to offer." As the stream of cars offloaded the passengers, Gabreski returned to Browarczyk. "What is this?" Hanging back to let the first group through, Browarczyk looked to Gabreski: "This is the sub office of Bartek International. It is the address they use occasionally when in other countries. It has never been listed as a business address here. It is listed as a business in Moscow to deal with both private security and the expansion into the arms export markets. This place, we think, brings both things together." On that he turned to follow the others into the darkened stairwell of the old building, part hostel and part office space. It was unlit towards the top of the stairs and spacious to the point where the stairs appeared to be the centre of the whole block.

The four at the front checked the rims of the door frames and the exterior. Precautionary and suspicious, they were obviously taking no risks. As Browarczyk arrived with the rest, he waved to his unit, at which the response was the door being knocked by the first man. The time given to wait for an answer was short as another of the unit moved in with an industrial lock drill, removing the lock at the front of the solid wooden doors. The professional caution of the team became evident as one by one they moved into the darkened hallway. The first three had handguns and seemed to be veterans of this type of work. They disappeared into the darkness, the shuffle of feet being the only indication of activity, silhouettes darting across monitors. They moved through the hallway, the heat from computer radiation could be sensed around the offices. Only the glare from a bank of computer screens lit the room. It had the stench of sweat and nauseous heat.

"Clear. Clear. Clear." Voices came from across the floor.

"They must have just left. They must have been keeping an eye on our movements." One of the unit sifted the place to check for evidence of who had been there. Browarczyk brought Gabreski and Lubeka over to the screens. Moss and Wójcik followed slowly, taking care not to be intrusive to the unit checking through the office desks and files.

"What do you think?"

Gabreski and Lubeka viewed the monitors. Gabreski was the first to respond, nodded to Lubeka for approval.

"They seem to have been hacking into the government's CCTV networks around the city." He pointed at the various interiors of state buildings. "They could get access to just about every camera and computer in the city with this equipment. You would need an IT specialist to get to the programmes used, but the targets are obvious. These are military, police and government offices." He moved along the monitors. Twenty in total. "This bank of screens is fed from drones in flight. They are gathering information on whoever they feel needs to be watched. If they had these in every city their information would be comparable to that of the government agencies. The CIA could not have done better than this." Lubeka cut across him.

Five smartphones were lined up neatly under one of the monitors.

"These are interesting." Gabreski lifted one of the live phones. "In England, they call these 'Mickey'. A monitor fed through to phones so that those observing can keep an eye on specific targets as they move. They are probably linked in to all the monitors and the drones. Very sophisticated indeed."

"They were simply able to watch us coming and going, and took off."

"At least we have located a security hub. I am sure this is not the only one."

"Yes, but how many more do they have?" Lubeka was wary.

One of the unit members revived a laptop which, in the rush, had not been shut down. "Sir, come and see this." The others followed Browarczyk as he navigated across the large office and into a side room. On the bottom of the screen there was a line of files. One was a file on Maria Braszak. Another woman's file was active, covering half the screen, with the other half of the screen filled with pictures from the previous evening, some taken from inside the restaurant.

Going to the document in which the file was contained, there were scores of individual files, each scanned from the old archive version, but each with updates on the people who had been interrogated in the 1980s. Some of the names were familiar, with updated pictures matched with the archive photographs. The archive pictures were of the young and frightened, new details were of the survivors, the pictures taken obviously under surveillance.

"Maria is that important to them. She knows who they are and, more importantly, where they are." Wójcik fed through the thought with a sense of concern.

"We will need to locate Maria as quickly as possible. She is their past coming back to haunt them." Browarczyk tapped heavily on his phone, the ringtone loud and distracting. He stated his intentions aloud.

"I will get the local police in her hometown to put a security circle on her house." He turned and walked towards a curtained window, pulling them across with one hand as he spoke to his office in Warsaw.

Lubeka and Gabreski flicked though the files on the PC. They were updated versions of the originals from Moscow, translated into Polish. For Gabreski, they seemed to be involved in a security gathering exercise, to locate threats and isolate the past in a manner that could be better managed for their purposes. For Lubeka, it was a hit list. These people, most of them women, some of them from the previous night, were being located to be silenced.

"This is too sophiscated to be exclusively Polish." Gabreski looked around the room.

"What do you mean?" Lubeka was intrigued.

"The languages used here move across the Eastern states. The technology is perhaps a year old, but comes from outside our circles. It has all been shipped in. Even the layout is not something I have seen in Poland before. This is a command centre. Easily constructed, relatively inexpensive and flexible, but more in line with what the state security services have in the US or Russia. The CIA centre in Brussels is very like this, technologically effective, but expendable, moveable. It is the operatives here who count, which is probably why they were confident enough to just pack up and leave. It does, however, leave a big question mark over who is running this. Who is supporting it and who is benefiting from it?"

"Okay." Browarczyk shouted. "We need to leave a team here and get our IT people in to break this up and get it back to Warsaw. We are contacting the President's office to inform them of the developments. I will need to get back to Warsaw… with Maria and the women." He paused and looked at Lubeka. "Kasia, would you go to Krosno to find her? One of my men will take you. She is not answering her phone. I am sure it is nothing, but she trusts you and your presence there will deter any threats to her. They have only left here, so you should be able to make it to Krosno before they can act. They will be hiding up for a while I am sure."

Lubeka responded assertively. "We'll go now. Are you okay to come with me?" She looked at her companions.

"Maybe Marianna and Jason should stay after coming straight back from the funeral. That would give us a presence here and they could work on any media that may come our way."

"Okay. Is that okay, Marianna?" Lubeka assumed that Wójcik could answer on behalf of the two of them.

"Sure. You need to get going."

Browarczyk gestured to one of the men who had been driving to take Gabreski and Lubeka out of Kraków the two and half hour drive to Krosno in the south. As some of the unit remained in the room, the rest of the party made their way down to the cars. At that stage, others had arrived in forensic suits, emerging from white anonymous vans lined up outside the building in Starowiślna.

"I will inform the President's office now. I am sure the rooms are still live with monitoring equipment." Browarczyk stepped across the road and paced up and down as he talked on his phone. A tramcar rattled by, blocking him from the rest and leaving the others in a state of anticipation as to what would happen next. Lubeka typed away on the phone, trying to locate Maria Braszak. As with the other attempts, there was just the answering machine.

"God. I hope she is okay. They seemed to have her in their sights."

"We will get down in a few hours. I am sure she is avoiding contact today, after last night." Gabreski tried to reassure Lubeka.

Browarczyk returned from his conversation on the other side of the road. "The President's office is moving to stall the bill on the privatization of drone use until this investigation is complete."

"That will give us some breathing space to find out who Bartek really is and where the Zomo and their friends are these days." Lubeka felt this was a positive result. Stepping into one of the cars, she could not help forcing one more point, shouting over the traffic at Browarczyk. "Get them to order an investigation into Lustration while you are still talking to them." Browarczyk smiled.

Gabreski got into the back of the car with Lubeka. They waved at Wójcik and Moss, Lubeka winding down the window to see if they were on the same track. "Can you get this to the public as soon as possible?"

"Yes, Kasia, we will have this live before lunch." Wójcik waved, an index finger pointing at Gabreski assertively. "You take care of her." With that, the car lowered from the pavement and bumped over the tramlines, driving off in the direction of the ring road and the motorway south.

The brightness of the morning made for pleasant driving, as they skirted the castle and made their way towards the south-east bound Księcia Józefa dual carriageway, onto the less impressively named E40. A product of membership of the European Union, the new road linked the centre of the country with the less prosperous regions that sat uneasily on the Ukrainian and Slovakian borders. Lubeka dozed off easily, her mind settling after the excitement of the morning. Gabreski went into a trance watching panel after panel of road supports that seemed to have no reason for being there other than to hide the road from the houses on the other side of wildly different decorated fences.

"Do you enjoy your job?" Gabreski broke the calm to engage with the driver.

"I'm Dawid, and yes. I get the chance to catch the bad guys."

"What is Aron like to work with?"

"He is very loyal to his men. We have worked for six years together and he has risen up the ranks continually. His grandfather was killed in the Warsaw Uprising. His mother ran the children's hospital. He is solid." The driver was protective of his superior officer.

"I don't doubt it. Duty runs through his veins then?

"As with all of us." The driver never broke his concentration on the road. The murmur of the engine returned in the background of the hypnotic hum of the trip.

"Would you like some music on, Professor Gabreski?"

"Sure. We could do with waking up before we get to Krosno." The driver scanned a playlist. Blue Café's melodic tones filled the car. Gabreski resigned himself to the pop and sentimentality. Lubeka was more in tune with this, opening her eyes to acknowledge a marker from her generation. It was a reference point for at least two in the car. Gabreski returned to his trance and the unfamiliar countryside, still lacquered white with the crystallized snow. The route was pitted with townland and farms, people who have lived there for generations, bearing the hardness and scars to prove it. This was rural Poland in its complicated and tragic splendour. Lubeka sang quietly to herself.

***

In Kraków, Wójcik and Moss had made it back to their office. The chatter around the local media was of a significant find by the Office of State Protection. Wójcik's desk was littered with old stories and neglect since leaving it the previous week. The others in the office were standing around the two flat television screens that dominated the open plan room. The noise rolled with conversations cutting through the space, more like a stock exchange than a gathering of experienced journalists.

Wójcik and Moss pushed through to the front of the huddle to see the breaking news across both channels, both screens.

> "The president's office has withdrawn the bill on the privatization of drone use pending an investigation into the use of drone technology by private companies in illegal surveillance practices in Kraków. This is a huge blow for the industry, who were hoping to secure lucrative international

contracts and benefit from the outsourcing of surveillance and security operations from a number of government agencies. There is also an ongoing investigation into the links between one company and illicit surveillance activities. According to an Office of State Protection statement, progress will not be made on the bill until such times as the investigation is complete. Speculation is rife that there is a connection between this company and the killing of journalist Beata Krolas in Warsaw."

Wójcik hugged Moss, the rest of the office chattered their way through the chaos of desks and mess of paper that criss-crossed the room.

"Beata would have been jumping with joy at this. It is her last punch at the old guard." Wójcik felt relief at the speed and impact of the morning. The fight was obviously going on behind the scenes, but the fallout of their work could be seen in a very real way.

"We can make another link by this afternoon's press briefing. We can take a swipe at them." Her mood resonated across the room. This was why she went into journalism in the first place. The buzz was addictive. Moss smiled and nodded his head, winking at her as he tried to clear away the scattering of sheets on his desk. Wójcik pulled her phone from her bag and relayed details of the report to Lubeka, speedily typing into the phone at a pace that could only have come with a familiarity with technology that she lived with day and night. The desktop computers roared up. They settled into the ambitious industrious hammering along with the rest of the office.

***

The road to Krosno narrowed to two lanes as the black Audi cruised into Jasło in the Subcarpathian Voivodeship.

"I need to stop for something to eat. It is near two and we need to get some sugar into us before facing whatever is coming in Krosno." Dawid worked his way through the narrow streets of the town, straining to get a view of places where he could pull up to get some food. Just on the outer edge of the town, he drove carefully into what looked like a new petrol station. Lubeka sat up. Gabreski worked into his pocket to try and find some złoty.

"This is where my family is from originally, before they were moved to Kraków." Dawid strained to educate the other two. "The town was totally destroyed by the Nazis in September 1944 to make a rubble barrier against the Russians. Everyone was sent to Kraków or the death camps. I am Jewish and I am Catholic, as all patriotic Poles should be. The town was here for six hundred years before the Nazis came."

Gabreski had nothing to say and did not feel the right to question any of it. This was the story of so many small towns in this part of the country. He thought of how the trauma had been passed down, generation to generation. The issues for these people were still alive, not just from the Soviet occupation, but long before that. These villages and towns had been trampled over for hundreds of years. Everyone came through this country. The tenacity of its people ensured that they always returned, resumed, survived. Lubeka was used to the stories of the war; every family, every community rehearsed their social memories as a way of bearing witness to the horrors of the past. Even her generation passed on the stories emotionally, bluntly, conveying the sadness. It had become habit when triggered by location or event. Dawid had been obliged to say his piece.

They navigated their way into a fast food cubicle, each of them burdened with packaging and smells. As with all of these places, the paper trail to the food was the most interesting thing about it. Lubeka checked her phone, receiving a text from Wójcik.

"Look at this. The president's office has stopped the bill on drone use and production. The security industry is being investigated." Lubeka read snippets of the text before diving into a response with enthusiasm, encouragement for Wójcik and Moss back in Kraków.

"That's movement. We now need to see what exactly has happened in Krosno and where Maria is." Both Lubeka and Dawid held their phones, typing furiously with a casual disregard for the others at the same table. On occasion, Lubeka would raise her head with a brief on what was being communicated. "Texting Maria... No response... Texting home to let them know where I am..."

Dawid interrupted the office-like conditions that pertained at the table of the fast food outlet.

"Colonel Browarczyk wants us to get to Krosno quickly. The local police cannot find Maria and have requested urgent support for a manhunt. We have located just about all of the women from last night and they are safe. Maria has been targeted." Dawid stood up while still eating. Both companions followed, lifting what food they could as they rushed towards the car. The station was filling up with children – setting a contrast between the joy of the day for some and the severity of the moment for others. Gabreski smiled as he pushed his way through the throngs of Eskimo clad little ones, all pom-poms, colour and noise. Lubeka gently hushed the children aside, partaking in the chaos, becoming part of the incoming party. The car was still warm when they got back in. The food quickly deposited in the car park bin, they could now focus their energies for the last few kilometers into Krosno.

Although recently it had become a destination for weekenders, mostly Poles from the north, the winter still controlled the traffic and business going through the town. Spiralling into its medieval town square, the place was known for a market that had been operating on the same spot by the Wisłok River for almost a thousand years. Beyond that, the glass factory dominated life in Krosno. It was the biggest employer, the main tourist attraction and cause for the small museums of the city to celebrate.

The darker side of the place was not as obvious and remained subdued knowledge among the people. It was occupied by the Russians during the First World War and looted. It was taken by the Nazis after eight days in Poland in September 1939. On 9th August 1942, the Gestapo ordered the Jewish community in the city – on that day – to make their way to the square by the train station, where they were force marched to a field outside the city. To a child they were murdered. Any members of the community who escaped that fate were sent to Belzec death camp for their apocalypse. Over two thousand Jewish people perished, one in three of the city's 1920s population. The need for a monument to their martyred community haunted the city, linked with the memories of a vibrant society that once thrived there.

The three in the car were aware of the history of the region. They knew of the difficulties that the region held, with its migrating young, its hidden histories and an occasional historical mention on the regional television stations. Lubeka had passed through the city on her honeymoon and was fond of its peacefulness and friendliness. As they drove down through the main thoroughfare, Podkarpacka, Gabreski was increasingly aware of how developed the city looked.

Many of the buildings seemed new, the European Union viewing the city as a major asset worth investing in. The remnants of the snow and the blueness of the sky were met in the middle by the sharpness of the chalked white renaissance architecture. It was unlike many other cities in Poland in that it had a freshness, a newness about it.

"Welcome to little Kraków." Dawid was returning to his knowledge of the area. "It has all the history, but none of the tourists, which is a good thing if you ask me."

"Do you know where we are going? I have some idea of the city." Lubeka was keen to bring her knowledge to the conversation.

"Yes, Kasia. We will go to the local police and see where they are with the search for Maria."

"Can the police here be trusted?" Lubeka returned to her habitual suspicion.

"We just need the information from them. And I think they are well out of the way of what is happening in Warsaw and Kraków. They work for the community here, not the state. And anyway, I hear the biggest crime around here is bikes being stolen. You are just down from Warsaw. Compare the difference."

Lubeka was silenced.

"They do not even have a proper station in this city. It is the perfect place for a peaceful life if you want one. The Komisariat of the local police is based just outside the city at Rymanów. We have to meet him and his people in the city square. They are already there working on this."

"Will we be here overnight, Dawid?" Gabreski was looking at the practicalities of a new investigation.

"Probably. We can sort that out later."

The car cruised past the old market and up the hill, past the monument to the Soviet dead of the Second World War and into the square. The expanse of the place hinted that this was an important regional power base at one stage. The colonnades and fountain in the middle spoke of a long gone splendour, the newness of the cobblestones and brightness of the painted buildings, a product of recent investment. The car bobbled across the square and towards two blue and white police cars at the far end. A cluster of heavily armed police hung around the cars. As the Audi drew to a halt, the Komisar approached the driver's door. The saluting looked like a collective nervous tick by all surrounding the car. Lubeka, Gabreski and Dawid emerged to don their coats against the chill. The introductions were brief.

"Professors Gabreski and Lubeka are here to help with the investigation into the disappearance of Maria Braszak. The files we discovered in Kraków suggest that she was being tracked by former members of the secret police. They are specialists on the files and know the individuals concerned. Please consider them as advisors to the Office." Dawid set out the *bona fides* of Lubeka and Gabreski.

"Also, Colonel Browarczyk will be joining us as soon as his business in Warsaw is complete."

The Komisar turned and took a pace away from the group, drawing Dawid into a more confidential arrangement.

"I need a quick word, Captain." Both men moved to the side.

"We have just had reports of two other women in their fifties going missing. They were also on a trip to Kraków last night." Dawid called Gabreski and Lubeka over. They stepped quickly to get a handle on the situation.

"We have two other women missing. Who are they, Komisar?"

"Karina Glinka and Hanna Back."

Lubeka gasped, knowing that these were the women they had met the night before, women who had broken their silence to speak to her and her colleagues. Gabreski questioned in an agitated but definite manner.

"Where were they last seen?"

"The three of them, we understand, had made it back to Krosno. Hanna did not reach home. Karina disappeared going out this morning. We have no information on Maria at all, given that she lived alone at the edge of the square. We need to know what you know about them."

Gabreski and Lubeka looked to Dawid for confirmation that contributing would help. Dawid nodded and moved to the side urgently tapping his phone.

"They were all ex-prisoners of the Zomo. They had gone to ground and only emerged to speak out in the past few days after the release of Russian files on the student interrogations of 1988. In the search of private security company offices in Kraków this morning, we discovered that the files of the prisoners were being updated, presumably for some sort of a hunt. What happens now?"

"We search the city. We do not think they have left, otherwise we would have some evidence of movement." The Komisar directed a detachment of his officers to set up road blocks on each of the main roads from the city. Turning back to the civilians, he pointed to the other side of the square.

"We can use the staff room of the city's college as an operations center. It has all the equipment we need to coordinate a search of the area."

The illumination of the lights and the disturbing whine of walkie-talkies dominated the winter air. When they arrived into the courtyard of the college, they were aware of major activity by the regional police. Staff cars were lined up and equipment was being offloaded into the marbled corridors of the college. As they moved towards the hub of activity in the staff room, they rushed by the normality of academic life, startled students still in the midst of their semester. They were met with a wall of laptops and copiers.

"What do you know about the people who are doing this?" The Komisar was desperate to get any supporting information, his question coming from a point of enthusiastic naivety.

"We suspect a rogue group of security service personnel who are in the process of being exposed. They seem to be getting more desperate as time goes on and as their business goes down the drain." Gabreski looked to Lubeka for acknowledgement at the summary. She nodded in agreement.

"What do they want in Krosno?"

Lubeka responded loudly. "They need to get to the women who know exactly who they are and what they have been doing. They need to silence as many as possible."

"How many women are we talking about?"

"At least twelve that we know of." The numbers had the dramatic effect of getting the Komisar to call the room to attention to relay the conversation.

"Check to see if anyone here has gone missing in the past day. Get a list of all holdings by private security firms in the region. Search properties that have links to the three women we know have disappeared. Get moving, these are dangerous people and we need to get to them before they get to others."

The energy of those within the office went into overdrive. Different teams emerged, breaking into various directions, moving out of the door to be mixed with a throng of students converging from the last lectures of the day. The artificial heat of the building and the radiation from the computers mixed with body heat and adrenaline. The darkness of the afternoon had descended onto a city lit up by decorative mock gas lights. The town square glittered with the multi-coloured lights that bound from the fountain, illuminating the restaurants that surrounded the two, and three, storey cloistered buildings. It was a very pretty place, quiet in the mystery that had befallen it.

Dawid drove Gabreski and Lubeka to the nearest hotel to book in. He was aware that the process may take some time and that there was a need for some respite from the potential trauma of the next day or so. The hotel was used to customers turning up on the doorstep. The university used it as a holding point for the legions of foreign students who came through the city during the year for courses and conferences.

"We will take any full floor that is available. There will be personnel who will be coming down from Warsaw."

This was the first time Gabreski and Lubeka had heard of reinforcements or knew of the need for reinforcements. They dutifully took their keys and followed the receptionist to the floor above the reception. The need for silence was foremost in Lubeka's thoughts, time to think, solace in the middle of the storm – answers. Gabreski took an alternative route, dumping what he had and descending to the small bar where Dawid was already reviewing material that was coming through from intelligence hubs across the country.

"Well, what do we have?" Gabreski joined him at the table.

"You need to look at this. We have located the updated files. They have been translated from Russian into Polish and have the pictures taken from last night. We also have lists of property holdings by numerous private security agencies in this region. The property portfolio is as strong as any other aspect of their work."

“Anywhere local?” Gabreski knew that a search was needed to target the places effectively and quickly. Dawid spun the tablet around to present Gabreski with a list of addresses.

“A lot of these are domestic dwellings.” Pointing to the screen he selected a few of note. “These are sales offices and financial centers.”

“Prioritize.” Dawid suggested that Gabreski give an idea of where could be targeted first.

“Please get Kasia down here, she will have a better idea than I would. She has been working on these people and their antics for years.” Dawid called across to the receptionist to get Lubeka down to help.

“We will have people and equipment here to get this search under way. Presume they know we are here. Colonel Browarczyk will be flying down in the next hour with backup.”

Lubeka arrived promptly to join the table and, without saying a word, scanned down the list to pick up any hint of where the women could be. She scrolled the addresses, stopping occasionally to pick up on the names of shops, street names, numbers that seemed irregular or familiar. Within seconds, she returned to one name that was out of context.

“‘OAP’ ‘ØAP’ with a strike through the O. That is Bulgarian for ‘lighthouse’ or ‘safehouse’. It is just down the street two minutes from here, beside the river.”

“That seems to be just an office which can be rented, an anonymous building. Anything else?”

“Here is another one.” Gabreski looked at a pattern.

“It is just an office again, but it is in Russian, ‘Mark’. Mark means ‘lighthouse’.”

Lubeka intervened: “The lighthouse is an insignia. They seem to use it as a business logo. I have seen it before... on the lapels or arms of their uniforms. It gives them an obvious base, wherever they move across the country. We are getting somewhere.” She pulled out her own tablet and scrolled across, occasionally tapping the screen. Pictures appeared of the 1988 riots in Kraków.

“Look. Here. Here it is.” Lubeka zoomed into the arm-patch of one of the Zomo unit. Distinct and clear, the stitched outline of a lighthouse could be seen.

“Okay, we need to do this now. List any you think we should search.” Dawid jumped up, tapping on his phone as he moved into the reception. The other two called out businesses or property names, copying, pasting and listing details.

“Let’s go. ØAP is just across from the old market. We will be met there by the others.”

The table went into a clatter of anxious activity. The staff watched on as the movement disrupted the quietness of their day. By the time they were settling into the car they could hear the police sirens from the town square echoing across the valley. The stillness of the evening was broken by the shutter of movement as cars met at the junction beside the old market. The office was located in a bland steel and glass office complex. A row of cars pulled up together. Lubeka and Gabreski held back as the police and State Protection unit rushed to the main door. The only indication of the occupancy was a small plaque with the name ØAP beside a logo of a lighthouse.

“Stand back. We need to force entry.” On this command, two of the police emerged with a ramming rod which shattered the lock on the front of the building. The police filed in, accompanied by Dawid’s men. Lubeka and Gabreski followed. The dust from the light piercing through the front door reflected in the sharpness of the evening. The noise of the battering met the pattern of the blue police lights which lit up the building.

"Casualty. Call an ambulance. This is an emergency." The police commander was first into the office and bellowed his authoritative command. Lubeka pushed by the crowd to reach the body of a middle aged woman tied to a chair, sitting in the middle of the room.

"God. That is Karina Glinka. That is Karina Glinka." Lubeka's voice could be heard on the steps outside. Some of the police rushed out to secure the building. The body had been there for some hours. The stiffness and contortion of the position suggested a severe amount of stress in her final moments. The lights filtering into the room lifted the lingering remnants of cigarette smoke, drifting and hanging on the stale and sickly perfumed air.

"She looks as if she has been strangled." Dawid immediately went into the analysis in the manner of someone who was natural to this scene, coping with emotions through studious professionalism. Her hair was tied back and her eyes stared at the opened door. Dawid looked into her eyes. Lubeka pushed through and bent over close to the body to whisper something in her ear. The others did not budge, but took this strange behaviour as a normal occurrence. Gabreski picked up the last whispers, gently confided: "...forgive us our trespasses as we forgive those who trespass against us. And lead us not into temptation, but deliver us from evil. Amen." ["...odpuść nam nasze winy, jako i my odpuszczamy naszym winowajcom. I nie wódź nas w pokuszenie, ale nas zbaw ode złego. Amen."] When she had finished, one of the policewomen, who had entered the room in the first group, touched Lubeka on the shoulder, an acknowledgement that it was their duty to take over from that point.

"They must have picked her up as soon as she arrived back from meeting us in Kraków. What have they done to the others? What about Maria?" Gabreski voiced thoughts that Lubeka was trying to avoid.

"We have support from Warsaw arriving at any minute. We need to keep the media at bay for the time being. So, please, no divulging the current situation." Dawid looked at Lubeka as the person in the room who had the closest links to the media. She nodded in response, the question was directed only at her.

"Sir, the tracks in the snow outside show a couple of cars have been through here recently. One has a wide tread snow tyre, which we think may be a four-by-four Land Rover or something like it. The road is also dug up a bit where the vehicle tried to get a grip in the snow speeding off. Someone is bound to have heard or saw this."

"Okay, that's what we are looking for. Get the road blocks up around the city and we will have helicopter support soon. This is an armed hunt situation, so warn those going out to search for the perpetrators." Dawid was decisive in the lead. Gabreski and Lubeka moved out into the car park.

"What do you think, Łuka?"

"They are killing their way through to the Ukraine. It is only seventy-five kilometers away. Once there, they have a free route to anywhere in the East."

"So this is it. If we catch this group, desperate as they are, we get answers on the rest of their network."

"I think so, Kasia." He shouted to Dawid. "Have you closed the road through to Ukraine?"

"Yes. We are also sealing the minor roads." In the distance, through the darkness of the night, a helicopter could be seen to be approaching the site. The group stood in the car park and watched as a Mi-24D camouflaged helicopter echoed around the valley, hovering over the car park for twenty or thirty seconds, blowing up the snow, before shifting to land beside the market. The whooping of the propellors and the vibration of the ground forced its power onto the still of the evening.

"That is Colonel Browarczyk. Let's go and meet him." Dawid instructed Lubeka and Gabreski to get into the car. The others in the team began to fan out over the back and sides of the building, torchlights flickering across the gardens and wasteland around the back of the offices. A small fleet of police cars and Jeeps circled their way out of the car park and drove the one hundred meters to the sportsground beside the market. By the time they arrived, the occupants of the aircraft had alighted onto the snow covered pitch and were running through to the railed opening that led to the road. Of the dozen or so who came off the helicopter, half were armed and dressed in Special Forces uniforms. Gabreski and Lubeka knew the fatigues from recent exposés of the training of this unit, and the attempts by the government to give the military more of a profile across Polish society. Browarczyk led the group to the site and immediately searched out the car containing Dawid, Gabreski and Lubeka. He made his way into the back seat beside Lubeka, looking at her, expectant of a remark. Lubeka held her comments.

"Well, Dawid, what is the update? We hear you have recovered the body of one of the women."

"We have one of the missing women in an office. She was strangled. They left quickly. They know we are after them and are panicking. We have a number of addresses we can check around the city."

Browarczyk cut across him. "We have raided offices in Kraków and Warsaw. The profile is the same across the country. They have holding properties which operate small security and finance businesses. They open for months at a time and then move on to emerge doing the same business somewhere else, different locations."

"We have closed all roads out of the region and have been watching irregular movement between the regional cities."

"Excellent. Professor Gabreski, what do we do now?" The bluntness of the question startled Gabreski.

"Well. This seems to be an endgame for them. They have killed and run. Killing poor Karina was an act of desperation. Are they still here? I don't know." Gabreski's question resonated with Lubeka.

"This city is where we will find out." Lubeka broke her reserve. "We have Hanna Bach and Maria Braszak to find yet. They live here. The Zomo have become even more savage in Krosno. If they get out, they will have had help. If they do not, they will drive it to a conclusion here."

"We are here to deal with that. That side of things, you leave up to us, Doctor Lubeka. What do we do now? What do you think?" Browarczyk sounded as if he had the answers to his own questions, but was looking for a second opinion.

"The natural thing to do when running is to move in a linear direction. To go to where they feel safe."

"And where might that be? Where do we go next?" Browarczyk was relentless. Lubeka retrieved her tablet from her backpack and proceeded to open her file on Krosno and the list of addresses. Her index finger ran through the list, drawing downward to an address located on the riverbank itself.

"If you are right, Łuka, we should aim for the office registered as 'Mark', which is at the end of this road and to the side of the river."

“Okay, that is where we go.” Dawid aggressively spun out onto the road. The other cars, along with two Toyota Jeeps, which had joined the trail with lights flashing, pulled out after them. The cavalcade sped along the merging dual carriageway by the side of the river and curved around by the city’s stadium. The Sat Nav in the front of the dashboard flickered and highlighted the direction. At the bridge, the Sat Nav gave directions to the back of the Pub Piwny, a wooden structure with a beer garden dominated by beer signs. “Turn right” flashed up on the screen.

“There is no right.” Dawid shouted, starting an argument with his Sat Nav.

“It must be the pub.” Browarczyk opened the car door before Dawid had time to stop.

“Wait here.” He went into the pub, only to return seconds later with a startled barman following him frantically pointing and giving directions. Browarczyk went directly to the Toyota, shouting orders to the Jeep full of Special Force personnel before jumping into his own car.

“It is down this lane. The barman saw a black Land Rover going in an hour ago.” As he spoke, the black-fatigued military team broke out along the river bank. The lights of the police cars lit up the trees and reflected off the gushing flow of the river, torrentially crashing down the side of a tight gravelled lane.

“Come on and take it carefully.” Browarczyk opened the back and front doors of the cars in an instructive and protective manner. Gabreski and Lubeka emerged, stunned by the industrial scale of the backing. The roar of the river and the careful movement of the security personnel complemented each other, flowing in the same direction. The shadowy figures skirted the sides of the lane and made it to a shed. It simply had a number on it, non-distinct and functional

– eight. The building was crudely constructed, but perfect for storage or hiding something beyond the view of the road. The corrugated iron cladding sparkled as torch lights criss-crossed the slatted frame.

"This is it." Browarczyk waved to instruct some of the team to go forward. The stillness of the building and lack of any vehicles outside belied any activity that had taken place in the vicinity. The first two of the Special Forces unit crashed through the door, breaking it relatively easily, leaving it ajar to take the spotlights piercing through into the darkness of the room inside. Staring at them from within was a seated figure, tied to a steel framed chair, her mouth covered in duct tape. This time there was the uncomfortable, gasping, struggling sign of life.

"That's Hanna Bach." Lubeka could not contain the knowledge as she ran towards the woman in the chair. "Let her go." Browarczyk instructed his men to permit entrance for Lubeka. She almost fell through the door, demanding to be a compassionate presence in the middle of a war zone.

"Hanna, Hanna. It's Kasia, it's me. Let me get you out of this." The plastic restraining tags were cutting into her wrists and ankles, where she had attempted to force her own way to freedom. "This is over, Hanna, you are safe." The woman relaxed into the chair, her eyebrows raised at the discomfort. The chaos around her worked to release her from confinement. Lubeka held her for a moment and then gently tried to remove the tape form her mouth. "We are almost there." Bach waited patiently, then, released, breathed in deeply to catch the fresh air from the opened door.

"They have taken Maria. Maria." This was what Lubeka did not want to hear. Browarczyk and Gabreski moved closer to Bach, crowding Lubeka who stood hunched with her arms around the woman. The questions came out together: "Where have they taken her?" "Who has taken her?" Browarczyk acknowledged Gabreski, gesturing for him to continue. "Where have they taken her?" "Up the lane... back to the old city. That way. I heard them driving away. They killed Karina. Thcy killed Karina." The tears were welling up in Bach's eyes. Lubeka hugged her tightly. "We know, Hanna, we know. We found her." The older woman steadied herself and continued. "They want the names of all the women. We knew they would come after us some day. They never forgot. They wanted the names of all our women. Karina refused and they tortured her." Bach began to cry. Grabeski looked to Lubeka in empathy. The emotion suggested that Bach had given them what they wanted. After all these years lying low, keeping a past life secret, under fear, her heroic past had come back in a forced reenactment of the Zomo's days of torture and interrogation. "I am sorry. I am sorry."

Browarczyk interrupted the huddle of bodies. "We need direction here. Where to next? We have closed the roads and if they have only just left, they must be around here somewhere." He stepped forward and went down on his knees in front of Bach, holding her hands, making sure that with each word he could get what he needed to act on. "I have three questions, Hanna. Is that okay?" He waited a second until Bach nodded and then continued. "What are they driving? How many are there? Do you know where they went to?" Bach responded slowly but concisely to the questions. "They drove us in one black Land Rover and one black Mercedes. I saw about five of them."

Lubeka went on her knees beside Bach and, looking to her eyes, presented one more question that was unresolved for all of them, bar the women. "Did you know any of them?" The silence lasted for minutes as Bach swallowed and looked around her. It was a conscious recognition of her stating her own fate if she was to disclose names. It was what she was tortured for. "Bolek Janowski." Gabreski looked to Lubeka. The severity of the revelation was mind shattering. She had mentioned an insider, a person who was at the forefront of the establishment and media's focus. They had seen him on television continuously over the past week, giving interviews on the need for security service liberalization. This was a big fish and he was all the more dangerous because he was in the process of being hooked.

"What about guns, Hanna. Have they got guns?" Browarczyk was realizing the scale of the threat, and needed to get a grasp of the fire power that his men were dealing with.

"Small guns. They all had handguns." Lubeka hugged Bach again and caressed her hair in a manner that a daughter would do to a sick mother.

"Kasia, can I have a mirror." Bach's voice was weak. "Hanna, I do not have one." Thinking a second, she grappled through her bag to take out her phone. "Try this Hanna." Pointing the phone video camera towards her. "One minute, please." Lubeka looked to the attendant onlookers and with embarrassment they turned, shifting their gaze. Bach straightened her hair and wiped the dirt from her forehead. "Please, Hanna." Lubeka gave her some lipstick and waited as she nervously applied the dark rouge. "Thank you, Kasia, that is better. Can I go home?" Lubeka waved to the policewoman who had been behind her to come over. "Can Hanna go home?" Browarczyk, hearing everything, intervened.

"Hanna, please let us take you to the station for some questions first. This is Policewoman..." He stopped and looked at the officer. "Lańska, sir." Her reply was disciplined. "Policewoman Lańska. She will escort you and take care of you. Would that be okay?" Bach nodded. Lubeka helped her up and towards the arms of the police woman.

***

Browarczyk consulted with Dawid for some time, while Gabreksi and Lubeka stood by the door of the cabin. "If they are preparing for a gun battle, Kasia, this is maybe not the best place for us to be." Gabreski's caution was natural and inquisitive. "We need to get to Maria. Where do you think they have taken her?" Cautiously, they exited the office. "They were going towards the town."

Moving out into the darkness of the night, the shifting vehicles redirected lights towards the river. Gabreski looked up and, hovering over their side of the town, was the increasingly familiar ring of green lights. "Look up, Aron, they are watching us. They can do this virtually. They have been tracking our movements." Browarczyk looked up and seemed alarmed by the technology. He called to his team. "They are watching our movements and know what we are up to. We need to take that thing down."

Gabreski relayed a thought to Browarczyk: "With the technology they are using, they are probably watching the drone as well. If they are working from cars, they will have the drone within the line of sight."

"Łuka, where is it?"

"If we can see it, they are giving their own location away by keeping it safely within view themselves. I would think, from its movements and what Hanna told us, they are in the center of the town somewhere. Probably around the town square."

Browarczyk relayed the position to his team: "Get as many to the town square as possible. You two, get into the Jeep." He pointed forcefully at Lubeka and Gabreski.

The trail of cars and Jeeps left the lane at speed, in sequence, along the river and past the pub. As they swung by the roundabout onto Józefa Piłsudskiego hill leading up to the town square, the Rynek, the rattle of gunfire could be heard echoing across the valley. It was the first automatic fire that that the city had heard since the Red Army came through southern Poland in the winter of 1944.

"That is a Beryl. You would know the beat of that rifle anywhere. That is ours." No sooner had Browarczyk turned to reveal his knowledge on the weapon when a mass of green lights crashed to the ground in front of them. The sparks, metal and clutter of the disintegrating machine splashed onto the bonnet of the Jeep. Browarczyk swerved to avoid wreckage bouncing off the road.

The crunch of the wheels and the rumble of the Jeeps disturbed Lubeka. Her thoughts were still with Maria Braszak being caught up in the middle of it all. She was frightened for her. This macho world of boys games and toys was deadly, destructive, all of it. Her focus was simple, to get Maria and get out of this world as quickly as possible. They held the hand rails of the doors as the Jeep spun into the square. It was dark. Blue flashing lights could be seen across different points of the square.

Within seconds a series of exchanges, shots, could be heard from different points of the small town. From the shadows of the cloisters at one side of the square, there was movement and tracer lights skirting up and down the darkest recesses of the renaissance buildings. The light show was complimented by the beauty of the fountain in the middle of the square, switching colours periodically. Browarczyk drove towards where he felt the core of the exchanges were taking place, abruptly halting at one edge of the square, twenty meters from a medieval Franciscan church. The other cars followed suit, pulling up in a semi-circle around the opening to the street. Policemen were holed up along the street, moving by stealth when possible and reacting to short exchanges of gunfire.

Lubeka and Gabreski stood beside the Jeep with the door ajar for defence. The sparks of the bullets coming from behind the walls of the church were limited in that they could only target a two or three meter square at the arched doorway at the side of the main entrance to the church itself, leading to a garden. Behind them, on the other side of the square, there was a similar standoff with another group of Special Forces personnel targeting the ancient globular copper belfry beside the parish church. Through all its six hundred years, it had survived continual conquerors' bloodletting. It held, sturdy against this most recent of threats. Sparks danced from its dome as the protagonists took refuge in a besieged stairwell. The battle was coming to a few points of detention, the two ancient churches becoming the loci of a generational standoff. In the intermittent periods of silence between exchanges of ten or fifteen shots at a time, there was an eeriness, as if the cloud of time was sitting in disapproval over the events of the night.

They had been here before. The spectre of time had touched the square in terror on previous occasions. Here, they rounded up the city's Jews and ghettoized them in the small enclave which police were now trying to calm. Even the buildings looked down disapprovingly. Peace was hard won and continued to be hard to defend. Gabreski's mind drifted in the time between the sparks of noise and the instance of violence. He had been here a few times before in North Africa and was caught waiting while the desperate and the professional battled it out to see who could control the moment. All the lashes of violence served little purpose. It merely prolonged the surrender. It was violence without cause, a pointless defence, a statement from an older world view directed towards the new. Its time had gone and this was a final bloody kickback from the past. He thought – get it done – their time needs silenced to give the people of today their peace.

In the middle of the trauma, Lubeka sat on her knees against the side of the Jeep, the door solidly in defence. She whispered into her phone. “Marianna, Marianna, we have found them. They are fighting back. Has the media heard yet? Marianna, get this out. A gun battle is taking place in Krosno between some remnants of the old regime and the Special Forces. Get it into the media network. Bolek Janowski and others have murdered Karina Glinka of the student resistance, tortured another. Maria is still missing.” Lubeka crouched down further and held her conversation as another loud volley of shots rang out. “They are outnumbered and outgunned. This is it, Marianna. This is it. Get it out there.” Lubeka did not flinch at the turmoil around her. She was steady in this environment, a result of living a volatile home life and being driven by a cause. She was excited and hopeful at the same time. Gabreski looked on to see if she was all right. She felt she would be more contented if she had one of the guns, and was in the midst of battle itself.

“Target down.” In a split second, one single shot rang out. “Target down.” One of the policemen shouted and a lull in the shooting took place in and around the garden of the Franciscan church. The Special Forces moved in under the arch and filed into the garden. By the time Lubeka and Gabreski reached the arch, there were two bulky leather-coated bodies lying at the corner of the church wall. One of the men was lifeless, the other moaning and retching. This sight was disconcerting in that no one moved to assist the badly wounded man. The police stood over the bodies, others fanned out, continually searching. Spotlights darted across the walled gardens to the crevices and trees that dotted the pathway.

Dawid kneeled down beside the wounded man. "Where is the woman? Where is the woman?" The man, holding his chest with a puncture wound weeping onto the leather, just stared. "Where is the woman?" Dawid pushed down on the man's wound. Lit up with the white force of the spotlights, the man's grimacing face went visibly grey with pain. Tears streamed down the side of his neck as he lay half on the snow-glazed grass and half on the pathway.

"No." Lubeka shouted loudly. "We can't be like them. We will find her. She is around here somewhere."

At that appeal, and more to do with witnesses than conscience, Dawid withdrew the pressure and stood up. The gunman was unconscious. "She might be with the other group at the belfry." Dawid walked away. Gabreski and Lubeka followed along with the Special Forces team, who were keen to make it over the square to the last evidence of a firefight.

The atmosphere was still and the square brightened with a mosaic comprised of the remnants of snow. It crunched as they moved carefully around the edge of the shops and restaurants that surrounded the square. In the middle of the violence that scared the night, the fountain continued to splash its colour into the air, a future peeking through the bitterness of the past. This was built for the children of Krosno and their party would continue. There needed to be a clearing up, an exorcism of a former generation's dysfunctional ways. For Gabreski, there had been too much blood shed in the beautiful little town, it deserved better. It demanded peace. For him, the future of these places survived through boredom, where children's minds could dance.

As they moved slowly around to the corner of one of the restaurants to where they could just about see the belfry, he considered his own childhood, its disruption, the fear and displacement. People need to be free from all of that. They need the oxygen of peace to develop. Browarczyk had already made his way over and was directing the operation. The coded banter of the radios crackled out around the cloisters. People who had been patiently waiting for the battle to end, huddled at the back of the restaurants. As they waited, in the middle of the chaos, Lubeka pulled a box of cigarettes out of her pocket and proceeded to light up. The police looked on in bemusement at this casual act of defiance.

Another succession of shots rang out from around the corner. The Special Forces detachment, who came over from the church, filtered out around the corner from the safety of the arches and the restaurants. The street lights towards the belfry were forced out with a swift volley of fire, the loudness startling the locals who had gathered towards the front door of one building to get out into the safety of a colonnade. Within seconds and one final burst of semi-automatic fire, the silence stayed, pitted only with muffled shouts from the street below. The radios of the police relayed the distinct message of "clear" repeatedly. It was done.

The police, followed by Lubeka and Gabreski, walked out slowly and cautiously into the tight street that fed through to the square. The street filled up with police and military.

"What about Maria?" Lubeka was eager to know from Browarczyk. Ignoring her initially, his bellowing conversation over the radio to his unit, criss-crossed the scenes. "Alpha Beta. Is location one secure?" "That is affirmative."

"Any sign of a woman?" The beeping of the radio was disorientating, operating from a number of the machines at the same time. "Negative." "Delta, Delta. Is your location secure?" "Affirmative. Two targets down and one unarmed." "Any evidence of a woman?" "Negative. Repeat, negative."

They stood in the street, the build-up of noise carrying across the square. The creeping normality started to bring residents onto the streets. "Cordon these areas off." Dawid hurriedly arranged for tape to extend around the sites to prevent the locals from wandering into the scene for the sake of curiosity, to reclaim their town.

"Łuka, what did they do with Maria?" Lubeka pushed her cigarette into one of the public bins and wandered out into the square. They knew that they left the office where Hanna was with Maria. "She must be here somewhere." The thought came to Gabreski that they could have dumped her in the river. He thought how horrendous that would be and decided to keep this to himself. Where was the hope in this? "Kasia, they needed her. They kept her as long as they could. There has to be a reason for that." Lubeka picked up on it. "Why would they dispose of a resource that they were keeping to interrogate? She was their biggest prize. She cannot just disappear."

Browarczyk barged through all the possibilities of the disappearance. "I have ordered a search of the river and riverbank in case they tried to dispose of Maria on the way up the hill." It was the first indication of such an act to be voiced. It took Lubeka by surprise. She looked to Gabreski for some assistance in finding her alive.

"We will check the area around the church where they stopped. Are you sure they did not stop somewhere else coming up the hill to the square?"

Browarczyk, while distracted by his unit moving in to secure the area, returned to Gabreski with a more definite response. "We are sure they moved directly up the hill without stopping. We were not far behind them; minutes I would think. They would not have had time to dispose of a body if they were preparing for a battle. The problem is that she has just disappeared."

"They need Maria. She was the only one who could positively identify them. She knows their past and who else was there. Why would they kill an asset like that?" Lubeka could not bear to think that they would have been so wasteful in their desperation to escape. They were in Krosno after all to get information from these women. Why dispose of the single most important person that they had caught up with. She refused to believe that they had killed her.

"Maybe so. But I am taking no chances. We will be searching all areas." Browarczyk looked different out of a suit. He was the same person, but his demeanour changed when the uniform went on. His authoritative gestures to his own unit and even his use of language altered. This was a toughened professional who operated when he had to on a vocabulary of verbs, in a colourless and clinical manner. Lubeka saw a different man to the one she had come to warm to in Warsaw. Humanity was wanting as he joined his colleagues in a hunt and kill.

As they pondered the track of the Bartek group across the town, spotlights targeted on the bottom of the belfry lit up two men being marched from the lane between the gates and the parish church. The lights illuminated a sandstone plaque that was positioned half way up the tower. '1637' in gothic carving. It was poignant that one of the oldest sites in the region would become the focus for a fight that had been continuing in various guises for seventy-five years. This explosion of violence was a marker in that long history. The belfry looked on as a totem of stability and an icon of time. As the men were brought past, Lubeka and Gabreski recognized Bolek Janowski, gaunt and exhausted. He was clearly the same figure who would justify anything for his cause, driving for an old guard and a corrupted ideology. The arrogance remained, visible and aggressive.

"Where is Maria?" Lubeka shouted at him as he was led away. He looked up in distain and marched on without saying a word. "Where is she?" Lubeka was getting increasingly irate and desperate. It was out of character, but she felt that the ill-fate of the heroic woman she met the night before had been a result of her own failings and her passions. Bolek Janowski walked on. Gabreski moved to hold Lubeka as she lunged toward him. Gabreski's reassurance give her some succour. "We will find her, Kasia. We are better than that." He flicked his head in the direction of the two men being led away.

"He will get off." Browarczyk watched stoically at the clambering of the police to secure the two men into their cars. "He had no weapon with him and will deny he was anywhere near the scene. His type are too skilled to be taken this easily." After a few seconds of reflection, he returned to the job at hand. "We need to search. Follow those policemen back to the church if you want to. We will get this street cleared and there is a trawl of the river under way." The various groups segregated and began to move in the directions ordered. Gabreski and Lubeka tagged in with the small team crossing the square to go back to the Franciscan church. The locals were emerging in large numbers, enquiring and standing around the square which had its peace broken so violently not an hour earlier. The chatter and life came back to the town centre as young people began to clutter up the sides of the scene, camera phones and flashes intruding on the dark and broken evidence of the events.

Gabreski and Lubeka pushed their way through the police lines twenty meters from the church to survey the area and waited until a policewoman approached. "Please tie in with us. If you notice anything out of place, please, let me know." The search began with a line of police in forensic suits moving slowly down the street towards the church, each trace of gunfire and shrapnel scrutinized, logged and photographed. The pace of work frustrated Lubeka.

"This is painful. We need to get answers here. Let's go." Dragging Gabreski, the two pushed through the ranks of the police and onward down the sub-altern stairway and into the church. Its nave was dark and medieval, the smell of polished wood and dust lifting through the draft that they had brought with them and the half opened door. The echo of the baroque interior carried with it shadows that were ghostly, casting and disconcerting. As the lights from the exterior fluttered though the window at the back of the church, shadows tracked their way through to the beams. Gabreski felt a chill go through him.

"We need to look in around the confessional and through the vestry. That is close to where they were shooting from. They should have passed by there." Carefully, Gabreski and Lubeka checked the crevices of the old church, the torch they had been given by the policewoman flickered its beam across the brick and wood supports, the statutes coming alive with ceramic eyes following them around the corners of the building. "This is eerie, Kasia." "That is Saint Anthony and the Sacred Heart. You should know that." The crucifix hung over the isle, creaking in its own echo around the vast space of the vaulted ceiling.

"We came here when we got married." The whisper got louder as Lubeka recovered control over the darkness. "We came in here for a while. I think I told you that. Andrzej lit a few candles." Instinctively, she blessed herself.

The front door of the church opened, as a stream of police came through to check the building. "We have found nothing yet, Doctor

Lubeka. We are going to concentrate on the river." The policewoman who was in attendance at the belfry was leading the search. The police picked up their stride and moved quickly around the pews and benches, with the spotlights stretching like anti-aircraft beams into the rafters. "Do you see anything?"

"No. We will finish up here and follow you to the riverbank." Gabreski's response was matter of fact, a sentiment that Lubeka resisted. "We need to check the parameters. I still cannot see how they lost her in the rush to escape." The police moved out as quickly as they arrived, bringing the church back to its sombre darkness. Lubeka went to the candle holder and lit a tealight from the few surviving from the afternoon vigil. She stood looking around, reflecting on what could have been and how lives change so quickly. This spot once was a moment of hope for her, on return it had become a place of isolation. Time had been lost to haemorrhaging, painful life experience. She stared at the flickering lights.

"Okay, Kasia, let's look in the Oświęcim Chapel and then move on. There is nothing more we can do here. It is just getting us depressed being here." Gabreski pushed her lightly to awaken her out of reminiscence. "We have got to get to Maria." They crossed the laminate flooring at the back of the church and climbed the few steps into the square chapel with marble baroque statues lining the walls, and a brightness that filtered through from the street.

"We went underneath the last time to see the coffins of Anna and Stanisław. That's them." Lubeka shone the torch on one of the paintings on the wall of the chapel, lighting up an ancient portrait of two adorned aristocratic young people from the seventeenth century, staring inquisitively at whoever ventured into their marbled monument.

"What do you mean underneath?"

“When Andrzej and I were here, you could get below this chapel to the tombs.” Lubeka walked out of the chapel and stood at the bottom of the steps. She stamped a laminate mat with her foot. An echo rang out across the church and resonated out of the side chapel. Gabreski followed her and watched as she got onto her knees and started to pick at the sides of the floor with her fingernails. As the sides lifted, she got more animated in her actions. “Don’t just stand there, Łuka, help me.” Gabreski did not question the motives and struggled to his knees to assist, using a pen to force up the flooring. Lubeka arose from her knees with a swath of laminate.

“There it is, Łuka.” Standing with a strip of laminate lifted to her waist, Lubeka revealed a trap door with a sunken bullring fixed as a hook. Gabreski forced the last section of the flooring away and the full trap door was released. Lubeka grabbed the bullring and lifted the full weight of the two meter strip of wood. Gabreski took the weight of the door with his back as Lubeka shone the light across the crypt. “Lift it against the railings of the chapel.” They pushed the planks of wood back to expose a stone stairwell. As the church fell silent again, they heard a shuffling from the crypt. Lubeka was less hesitant than Gabreski to make it to the bottom of the steps and forced open the grill. She had been there before and forewarned of what to expect. Moving down into the darkness, her light caught the wooden coffins of Stanisław and Anna, lying for over four hundred years, side by side – a testament that in death time cannot separate what was for a fleeting moment wonderfully alive.

“What was that?” Gabreski was spooked by the reflection from the far coffin, a shard of light startled him in its unexpectedness. The sound of shuffling became more pronounced. “Quiet, quiet. That flash is the window of Stanisław’s coffin.” They moved further inside towards the noise.

Instantly, the torch caught the whites of eyes staring fearfully at them and a body wedged between the coffin plinths. For Lubeka, it was recognizably Braszak. “Maria, Maria. Łuka, get help. It’s Maria.” Gabreski turned and scrambled up the stairwell. His voice resounded around the open church door. In moments, the sound of the police clambering to their assistance brought a stream of light through into the church. In the crypt the single beam from the torch moved up and down the bound body of Braszak. Tears streamed down her face. “It’s me. It is Kasia. You are safe now.” Lubeka forced the tape from the head of Braszak and held her between the two coffins. “Kasia, did you get them? Please.” Braszak was weak, bruised, but alive. “Yes. We got them, Maria. We got them.”

Epilogue

3rd December

The grave of Andrzej Lubeka was already sunken and settled after the thaw of the past few days. The tips of ice could be still seen on the high ground on the rim of the cemetery in Kraków. The flowers had wilted, the smell of sodden mud bringing back memories of the depth of loss. Lubeka and Wójcik stood quietly. They listened to the wind cut through the graves and found a calm in the whispers of nature. Lubeka's world had been broken absolutely and she was numbed by the emptiness of it all. The total emotional drain of the past weeks had taken its toll. For her, in hindsight, Andrzej was one of the last victims of the old regime, for all his faults. He was failed by his government, its austerity and joblessness. Failed by a society who judged too harshly. He was one of many still languishing in the past, in the hope of change. For some, hope came with stubborn hard work and luck, or by resorting to emigration. For so many others, the wait continued.

Gabreski struggled through the cemetery, trying to avoid the clumps of mud left from the previous week's burials. Slowly, he made his way though, stepping from one clump of sodden grass to another to avoid the mud. He kissed Wójcik on the cheek. Lubeka bent awkwardly over the mound to receive a kiss on the cheek. Gabreski shook her lightly from her shoulders.

"Are you okay?"

“I suppose so.” The non-committed, dissipated answer demanded silence. Gabreski obliged as they stood, the bitter northern wind driving through them.

“The war’s over, Kasia. The President’s office has agreed to a Truth Commission. Finally, we will know what happened in that autumn of eighty-eight. Those good women will be freed from hiding once and for all, and we will have the government people tracing the names, not us. It won’t be left to the likes of you and me, or poor Beata.” “We will see.” Lubeka positioned herself directly facing Gabreski. “It has been a high cost for me, Łuka.”

“I know, Kasia. I know.” She returned to staring through the cluster of wilted flowers.

“What are you going to do now?” Gabreski changed the subject.

“I can’t stay here. I need to get away. I need to find peace of mind somewhere.”

“There is always London.” Gabreski speculated with the suggestion, voiced as an offer rather than a destination.

“I liked the sound of Dublin. They all speak Polish there. Or Chicago. Well, somewhere where we are going to be welcome.”

“Okay, Kasia.” He held his thoughts as he realized that he had become a part of a long nightmare for her. They stood and listened to the wind, the afternoon breeze and a long winter that was only just beginning.

“I have to go, Kasia. I have a flight to London in two hours.” Gabreski reached over and brushed a loose lock of Lubeka’s hair behind her ear. He leaned over and kissed her on the forehead, holding it for a second. “You take care of yourself.” She said nothing, her eyes not breaking the gaze. “Watch out for her, Marianna.” Gabreski hugged Wójcik, shaking her as if to present her with an order. He turned and walked away.